Praise f

"Dangerously funny stuff."
Janet Evanovich

"Simple sexy sport may be just what the doctor ordered."
Publishers Weekly

"Lois Greiman is a modern day Dorothy Sayers. Witty as hell, yet talented enough to write like an angel with a broken wing."
Kinky Friedman, author of *Ten Little New Yorkers*

"What a marvelous book! A delightful romp, a laugh on every page."
MaryJanice Davidson, *NYT* best-selling author of the Undead series.

"Amazingly good." (Top Pick!)
Romantic Times

"L.A. psychologist, Chrissy McMullen is back to prove that boobs, brass, and brains make for one heck of a good time…laugh out loud funny…sassy…clever."
Mystery Scene

"Excellent!"
Library Journal

"Sexy, sassy, suspenseful, sensational!! Lois Greiman delivers with incomparable style."
Best-selling author of *To the Edge*, Cindy Gerard

"Move over Stephanie Plum and Bubbles Yablonsky to make way for Christina McMullen, the newest blue collar sexy professional woman who finds herself in hair raising predicaments that almost get her murdered. The chemistry between the psychologist and the police lieutenant is so hot that readers will see sparks fly off the pages. Lois Greiman, who has written over fifteen delightful romance books, appears to have a great career as a mystery writer also."
thebestreviews.com

"Ms. Greiman makes a giant leap from historical fiction to this sexy and funny mystery. Bravo! Well done!"
Rendevous

"A fun mystery that will keep you interested and rooting for the characters until the last page is turned."
Fresh Fiction

"Fast and fun with twists and turns that will keep you guessing. Enjoy the ride!"
Suzanne Enoch, USA Today best-selling author of *Flirting with Danger*

"Lucy Ricardo meets Dr. Frasier Crane in Lois Greiman's humorous, suspenseful series. The result is a highly successful tongue-in-cheek, comical suspense guaranteed to entice and entertain."
Book Loons

UNCORKED

Uncorked
By Lois Greiman

To Caitlin Alexander, the best editor (and possibly the best person) in the universe. Thanks for being you.

Special thanks to Lori Speer, Northampton Police Department Court Queen, for answering a barrage of last minute questions. Any mistakes made are solely the fault of the author.

Chapter 1

If love is blind, why is Victoria's Secret still making a killing?
—*Christina McMullen, while eating red velvet cupcakes and agonizing about her expanding waistline*

I picked up my cordless on the third ring. Since the demise of my caller ID, answering the kitchen phone always felt somewhat like playing a fun-filled little version of Russian roulette. The call a few minutes earlier had been from my mother, one Constance Iris McMullen. The ensuing conversation had made me as skittish as a scalded cat and a little breathless. "Hello?"

There was a slight pause during which I wondered about the identity of the caller. Maybe one of those sleazy heavy-breathers, I thought, but I wasn't that lucky.

"There's only one thing I can think of that makes you that breathless." The voice belonged to Lieutenant Jack Rivera, police officer, ex-lover, jackass. I had, at one time, been deluded enough to believe we might someday pick out china patterns together, but six months ago I found him slapped up against a bleached blonde with a triple-digit bra size and a double-digit IQ.

After that, I considered picking out a nice hit man who knew how to keep a secret.

Not that I'm bitter. I'm a trained psychologist…and classy as hell. I don't do bitter.

I pursed my lips and concentrated on being haughty. So what if his voice was as deep as a Dostoyevsky novel and shadowed with a shitload of mouth-watering innuendo? So what if just the sound of it conjured up a hundred lurid memories that burned the back of my mind like a George Foreman grill and sent my nerve endings into a feeding frenzy? I'm an adult. I'm a professional.

"What's the matter, Rivera? Skank Girl busy on her street corner this evening?"

Okay, maybe there was a teeny bit of bitterness.

I heard him draw a breath and imagined him leaning back, chest expanding. "You know they have pills to help with that pissy PMS problem, don't you, McMullen?"

"Do they have pills to get rid of cheating bastards, too?" Maybe there was a lot of bitterness. I closed my eyes to the sound of it, letting an errant draft from my little desk fan cool my rancor and soothe my thoughts. But he spoke again.

"I thought you'd have the answer to that one. After all, you're a trained psychotic."

"Psychologist," I corrected irritably. "And if you continue with this obsessive pursuit of me, Mr. Raver, I'm afraid I'm going to have to report this harassment to your superiors." Doing my woefully inadequate best to ignore the memory of his blistering betrayal, I pushed a wet tendril of hair behind my right ear. It was currently a deep mahogany hue. No one knows what color it would be without chemical assistance. It's highly probable that even fewer people care.

"I wouldn't bother calling Captain Kindred if I were you," Rivera said. "No use confirming his suspicions regarding your mental condition."

"Ahh," I said. "How I would love to sit here and listen to your slanderous invectives, Lieutenant Riot, but I have a date." I gritted a plastic smile. Still damp from the shower, I was as naked as a jaybird, but the weatherman, bastard that he was, had dished up a hundred and eight degrees in L.A.'s dubious shade and I didn't plan to wear clothes again until the morning commute. And maybe not even then.

"A date?" He spoke the words slowly. "Tonight?"

Was there a tightness to his tone? Could that tightness be jealousy? Be still my evil little heart.

"Yes, tonight," I said. I was lying, of course. It was 10:27 on a Tuesday night and I had just finished watching McLintock. I was on a John Wayne kick. Hell Town would have to wait until tomorrow. "I just got out of the shower."

"What are you wearing?"

My heart did the happy dance in my chest. I'm not too proud to admit that I would have paid in plasma to make him jealous.

"I usually shower naked," I said. "A little eccentricity I have, but that's the way I am."

“You’re naked in the kitchen?”

I raised my brows and almost laughed out loud. He was jealous. I was sure of it. “I’m hanging up, now,” I said.

“Are your curtains closed?”

“Stooped to being a Peeping Tom, have you, Reaver? Or just—”

“Are the damn things closed?” he asked.

I lowered my brows, some of my glee disappearing at the memory of him saving my ass on more than one occasion. “Of course they’re closed,” I said, but there was something in his voice that made me glance at each one, just to be sure. And maybe there was an inch or two of window showing beneath my rust-colored kitchen blinds. Still, it surely wasn’t enough for anyone to have seen me. Nevertheless, I pulled a napkin from the table and draped it in front of my body.

“So you’re still trying to get yourself killed,” he said.

“What are you talking about?” My voice had gone from professional to constipated. “What’s the matter with you?”

“Your usual wardrobe is dangerous enough, McMullen. You don’t need to be parading around naked for any passing pervert to see.”

I shot my glance from window to window again. Maybe there was some space between the living room drapes, too, but I kept my voice calm. Sunland may not be Disneyworld, but it’s not exactly the Gaza Strip either. “Luckily, I only know one pervert sick enough to try it…and he's a cop," I said.

"Don't be naive, McMullen. I'm a Boy Scout compared to half the men in this city."

"Naive! Are you forgetting what line of work I'm—" I began, but he snorted.

"Work!" he said, then chortled. "You think sitting around discussing some bored CEO's luncheon options is work? Try running down a hopped-up asshole who just raped a woman idiotic enough to leave the curtains open on the ground floor of her Tudor."

I glanced around at the ground floor of my Tudor, swallowed and did my best to convince myself I wasn't nervous. "And I suppose you believe leaving one's drapes open warrants rape."

"I think even you should have more sense than to prance around in the buff for half the world to see." His voice had risen a few decibels.

Mine rose a few more. "You're just mad that I caught you in the act with that stupid hussy who—"

"I'm mad because you're a raving lunatic. Put some damn clothes on and shut your drapes!"

I felt a heady meld of rage and revenge zip through me. Some people are good at taking advice. And some people are Irish.

"As it turns out, Rivera…," I said, fluttering the aforementioned napkin in the breeze created by the living room fan. "It just so happens I'm wearing a little something I got for a graduation party." The napkin had the year 2012 emblazoned across its cherry red expanse and had been purchased for my secretary's youngest son. One corner sported a dab of frosting retained from the congratulatory cake I had consumed earlier in the day. I licked it a little, then stuck it to my decent-sized right boob.

Rivera was silent for a moment. "So you're not naked?" A shot of something that felt like aged rum but might have been estrogen splashed through my system.

"Well…maybe it would be more correct to say I got it at a graduation party," I said.

He paused. Possibly he was thinking. It happens sometimes even with L.A. cops. "Did it come with cake on it?"

"Give the officer a medal," I said. "Now, if you'll excuse me, I'm expecting my boyfriend in just a few minutes. Perhaps I should be wearing something that doesn't say 'Congratulations' on it. That might seem a bit suggestive."

I heard him inhale softly. "What's the lucky bastard's name this time?"

I smiled into the middle distance and tried not to enjoy myself too much.

"That's no longer any of your business, Rivera."

"Are you going out?"

"Also in the none-of-your-business category, I'm afraid. Now I really must go. I believe he's already arrived."

"I don't see his car."

"That's—" I began, but suddenly the implication of his words reverberated through my system like an L.A. earthquake. My eyebrows shot into my hairline, and my heart, just getting accustomed to Rivera's sex-steeped voice, slammed against my ribs like a gong. "What?"

"Is he too broke to afford wheels, McMullen? You don't have to pay his bus fare, do you?"

Anger followed the estrogen like a wild flume through my system. Maybe it was because Rivera seemed to be spying on me. On the other hand, it might have been because I was about to get caught in a lie. "You're outside my house?"

"If you'd close your damn drapes you wouldn't have to worry about who's out here."

"You're spying on me?" My voice had risen into the range where only canines and arachnids could hear me.

"Not spying. Observing." He sounded smug enough to smack. "I'm a cop, remember?"

"I remember you're a two-timing cheat who can't keep his dick in his pants," I snarled. Marching buck naked to the curtains in the darkened little office at the front of my house, I yanked them aside and peered into the street. It was entirely empty except for my own antiquated Saturn. The car had a faulty air conditioner, iffy door latches and a trick trunk, but it was still more trustworthy than most men I knew.

I drew a deep breath through my nose and primped a tight smile. “You used to be quite an excellent liar, Rivera.”

“I’m thrilled you think so.”

“And I’m thrilled to have had this lovely chat, but I have to go now. Looks like my date just showed up.” Smacking my palm with my lips, I blew a noisy kiss to my fictional suitor. Then I pulled the drapes sloppily closed, not particularly caring who saw what.

“So you’re planning to give the whole neighborhood a show?”

“Not the whole neighborhood.”

“Chrissy.” He gritted my name, trying to hold his temper at bay. I grinned at his lack of success and made my tone sassy.

“It’s not easy keeping a man’s interest, Rivera. A girl’s got to go the extra mile sometimes. But you know that, don’t you?”

“For God’s sake, McMullen!” Rivera said, sounding pissed enough to pop an artery. “Put on some damn clothes.”

“He’s always so classy. And early,” I said. “Impatient I guess.”

“I mean it,” he growled. “Do you know what kind of sick bastards we see every night at the precinct?”

“Don’t be so hard on yourself, Rivera. You're maybe not as sick as you think you are.” I rustled the drapes vigorously, as if I were peering outside.

"Hmm, it looks like the good doctor is driving a different car tonight."

"Damn it, McMullen, it's probably not even him. Close the fucking drapes." In the background I could hear his chair complain noisily, as if he'd just sprung from its seat. I sneered, knowing he wasn't spying on me at all. Lying bastard.

"You must stop judging people by your own standards," I said. "My man has four or five vehicles. I never know which one he'll choose to pick me up in. This one's an SUV. An Escalade, I think." I wouldn't know an Escalade from an escalator, but my Irish was up.

"Fuck it, McMullen, is there really a vehicle parked outside your house?"

"I know you thought I would languish here alone after you cheated on me with every bimbo from her to the Potomac, Rivera, but as it turns out—

"

"Give me the make, model and color?"

I laughed. "I understand that you're jealous, but you can't put every guy in jail that shows a passing interest in—"

"Which direction is it facing?"

"Good-bye, Lieutenant. He's getting out. I have to go. He probably…" I paused, then caught my breath as if surprised.

"What? What's wrong?"

"He looks even taller than usual tonight."

"Are you still standing at the damn window?"

"His face is kind of shadowed from this vantage point, but I'm…" I let my voice falter a little. "I'm sure it's him."

"Give me a physical description!" he barked, but I laughed. It wasn't all together forced. I'm ashamed to say that I was having a hell of a good time at his expense.

"What?" I asked, voice Marilyn-Monroe soft.

"What does he look like?"

"Who?"

"The man approaching your house!"

"You want a physical description of my boyfriend? That's not very healthy, Rivera. Even for a—"

"Are you sure it's him?"

"Of course it's him. I'm sure it's… I do wish my security light was still working."

I won't burden you with the string of obscenities that followed that little lie. Suffice it to say they were fairly inventive. I stifled a laugh.

"Give me his height, hair color and any scars or other distinguishing—"

"He's tall and handsome and…Oh!" I said with a little gasp.

"What? What is it? Talk to me, Chrissy."

"Another guy's getting out."

"There are two of them?"

"He's tall, too."

"Lock your doors!"

"What?"

"Lock your fucking doors. Then call me from your cell phone. I'll be there in thirteen minutes. Don't let anyone in. Not even me. And for God's sake put some clothes on before—"

I could no longer resist. Laughter bubbled up like venom. His words stopped in mid sentence. I could practically hear his mind buzzing. I'd bet my PhD that none of his thoughts were pleasant.

"McMullen?"

I barely managed to stop laughing long enough to answer. "Yes, Lieutenant?"

"If there are no murdering gangbangers parked in front of your house, I'm going to kill you myself."

"Isn't that frowned on?" I asked. "Even in L.A.?"

"I'm sure the judge will understand my predicament if he's met you. Lock your fucking doors."

"They are locked!" I snapped. "You think I'm an idiot?"

He snorted. "Check them!"

"I don't have to take your orders anymore."

Now his snort was more like a guffaw. "As if you ever did a reasonable thing in your entire life! If I had a nickel for every time you took some dumb-ass risk, I'd be up to my eyeballs in—"

"I don't take dumb-ass risks."

"Yeah?" The single word was sharp with emotion. "How about the time you confided in Hawkins?"

I stifled a wince. Dr. David Hawkins had been a trusted colleague. Memories washed over me in fresh waves of panic. I glanced at my La-Z-Boy, remembering him sitting there, uninvited. That had been just minutes before the good doctor tried to kill me with a fillet knife.

"Check the door, Chrissy," he ordered again.

"No," I said, heart pounding and the entirety of my attention focused on that damn lock. But my tiny foyer was too dark to allow me to see if it was secured. Stiff legged, I pattered silently to it on bare feet.

And at that second, it burst open.

Chapter 2

A gentleman, he is but a wolf that is patient, si?
—Rosita Rivera, whose former husband was a politician and a gentleman

I screamed and lunged backward, ready to run like hell. But I had so little space, and the intruder was already leaping toward me.

I stumbled sideways and grabbed the nearest thing I could find. A framed picture came away in my hand. I swung with every ounce of terror I possessed. The attacker ducked. My impromptu weapon whistled over his head. He lunged at me. I dropped the picture and turned to run, but he dragged me down. I fell to my knees, him on top.

I screamed bloody murder. He smothered me with his hand. I bit. He swore. I struggled, almost got away and was dragged back to the floor. But I wouldn't go down without a fight. Squirming onto my back, I brought my knee up with all the force I could muster. It slammed against his crotch with satisfying momentum. He grunted and froze. For a moment he was poised above me, then he toppled sideways, falling onto the linoleum like a beached mackerel. I scrambled to my feet. In a heartbeat I was racing toward safety, but he croaked something guttural and terrifying.

I almost made it to the back door before I realized he'd spoken my name. I grabbed the spinning desk fan for protection and pivoted toward him.

"Holy shit, McMullen!" The bastard's voice was harsh with pain. He lay in a fetal position on the floor, hands tucked between his legs, eyes scrunched shut. "How many times do I have to tell you to set your damn security alarm?"

I backed away a few steps. My hands were just steady enough to flip on the lights.

A well-built, dark-haired man lay writhing in my hallway, but not in a sexy way. More in a dear-God-you've-just-crushed-my-nuts sort of way.

I canted my head at him, sucked in a breath and said, "Rivera?" His name escaped like a question, but I knew it was him. Telling me he was outside my house so that I'd believe he was miles away, then yanking open my door and scaring the bejeezus out of me was just the kind of thing he had done on numerous occasions. But I wasn't quite ready to relinquish the fan. "Is that you?"

"Of course it's fucking..." He sucked in a careful breath, calmed his voice. "Of course it's me." A muscle jumped in his cheek. He'd once called it his Chrissy tick. "Who the hell did you think it was?"

"Well..." I tried a sardonic laugh. It sounded a little asthmatic. Adrenaline was mixing dangerously with a dozen other hormones in my overexcited system, and my hands hurt from gripping the fan with such ferocious intensity. "Certainly not you. You said you were watching my house."

Turning his head with painful carefulness, he rolled dark, questioning eyes up at me.

"I assumed you were lying!" I shrieked.

"Are you totally nuts?"

"Me? I'm not the one who habitually attacks me in dark allies or—"

"I'm just trying to make sure you're prepared."

"Prepared! Are you—"

"Stop!" shouted a voice, and suddenly another man lunged through the doorway. I jerked toward him, still in battle mode, fan lifted high. But my neighbor, Mr. Al Sadr, was carrying a baseball bat in both hands and failed to notice me. "Do not move or I shall—" he began, then came to a screeching halt and stared at the body on my floor in blinking uncertainty. "Lieutenant Rivera?"

"Fuck." His response was more a groan than a spoken work.

"What has happened here?" Mr. Al Sadr's face was a meld of concern and curiosity not entirely unknown to me. I first became familiar with that particular expression when, as a four-year-old, I decided to become a professional golfer and hit my brother's left eye dead on with a nine iron.

"I didn't know it was him," I said.

"Miss Mc—" Al Sadr said and turned toward me, but in that instant his eyes popped wide and his bat dropped to the floor with a metallic clatter.

"What?" I raised my own weapon in instinctual defense and jerked back against the wall. "What is it?"

"Holy shit!" Rivera muttered. He almost sounded more tired than wounded.

I jerked my gaze to him. "What?"

"Get some fucking clothes on," he hissed, and in that moment I once again realized my state of undress.

I felt my face heat all the way to my scalp.

"Christina!" called a heavily accented voice from outside. "Christina McMullen, is all well?" A second later Ramla Al Sadr, too, burst through the open door, holding a can of pepper spray and looked ready to do battle.

At that juncture I rather hoped I would die, simply pass away and move onto the hereafter.

"Christina…" She blinked at me, big eyes dark and round beneath her brightly colored hijab. We have a history. Some of it's good. Most of it's weird. "What has happened here? Are you well? Why are you without the clothing?"

My weapon was beginning to droop toward the floor. "I didn't know it was him," I said again, but my tone had lost its sterling edge and sounded a little defensive.

She turned toward the supposed villain, who remained on the floor, knees clamped together. Her eyes grew wide again. "Lieutenant Rivera?"

"Hello, Mrs. Al Sadr." His words sounded a little more normal but still had a good deal of that am-I-dead-yet tone to it.

"Christina, what have you done to him?" she asked and rushed forward. She'd liked Rivera ever since he'd been instrumental in saving her sister from an abusive husband, but I'd been instrumental, too, and I never elicited the kind of adoring glances he did.

"I didn't know it was him," I repeated.

"There is another whose testicles you wished to crush?" she asked, glancing up at me as if I was the bad guy.

"No. Well, yes, but—"

"Good God, McMullen, will you put on some clothes?" Rivera hissed again.

I glanced down, glanced at Al Sadr, glanced at his wife.

"Excuse me," I said, and setting the still-spinning fan carefully back in its allotted position, I slunk along the wall toward my bedroom.

By the time I had dressed and worked up enough nerve to reenter my own kitchen, Rivera was sitting alone at the table. He looked up, eyes dark and malevolent over the chipped coffee mug that housed my favorite maxim: Mornings are for masochists.

"I didn't know it was you," I said.

He exhaled something that sounded like a chuckle. "I guess things could have been worse, then."

I swallowed, cleared my throat, tried to do the same with the guilt. "Ramla made you coffee?"

"Tea," he said. "She couldn't find any coffee."

I nodded. That was probably because I didn't keep any in the house. I didn't believe in wasting my daily allotment of caffeine on such an inferior form. It's chocolate or die for me. "How are you feeling?"

"My balls were just rammed up my esophagus," he said. His Chrissy muscle twitched again. "How do you think I feel?"

His tone made me a little testy. I mean, seriously, the man had just broken into my house and scared the hell out of me. "Like an ass?"

He stared at me a second, then snorted and took a sip of tea. He didn't like tea. The thought improved my mood a little.

"Remind me not to worry about you anymore," he said.

"You don't worry about me," I countered, and remembered to hate him. It was easier when he wasn't curled up on my linoleum like a dying salamander. "We're not seeing each other anymore. Remember?"

His eyes were as shadowed as midnight dreams. "That's right," he said, but there was something in his tone that threatened to suck me in, to roll me under. Fortunately, at that precise moment, I remembered with unexpected clarity that my current boyfriend, one Dr. Marcus Jefferson Carlton, had an IQ of 141. He was a published author, an accomplished yogi, and a dynamite chess player. Unfortunately, he was also incommunicado while he was traveling in another country with no one to keep him company but Sam, his trusty publicist.

"What are you doing here anyway?" I asked.

He shrugged. "Hoping this tea will put out the fire in my balls."

"I really did think you were someone else."

"Yeah? You always greet your new beau with a knee to the gonads?"

I gave him a snotty smile and preened my tone to match. "Not at all. Dr. Carlton is a perfect gentleman."

"Is he?"

"Yes."

He chuckled a little. "Well, I guess opposites really do attract then, don't they?"

"What the hell's that supposed to mean?"

He caught my eye again. "You swung at me like I had Spalding tattooed on my forehead, McMullen. Sometimes perfect gentlemen take offense to that."

"Well, perfect gentlemen don't come crashing into a woman's house like a crazed gorilla."

"I never claimed to be a gentleman," he said, and something about his tone made me remember the first full night we'd been together. Part of it had been spent at the very table at which we currently sat. Part of it had been spent on that very table. Holy crap, I thought, and wiped away the memory with a sweaty imaginary hand.

"Well…" I got my snotty tone back with some difficulty. He was looking all lean and masculine. I can't be trusted with lean or masculine. "It's late. I'm sure you have to get to work tomorrow," I said, and turned away with resolute good intentions.

"I'm taking the day off."

I practically stumbled over my own feet as I turned back toward him. "You? The dark detective?"

His scowl deepened. "I've taken time off before."

"I must have been busy that hour."

"You still pissed because I didn't have more time to screw you?"

For a second I almost considered remaining above such adolescent banter, but the moment passed like a bullet from a semi automatic. "I'm pissed because you had time to screw everyone…" I stopped myself. I didn't really know if he had slept with everyone or not. But it didn't matter anymore. I was perfectly happy with my current guy. He was intelligent, intuitive and well read. That was so much better than irritating, insane and, well—

"I didn't sleep with her," he said.

Anger spouted up in me like Old Faithful on Viagra. "Well, I'm sorry if I interrupted before you could get the job done."

"I told you before," he said. "I was questioning her."

"Really? It looked more like mouth-to-mouth."

"I was on a case."

"What case?"

"A case that I can't talk about."

“Do they always tell you not to talk about who you sleep with?”

"Listen, I think we've got a bad cop in the department. Things aren't…" He stopped himself, rose abruptly to his feet, barely wincing at the sudden movement. “I guess this was a bad idea.”

“You bet your nuts it was.” We stared at each other. I knew better than to open my mouth again, but the words came nevertheless. “Why’d you come here anyway, Rivera?”

He turned away. “I shouldn’t have bothered you.”

I drew a slow, steadying breath. “Maybe I shouldn’t have kicked you in the balls either.”

He snorted, narrowed his eyes and turned back. “Is that an apology, McMullen?”

I shrugged a little. “Probably the best you’re going to get.”

He smiled and lifted his hand. For a moment I thought he was going to touch my face. I braced myself for the impact. But he took a step back and sobered immediately.

“Andrews is getting out of jail,” he said.

The floor jolted beneath my feet. I felt the blood rush from my face, felt my knees buckle. “Jackson Andrews?”

“Yeah.”

I sat down hard in my kitchen chair. Andrews had had his hand in numerous criminal activities but was best known as the inventor of a dangerous blend of chemicals called Intensity. From the little I knew of the situation, his incarceration had done almost nothing to slow its distribution. "When?"

"Today."

"Today!" I jolted from my trance. "Shit, Rivera. That means…" I could barely force out the words. "He's already loose."

He nodded, sober as a nightmare.

"Couldn't you have waited a little longer to tell me?" The words were weak. It's a bad sign when I can't even issue sarcasm with decent volume.

"I'm sorry," he said, and wonder of wonders, he actually looked sorry. "I didn't think you'd want me to…" He paused, atypically uncertain. "I didn't want to interfere in your life."

Since when? I wondered, but I didn't say it out loud.

"When you said there was someone parked on your street, I…" He blew out a slow breath, shook his head once. "I need you to keep your security system armed, Chrissy."

I nodded. "I really did think I had the door locked."

"You did."

I stared at him.

He glanced away. "I had an extra key made before we split up."

"You have a key?"

"You were always getting yourself in scrapes. I wanted to make sure I could get in if I needed to."

I tried to dredge up the appropriate amount of rage, but I was tired.

"You have to be more careful." He sounded tired, too.

"Okay." I try not to be compliant. Hell, sometimes I try not to even be reasonable. Or maybe that's just what my God-given DNA demands of me. But Jackson Andrews was certifiably insane. And the thought of him on the loose made me want to move to the Dominican Republic with a bodyguard named Hercules, or maybe Death Ray.

"And keep your drapes pulled," he added.

"All right."

"Do you still have the gun Manderos gave you?"

I shook my head. Blood was beginning to return to my cerebellum. My face felt warm. "I didn't have a permit. I couldn't keep it. It's against the law for me to carry—"

"I don't give a shit!" He spat out the words. I refrained from taking a step back, from fainting at his admittance. Rivera was cop to the core. He probably had his badge tattooed on his spleen.

He glanced away, jaw set. "You need some protection."

"I have Harlequin." I jerked my head toward the backyard, where my Great Dane was probably hiding behind one of the two landscaping boulders that graced my humble property. Harley doesn't like controversy.

Rivera turned his head at the mention of the dog I'd once thought of as our love child. "He's too big to carry in your purse."

"So is a knee."

He scowled. I nodded toward his balls.

"But it's pretty effective in a pinch."

He didn't laugh, but some sort of light shone in his dark coffee eyes. If I tried really hard, I could almost believe it was admiration. "Where's your spray?"

I tilted my head.

"The pepper spray I got you. Where is it?"

"In my purse."

"Get it."

"Listen, Rivera…" I was getting angry again. I mean, I know I hadn't been all sweetness and light thus far in this little transaction, but kneeing him in the groin had been an honest mistake. Really. And he had no right to tell me what to do. "It's very nice that you still carry a torch for me but—"

"Show me the pepper spray and I'll let you get to sleep," he said.

Sleep, he knew, was tantamount to chocolate on the Richter scale of pleasure for me.

I went to get my purse. I like to leave it in a heap on a kitchen chair. Retrieving it from said chair, I plopped it atop the table. Then I rummaged through it for a while, found a cherry sucker I'd gotten from my bank, two tampons that had escaped from their little protective sleeves and a tube of lip balm I'd mourned the loss of long ago. But no defense spray.

"I must have put it in my jacket pocket," I said, but when I glanced up, Rivera was glowering at me, eyes angry and body language unspeakable.

"Get it," he said.

"I left it at the office." I was just lying now. I had no idea what I had done with the damn pepper spray. I'm not an idiot. Really, I'm not. But I don't like to spend a lot of time on paranoia about being mugged by some lurking psychotic. It's hard enough just to pay the bills and keep my bathroom scale from performing treason.

"You lost it, didn't you?" he asked.

"No, I didn't lose it."

"Then get it."

"I told you—"

"God dammit, McMullen!" Stepping forward, he grabbed my arms.

And suddenly all the air was sucked out of the house. Maybe it was sucked out of the entire universe.

"What are you trying to do?" His voice had gone deep and dangerous again. His lips were a hard, straight line.

I swallowed, watching those lips. "I don't know what you're talking about."

He seemed to be watching my lips too. "I need you to—"

I blinked, shivered, tried not to be an idiot. "To…?" I said, but just then he slammed his mouth against mine.

Chapter 3

Violent mood swings—try 'em, you'll like 'em.
—*Crazy Bet, who may not have been quite as crazy as she seemed*

I tried to stop him. Tried to pull away, but the kiss was burning a hole straight through my lips to my pituitary gland. And that's where I keep the command center for my hormones. They were coming alive like Pop Rocks in battery acid by the time he pushed me away.

"God dammit, McMullen! What the hell are you trying to do to me?"

My mind was a jumble. My knees felt unhinged and my emotions were roiling like the Red Sea. That's the only explanation I have for my next action.

I slapped him. That's right. I slapped him across the face like a wide-eyed starlet in a grade-B movie. One minute I was standing there, limp as a lettuce leaf in his arms, and the next I was cracking him across the cheek with all the force made possible by terror and estrogen toxicity. The strike of my palm against his face sounded like a gunshot in my tiny kitchen. He didn't even flinch. I slapped him again. Nothing changed. He didn't step back, didn't turn away. If anything, his eyes just burned a little brighter.

Rage ripped through me, exacerbated by disappointment, guilt, and a shitload of emotions I wasn't prepared to address.

"What am I trying to do to you?" The words were raspy. I was leaning toward him as if braced against a bungee cord.

That muscle in his jaw jumped again. "I didn't plan to come here."

"Then why did you?"

He stared at my lips, then let his gaze slip lower. I was conservatively dressed in a baggy T-shirt and frayed denim shorts, but I might as well have been wearing a blood red corset and thigh-gripping garters. I swear he could see through my shirt all the way to my breast bone. And my breasts. Which were unfettered. I said I was dressed conservatively. I didn't say I was crazy enough to wear a bra in triple-digit temperatures. But my nipples were puckering despite the heat. I'm sure it had nothing to do with Rivera, though he seemed to have come a step closer somehow.

"Why do you think, Chrissy?" he asked, and raised his dark mocha eyes to mine. They were steaming. Swear to God, steaming like a sweet demon's.

I swallowed, cocking back my head a little. I was getting that feeling again. That horrible weak-kneed feeling that had nothing to do with released criminals or unbridled fear. But I checked my wobbling instincts and made a play for a snappy comeback.

"I think you must have had a slow day at the precinct," I said. "Run out of jaywalkers to waterboard?"

"That's right," he said. "So I came to torment you."

"Well, you can just go find someone else to play with. I don't need you making—" Just then he took that tiny step that separated us. Every nerve ending sizzled like Jimmy Dean's finest. And that was even before he kissed my neck.

My knees tried to buckle, my head tried to pop off my neck and roll onto the floor, but I was ready for their traitorous ways and braced myself against the weakness.

"Making what?" he whispered. His breath felt cool against my overheated skin.

I tried to think. Tried to move away. Neither attempt was wildly successful. In fact, I may have gone catatonic and somehow slipped even closer to him. "Making a mess of my life," I breathed.

He slid his fingertips up my arm. "Doing okay with that on your own?"

I stifled a shiver, but my voice sounded funny when I spoke. "I'm not on my own," I said. Or maybe I croaked. I hate like hell to admit it, but it might very well have been a croak.

"That's right." His gaze shifted to mine, somber as a dirge, sharp as a firecracker. His hand slipped into the baggy sleeve of my shirt. "What's the lucky bastard's name again?"

I opened my mouth to answer, but just then he brushed his thumb across my left nipple and I was entirely too involved in remaining upright to form any sort of articulate answer. My lips felt dry. I licked them.

"McMullen?" The whisper washed against my face. "What's his name?"

I wanted to answer, but my larynx seemed to have forgotten how to function. He had slipped his hand out of my sleeve and by some kind of forbidden magic seemed to be stroking my belly beneath my shirt.

He tilted his head at me. His devilish lips cocked into the semblance of a grin. "You haven't forgotten, have you?"

"Of course I haven't forgotten." Turns out my larynx worked after all, but only in a manner that issued a grating sort of demonic sound.

His mouth hitched up a little farther, highlighting the narrow scar that sliced through the right corner of his lips. "Who is he?" he asked.

My shoulder blades were pressed up against the wall now. We were skin to skin. "Why do you want to know?"

His knuckles bumped down my midline, over my navel, lower. I suppressed a shiver and refrained from closing my eyes and passing into delirium.

"I want to make sure he's good enough for you." His fingers slipped into my waistband.

"He's good," I rasped.

His lips may have jerked just a little, but his diabolical fingers didn't stop their downward quest. "Does he make you squeak?"

"What?" The word was little more than a breath against his face. He tightened his jaw and took a steadying breath.

"You squeak," he whispered. "High pitched and almost silent when you come." His fingers flicked open the button on my shorts.

I closed my eyes and chanted the rosary to myself. "I do not."

"Maybe not with him." He moved a fraction of a millimeter closer. I would have sworn there wasn't that much space between us.

"Not with anyone."

"There are others?" His tone was gritty, his body hard as hell against mine.

My mind was beginning to spin like water twirling down a toilet. He had moved his hand around my waist and was trailing his fingers down my spine. I arched my back, involuntarily pushing my breasts against his chest. "I don't need any others."

"Nameless is that good?" he asked and slid his devilish fingers inside my shorts.

"He has a name." I just wished to God I could remember it.

"Is it Francois?" he whispered.

"You wish," I rasped. Francois just happened to be a certain battery-run appliance I keep in a drawer beside my bed. In my current overheated condition I had no idea how Rivera knew of its existence, much less its name. “I don’t need that anymore.” That was an out-and-out lie. I’d had an impromptu date with Francois less than twenty-four hours earlier. But apparently he hadn’t been quite up to the job of dousing the inferno. “I threw it out.”

“Really?”

No, I thought and prayed he wouldn’t look in my drawers.

“I kind of feel sorry for it,” he said, squeezing my ass with one long-fingered hand.

Desire sparked off in every direction like embers from a forest fire. I managed to remain earthbound. “I think you’re just feeling sorry for yourself.”

He lifted one brow.

“Because I don’t need you.” I panted.

He grinned. “What are you feeling?” he asked, and pressed his considerable length against my thigh.

I did my best not to push back. Sometimes my best sucks the big one. “Nothing.” The word was little more than a gasp as he slid his cock closer to my core.

He shook his head once, eyes never leaving mine. “You used to be a pretty fair liar yourself, McMullen.”

“I’m not lying,” I lied.

“That’s just because you prefer to do it standing up.”

It took me a second to understand his meaning. To which I shot back, “Shows what you know.”

“I know you,” he whispered.

“And you let me go.”

“Fuck that,” he said, and tightening his grip on my ass, pulled me marginally closer. “You’re the one who called it off.”

I laughed. It sounded like something between a hyena’s wail and the bray of a wild ass. “What did you expect me to do, Rivera? Shrug? Laugh? Oh, well, yeah, my boyfriend sometimes sleeps with other women. Sometimes sleeps with whores with big boobs and—”

“I was undercover!” he snarled.

“Under the covers, you mean.”

“Holy shit, McMullen, I never slept with her,” he said, and slid both hands into my shorts.

I refrained from devouring him whole.

“How many times do I have to tell you I’m not interested?” I asked, but my fingers seemed to have become twisted in the hair at the back of his head.

“Nameless have you that enamored, does he?” he asked, and sliding his hands lower, he effectively displaced my sloppy shorts.

“He has a name."

“I don’t believe you.”

“That’s because you’re a psychotic narcissist with sadistic tendencies.”

“Quit talking dirty,” he warned.

“You’re sick.”

"You're horny," he said, and dropping his head to my left nipple, sucked it through my shirt.

I shrieked. He snarled. Harlequin howled at the door.

Maybe it was the thought of our erstwhile love child finding us fornicating on the kitchen floor that broke me from the spell. Whatever the case, I found my head and scrambled away, bouncing along the wall like a skittering virgin. "Marc!" I yelped. "His name's Marc."

Rivera followed me with smoldering eyes. A dozen emotions burned in them. None looked safe. Several looked as naughty as hell. "Marc what?"

I eased around the kitchen table. "I'm not going to tell you."

He followed me slowly. One may have been able to call it stalking. "Mark Wahlberg?"

Good God! I wished. "I'm not making him up, Rivera."

"Mark Harmon?"

Harmon was a hottie, but I kept strictly to reality. "He's a doctor."

He stopped in his tracks. His expression changed from hot-charged horniness to anger in the drop of a pair of boxers. "Not another nutcase psychiatrist."

I blinked at him. "What are you talking about?"

"If I remember correctly, your last psychiatrist friend tried to kill you with a hunting knife."

"That's not true."

“He was in this house, planning to kill you with a—”

“Fillet knife.” It felt good to correct him.

He raised a brow.

“It was a…" I began, then realized the stupidity of our current argument. “Marcus is a very capable doctor.”

“Capable,” he said, and laughed out loud. “Is that what you’re settling for these days?”

“Screw you!”

“I’m game if you are.” He took another step closer.

I tried to move away, but my legs were stuck on the screwing idea.

It was then that my phone rang from inches away. I jumped, squawked, then grabbed it like a lifeline, knowing it was Elaine even before it reached my ear.

“What’s wrong?” She spoke before I had the chance to say hello.

“Laney!” My tone was desperate. My throat ached with need. “Rivera’s here.” I don’t know what I expected her to do about it. I don’t even know what I *wanted* her to do about it, but she didn’t hesitate an instant.

“Let me talk to him.”

I removed the phone from my ear and handed it to him, hands shaking like a heroine addict’s.

He deepened his scowl, eyes steady and onyx dark, but he took it. “Yeah?”

I could hear Elaine's voice on the far end but couldn't make out the words.

Rivera stood in silence for several seconds, listening, brows lowered, then, "I know."

Laney's voice could be heard again, slow and reasonable.

"I didn't plan it."

His body was taut. His lips twitched. He closed his eyes.

"All right," he said finally and handed me the phone. "Arm your fucking alarm," he said, and after one last smoldering glance, stalked out of my life.

Chapter 4

A true friend is one who's happy when you do good and is ready to plan a kick-ass prank when someone else does.
—Chrissy's brother Pete, while in high school…though the ensuing years haven't changed his philanthropic philosophy much

I stared after him for several seconds, then dropped into the nearest chair, exhausted and numb.

"Mac?" I could vaguely hear Laney's voice through the phone that drooped in my right hand.

I did a little more staring and blinking before I managed the Herculean task of pressing the phone back to my ear. "Yeah?"

"You okay?"

I shrugged, though I was pretty sure she couldn't see it from where she was. Which was on location in Matamata, New Zealand. Elaine Butterfield is a kick-ass actress, my best friend since grade school, and something of a weird-ass telepath, but generally she can't see my body motions unless she's there in front of me. I wished rather desperately that she was there right then, but she'd gotten married about a year earlier and tended to spend a good deal of time with her husband, a dweeby little nerd named J.D. Solberg.

"Yeah. Sure." I stared at my back door for a second and whined. It took me a moment to realize it wasn't me that sounded like an abandoned pup. It was Harley. Rising like an automaton, I trailed off to let him in. He slunk inside, swinging his boxy head left and right in search of Rivera. It's a well-known fact that even the most neglected kids love their deadbeat dads. "I'm fine."

"Is he gone?"

"Looks like it." I tried to buck up. "What'd you say to him?"

"I told him the truth."

"That he's a jackass?" I said, but I didn't really think he was a jackass. I thought I *should* think he was a jackass, but when I considered his ass I rarely had the equus asinus in mind.

"That you deserve more than a panting reunion once every few months," she said.

"Uh huh." I nodded dismally. "But did you threaten him with some kind of bodily harm or something, too?"

"I said he was being unfair to you."

This was kind of a disappointment. I mean, it's not as if I wanted Rivera hanging around or anything. But I would have preferred to know he wasn't that easy to dissuade from the whole panting reunion thing. Although, I have to admit, Brainy Laney Butterfield has amazing powers of persuasion. She's been convincing men to act like idiots ever since the advent of her boobs.

"I'm sorry," she said.

"For what?"

"That he left."

“Are you kidding me?” I said, and snorted. It was a first-class snort despite my exhaustion. “You did me a huge favor. I didn’t want him hanging around here.”

She remained silent. I fidgeted in the quiet. I’m never comfortable lying to Laney. She could make me fidget from another solar system. Silence is kind of like her own personal truth serum.

“Well…” I paused and sat down. “Most of me didn’t want him here.”

“My apologies to those bits that did.”

“Yeah, well…” I breathed deep and rotated my neck, beginning to relax a little as I fiddled with Harley’s ear. His search for Rivera had been fruitless and he had come to plop his snout on my thigh and give me the droopy eye. “Those bits are fickle.”

“And happy with Marc, right?”

I sat up a little straighter. Harley rolled his eyes up at me but didn‘t move his head. “Of course they’re happy with Marc. They’re thrilled with Marc. Did I tell you he sold out at the bookstore in Pinsk?”

“Do you mean Minsk?”

“No.”

“Okay. Well…that’s…exciting,” she said, and for a moment I almost wondered if she was being sarcastic. Laney does sarcasm so well it’s sometimes difficult to detect. I’m not always so subtle. “I’m just not sure what that does for your fickle bits.”

"My fickle bits are unimportant, Laney. Because I've changed. Grown up. I'm classy now."

"Instead of Irish?"

I ignored her. "I've learned to make chicken marsala."

"Really."

"I wash my car on a regular basis," I said, and didn't bother to add that my less-than-classy automobile sometimes rebelled by popping an orifice open at rather surprising moments…such as when I was driving down the interstate.

"Wow."

"And I'm reading…" I glanced toward the dog-eared romance novel on my coffee table, then searched for the classic I had begun six months earlier and lost a half an hour after that. "…The Sun Also Rises."

"Yikes."

"Because I now realize that cerebral stimulation is so much more important than a couple moments of gasping pleasure."

"Just a minute," she said, then spoke to her husband, who was, apparently, in her vicinity. "J.D., honey, send some burly guard to Mac's house will you? I think there's someone there impersonating her."

I tucked my bare feet up under my bottom against the hard wood of the chair. "You're hilarious, Laney," I said.

"Yeah. When I'm finished with this film, I'm thinking of doing a stand-up routine in Vegas."

“Really?”

“No. Mac, listen, are you all right?”

“Of course I’m all right.” I imbued my tone with a marvelous blend of surprise and hauteur. “It’s not as if I’m languishing here alone without Rivera around to harass me.”

“I know.”

“I mean, he was always so high-maintenance anyway.”

“He did bring a certain level of excitement to the picture.”

“And now I have…” I paused. My mind had suddenly gone blank.

“Marc,” she said.

“Yes! Marc. He’s terrific.”

“Isn’t he just?”

“And brilliant.”

“I know.”

“And attractive.”

“He is.”

“And he’s sensitive.”

She sighed. “And there lies the problem.”

“I have no idea what you’re talking about.” I tried to sound offended, but mostly I really didn’t want to know what she was talking about.

“I love you, Mac, but you don’t do sensitive.”

“What? Sensitively lies at the very core of what I do. Who I am. I adore sensitive.”

“Mac, honey, think about it. You were raised with a family whose main form of entertainment involved noisy bodily functions.”

"That's not true."

"Peter," she said. "Could he or could he not sing the national anthem with body parts other than his lips?"

I gritted my teeth into a smile. "Well, I like to think Pete is not indicative of my family's—"

"And didn't Michael have some special skill he liked to—"

"I don't see what that has to do with—"

"Belching!" she said. "He could project belch. Make it seem like someone else was doing it. Usually the shy little girl that sat next to him in English, or the teacher who had just finished lunch. But I think James was the real champion in this little contest. What was his talent? I can't quite seem to—"

"Listen, Laney!" I snapped, then calmed my voice and drew a cleansing breath. "The McMullens may not be Illinois's founding family, but it's not as if we're knuckle-dragging Neanderthals." I thought about that for a moment, remembered my brothers cackling gleefully as they planned yet another hilarious prank, and moved on. "And even if we are, that by no means precludes me from being able to become close to someone who is articulate yet—"

"Shadow puppets!"

Shit!

"He could make shadows with his hands that looked like copulating—"

"So what!" I may have shouted the words. Fucking barbarian brothers. I hated them all.

"Maybe that's why I appreciate sensitivity so much. Maybe that's why it touches my soul like nothing else."

"Touches your soul?" Her tone was Sahara dry.

I squeezed my eyes shut. "Did I tell you Marc wrote me a poem?"

"A poem?" She sounded increasingly dubious, bordering on disbelief.

"Yes. It was wonderful. Soulful and eloquent and endlessly…creative."

I could almost hear the wince in her voice. "You didn't laugh at him, did you?"

"Of course I didn't laugh at him."

"Not even a little?"

"No!"

"No snorting or eye rolling?"

"Laney!"

"What? You hate poetry."

"I do not hate poetry."

"You told me you hated poetry."

"I said I didn't understand poetry."

"You slept through the entire free verse class in middle school lit."

See, there's the problem with having lifelong friends. They have memories like pachyderms. "Well, those were boring."

"And Marc's wasn't?"

"Absolutely not."

"What was it about?"

Oh hell! I had no idea what it had been about. It had been thirty-seven stanzas long. Thirty-seven!

No one should be expected to stay awake that damn—

"Mac?"

"It was about the sea."

"The sea."

I waved a wild hand at nothing in particular, then brought it back to rub my eyes. "It doesn't matter what it was about. Marc's wonderful."

"I know."

"He's smart and…well read…and neat."

"And there's nothing more fun than a man who organizes his socks."

I paused for a moment, realized she was being facetious, and launched into defense mode. "I don't need fun, Laney." I jerked to my feet. Harley stood, too, looking offended. "I need…"

"What?" she asked. "What do you need?"

"Stability and maturity and…" I motioned vaguely toward the world at large.

"Sex?"

"Sensitivity!"

"Screw sensitivity."

"Laney!" I had rarely heard her use such foul language. Her father the preacher would turn over in his grave. If he had a grave. Which he did not because he was still alive.

"Or have you already?" she asked.

I gasped, eyes wide. "Are you asking if I've slept with Marcus?"

"Yes."

I pursed my lips, scowled at the cupboards. "We haven't quite gotten around to that yet."

"Haven't gotten around to it."

"I thought it was a good idea to wait."

There was a long, pensive silence. "Can I ask why?"

"And this from a preacher's daughter!" I tried to sound disapproving. But it was like scolding a nun. Laney was, and has always been, my moral compass. "Because it's the right thing to do."

"Mac," she said, and sighed, long and slow, "you propositioned our calculus teacher."

I felt my face flush. "Well…it wasn't as if I was a student at thc time."

"The last cords of Pomp and Circumstances had barely died away."

"That's simply not true."

She remained silent. I looked down at my bare feet, shuffled them a little. "Okay, it's true," I said. "But he was hot, and I've changed!"

"You're still Christina McMullen, though, right?"

"The new, improved version."

"And the new, improved version doesn't like sex?"

Just the word sex did bad things to my corked-up equilibrium. I squirmed a little.

"Is that why you've abstained?"

"If you must know, it's because we don't want the physicality to get ahead of our emotional growth," I said.

"Are you serious?"

"Yes, I'm serious."

"He said that?"

"Y…" I caught myself. "We decided that together."

She was silent. I was determined to wait it out. After all, I had the moral high ground. "What?" I snapped finally.

"I'm trying to imagine Rivera saying such a thing. But I can't, not in my wildest dreams."

Some weird-ass emotion zipped through me like an out-of-control lightning bolt. "What's Rivera doing in your dreams?" I snarled.

There was a moment of stunned silence, then a very slow, "What?"

I dropped my head into my free hand. It was so clear suddenly. I was obviously losing my mind. Possibly from the lack of sex. The day I worried about Brainy Laney Butterfield, the most gorgeous woman in the world, lusting after a guy I was interested in was the day the earth disintegrated into whipped cream and we'd all have ice cream sundaes. "I said…" I shrugged. "Turns out I'm nuts."

"Oh, Mac," she sighed.

"See, it's a good thing Rivera left. He obviously makes me crazy."

"Well…it's nice to have an excuse."

I exhaled carefully, sat back down. "You know the truth?"

"Probably, but tell me anyway."

"When he kissed me—"

"He kissed you?"

I nodded to no one. "I thought my shorts were going to fry right off my ass."

"I'm sorry I ruined that for you. It sounds very entertaining."

"You probably saved me from second degree burns. He's—" I stopped myself before things got any weirder. "I'm better off without him. Right? I mean, no one needs all that drama."

She didn't answer. I felt my defenses weaken and fortified them with the kind of self-help talk Cosmopolitan dishes up like M&Ms.

"Definitely! I'm definitely better off without him. He doesn't even know the meaning of monogamy."

"Are you sure?"

"I quizzed him," I said. "He didn't know what sesquipedalian meant either."

"Chrissy—"

"He cheated on me!" I spat out the words.

"He says he didn't."

"He's lying."

"His captain confirmed his story."

"You know how cops are. They stick together. It's their code."

I thought she was going to speak, so I rushed on.

"I know a lie when I hear one. I'm a psychologist. Do you know how many pathetic women I see who eat shit day after day after day? I mean, they know they're being played, but they're so insecure…so afraid of being alone that they pretend everything's fine."

She was silent. The quiet took a little steam out of my sails.

"I'm not afraid of being alone," I said, but my voice was very soft.

Still she said nothing.

"Hell, I like being alone," I said, picking up a little steam again. "No one to tell me what to do." Harlequin plopped down next to my chair. "No one to feed me a bunch of lies."

"Are you really sure he was—"

"I'm not going to be one of those women, Laney."

"Okay, but you two seemed really good at the wedding."

I stifled a sigh. Laney's wedding had been a magical time, a couple of days sprinkled in fairy dust and frosted with chocolate dreams. Despite the fact that the most amazing woman in the world had vowed to love, honor and cohabitate with the geekiest geek on the planet, their wedding had been idyllic. The setting had been majestic, the bride radiant. As for Rivera, he had been charming, attentive and sexy.

"He was different then," I said.

"Was he?"

"Yes. Maybe it was just because he didn't have any of his old flames there to pant over. But as soon as we returned to L.A., he changed back."

"Or you did?"

"What?" Something twisted in my stomach. It wasn't guilt. I mean, I had nothing to feel guilty about. It wasn't as if I had done anything to sabotage our relationship. He was the one with the roving eye…and roving other stuff, too. "I was the same as always. My usual fabulous self. But listen…it's late." I glanced at my wrist. Which was just ridiculous. My watch had broken years ago. "I have an early appointment in the morning."

"Chrissy—"

"Lori Bernstein." I felt fidgety again and glanced into the quiet darkness of my living room. "She's as kooky as a windup clock. Thinks her cat is spying on her." I stroked between Harlequin's ears. "Has to talk in code when he's around."

"Mac—"

"Then there's Howard Lepinski." Howard was a peculiar little man with an eccentric sense of fashion and an odd need to discuss luncheon options. "Do you remember him? He's just as screwy as…" I paused, remembering the change in him. "Well, actually, he's doing pretty well." I scowled at nothing in particular. Harlequin stared at me with adoring eyes. If I ever found a man who looked at me like that, I'd take him home, tie him to my bedpost and feed him sugared dates. "He's in love." Something twisted in my stomach. It wasn't jealousy. That would be stupid. "Did I tell you that? And she loves him back. Canary yellow socks and all. It's like a scene from a Joss Whedon—"

"It's all right to be scared."

"What?" I said the word with some emphasis. I'm a lot of things. Crazy, perhaps, being up toward the top of the list. But I'm not a coward.

"I was scared to fall in love with J.D., too."

I made a face, sorry she wasn't there to appreciate it. "That's because he's a dweeb."

"You need to talk to Rivera."

I swallowed, then snorted. "I *have* talked to Rivera."

"Shouting is not the same as talking, Mac."

"I talked. He lied."

"You don't know that."

"I do too know—"

"Mac!" The word was sharp. I can count the number of times on one elbow that I've heard Laney raise her voice. It shook me to the core, but I forced myself to defend my position.

"Marc uses a coaster with his beverages." The words were little more than a whisper.

"You are never going to be happy with a coaster man, Mac. That's why you're still with him."

I shook my head. "That doesn't even make any sense."

"He's safe."

"What's wrong with safe? There's nothing wrong with safe."

"There is if you're an adrenaline junkie."

"I'm not an—"

"It's what drew you to Rivera in the first place."

"That might be true." I remembered the first time I met him. He'd accused me of murder. I considered braining him with my stiletto heel. Typical everyday boy meets girl. Except that the boy had magical hands and a smoldering gaze that sucked me in like the eye of a tornado.

"I know he's a lot of work," she said. "Volatile and intense and kind of crazy."

"Kind of?"

"But there's more to him than that. You don't want to believe it, but you know there is."

"Are you kidding me? He's as shallow as a foot bath. And a royal pain in the ass."

"He's hard-working and sexy and—"

"He's nominally attractive."

She didn't even bother to laugh. "And moralistic in his own way."

"Then why won't he explain that b…" I stifled the word I intended to use. Insults would only make Laney believe I had strong feelings on the subject. I still remembered the blonde's face, her hair, her rocking body. I hate memories.

"He's stubborn," she said.

"He is—" I agreed, ready to mount my high horse, but she interrupted.

"Just like you. This is never going to be a smooth ride, Chrissy. Not for you. Not for him."

"I want a smooth ride."

"No, you don't. You think you do, but you don't. You need a challenge and depth and intensity."

"Marc can give me those things."

"Rivera cares about you."

"Marc cares about me."

"Really?" She was beginning to sound tired. "What'd he get you for your birthday?"

I felt my stomach flutter, tossed my head, fiddled with Harley's collar. "What does that matter?"

"Just answer."

I straightened my back. "He got me something really lovely, actually."

"Lovely?"

I rolled my eyes, knowing I'd used the wrong adjective. I should have said "cute" or "nice" or even "nifty." And I definitely shouldn't have gone for an English accent. I sounded constipated. Even more so when I spoke again. "Listen, I'd like to sit here and let you defame my boyfriend, but it's late and I—"

"Was it a scarf?"

"No, it wasn't a scarf." Now I sounded affronted and constipated.

"Was it roses?"

"No."

She sat in silence. I fidgeted again. "Okay, it wasn't *just* roses…there were carnations, too."

She inhaled softly, as if choosing her words carefully. "It doesn't seem like he knows you very—"

"It's better than cacti!" Once when I'd been hospitalized, Rivera had brought me a cactus. A saguaro to be exact. I'm not sure what that means, but I don't think it's good.

"It's growing nicely."

I scowled at nothing in particular…or everything in general. "Damn thing won't die."

"If someone climbed over the fence Rivera built for you, they'd have to be careful of the cactus. And that's not even counting the dog he bought you."

I glanced down at Harlequin. I could disparage the cactus, but not the mutt. He had Eeyore eyes. No way could I disparage a mutt with Eeyore eyes.

"Or the pepper spray he makes you carry around."

"So he's paranoid," I said.

"He worries about you."

"I don't think paranoia is a real good reason to stay with someone."

"Geez, Mac, in a couple months he'll probably be digging a moat around your house and putting armed guards on the parapets."

"I don't have any parapets."

"He'll build them."

"I don't even know what parapets—"

"I just want you to be happy."

"I'm happy with Marc," I said.

She didn't sigh like a long-suffering mother hen, but I thought I heard it in her tone. "Okay. Well, I have to go. They want to start shooting the dueling scene before the fog lifts in the morning. Call me tomorrow, will you?"

"Okay," I agreed, and hung up, singing Donna Fargo's old hit about her inexplicable and kind of ridiculous euphoria.

Chapter 5

Families—a funny little version of hell.
—Phillip Murray, who didn't really find families all that amusing

"I met someone." Phillip Murray sat in the winged client chair in my office in Eagle Rock. He was not a large man. Five eight in his stocking feet, he was slim and plain and unassuming, until he smiled. Then the heavens opened and the celestial choirs could be heard singing their alleluias. It was a no-holds-barred, devious, beatific, angelic demon grin.

"Someone special?" I asked.

He shrugged, but his eyes were sparkling and his lips were tilted up a little, crinkling the corners of his mouth.

I couldn't help but smile in return. Maybe that's why the world was falling in love with him. He'd started out doing commercials for hand cream and car wax but was beginning to get some small parts in some big movies. "Who is he?"

"His name's Gregory. Greg. Greg Fremont."

"Is he an actor?"

He rolled his eyes. They weren't bad either. An interesting mercury with flecks of steel gray, fringed by dark lashes that were thick enough to carpet a hallway. "I'm gay, Ms McMullen," he said, "not stupid."

"So…not an actor," I guessed.

"He's a mechanic."

"Really?" I asked, although I'm not sure why. Maybe my head wasn't totally in the game. I mean, the previous night had been a little more exciting than I needed it to be. After Rivera's departure I hadn't slept well. And by that I mean I'd awoken once before my alarm sounded. For me, insomnia is when I'm still conscious when my head hits the pillow.

Phillip cranked up the right corner of his mouth, eyes sparking mischief. "Homos can be mechanics, you know."

I nodded. "I hear they can even work in construction these days."

He raised his brows at me. The room went silent. "Are shrinks allowed to say that?"

"I—" I considered defending myself. For a moment I even thought about telling him I'd been fretful and crazy and horny all night, bedeviled by weird dreams that involved parapets and, strangely enough, moats filled with whipping cream. But I'm a professional. "No. They're not," I said. "I'm sorry."

He laughed. And that was another thing that made him über likable. He had a deep, rich belly laugh that would better suit a man with a beard and a reindeer sleigh. It was the kind of laugh that made you want to sing along. "I'm not offended."

"Thank you. I really am sorry."

He shrugged. His shoulders were moderate-sized and covered by a well-fitted polo shirt that revealed just enough golden skin at the V of his neck. “I think you’ll agree that I have bigger fish to fry. Like the fact that I’m certifiably insane.”

“You’re not insane,” I assured him. He was, however, somewhat troubled. Apparently it kind of messes with your head when your parents give you up for adoption and keep your two siblings. Personally, I had often fantasized about being part of that scenario. Growing up in someone else’s dysfunction would have probably been therapeutic for me. But maybe Phillip was made of more sensitive stuff. He’d always known he was adopted, but he’d only learned about the other two children seven months ago. Five days later, he’d shown up at my office with a box of Crispy Creams in one hand and a gun in the other. He’d been showing up every Wednesday at four o’clock sharp ever since.

“What am I, then?” he asked. There was laughter in his voice, but a sober backdrop lit his pretty, heavy-lashed eyes.

“Sounds like you’re in love,” I said.

He gave me an exaggerated look that suggested both surprise and reproach. “I don’t believe in love.”

I raised my brows. “You don’t believe it exists or—”

“I think it’s a euphemism for lust.”

“Really? Then how do you explain couples who stay together for sixty plus years?”

"Dementia?"

I didn't laugh out loud. It didn't seem like it was my job to encourage such talk, but I did smile a little. "What about your mother?"

I watched his reaction. He was quite an accomplished actor and could almost hide it, but I saw his jaw tighten just the slightest amount. "Obviously she wasn't a believer either," he said.

I let the words lie undisturbed for a moment, then, "I meant your adoptive mother."

"Oh." There was a shitload of complexity in that one word, an intriguing blend of gratitude, guilt and confusion. His shoulders slumped, and his expression softened.

"Do you think she believes in love?" According to Phillip, he'd been an undersized asthmatic with an over-sized attitude when Lisa Murray had taken him in.

"She doesn't count," he said.

"Because…"

"She also believes in the tooth fairy."

"Phillip—"

"She *told* me there was a tooth fairy." He shrugged and grinned. That grin had probably gotten him out of more trouble than most people get into.

The man was too charming for his own good. I kept a somber expression. "She also told you that she'd love you whether you were an ax murderer or an actor."

His wince was almost imperceptible, which, strangely, seemed to make it more powerful. "Do you think I made the wrong choice?" he asked.

"The point is," I said, "she loves you."

"Well, that's because she's…" He paused. Irreverent and sharp-witted as he was, he couldn't manage to belittle his mother's enduring adoration. "Okay, maybe love exists, but only as it pertains to a mother and child."

I stared at him, using my wise face. My smart-ass face was tired.

"And…" He opened his hands, palms up, as he worked his way carefully through the quagmire. "Maybe it doesn't have to be a biological bond."

I nodded like an ancient sage. "Okay, if love exists and it doesn't have to be biological, doesn't it seem probable that it can also exist between two adults?"

He narrowed his eyes and seemed to be ruminating, then said with absolute certainty, "Nope."

"Really?"

"Think about it." He leaned forward, animated and earnest. "How many marriages break up?"

"Just because they break up doesn't necessarily mean they don't care about each other."

"So they can be in love and still want to kill each other?"

I actually thought that was feasible, but I also thought he was trying to hijack the conversation. "I think they can have considerable differences and still have a strong emotional bond."

"In other words, they can want the other person's head on a spit." Phillip was currently a plebe in a miniseries set in ancient Rome, and sometimes the setting colored his language. "Well, hell, if that's the case, I've been in love a half dozen times."

"Okay." I decided to work from where we were. "So are you in love now?"

"I don't think so. I haven't considered killing Greg once yet."

"Tell me about him."

He put the pads of his fingers together and stared into the distance. "He's oddly fond of the combustible engine."

"And you still speak to him? That must tell us something." Phillip didn't own a car. In fact, he was quite an outspoken proponent for public transportation, which, actually, was one of L.A.'s better jokes on humanity. Citizens of the greater Los Angeles area have been known to drive from their garages to their mailboxes just to get the frcc coupons that doomed rainforests from Brazil to Alberta. But Americans' penchant for vehicular overuse was only one of Phillip's causes. Institutions such as the Humane Society and Greenpeace considered him a demigod.

"Well…" He shrugged. "He's got a really nice head of hair."

"Hair?"

He grinned a little. "That might be code for ass."

"How about his personality?"

He canted his head. "His what?"

I gave him a look.

He sighed. "The man's a Neanderthal. He lives in a cave."

"Literally?"

He returned my look. "No. But if there were any unspoken-for caverns in L.A., I'm sure he'd take up residence. His apartment's a mess."

"And that bothers you?"

He shrugged. "Not as much as his accent. It sounds like he just escaped from the Hazard County demolition derby."

"Anything else?"

"He dresses like a redneck time traveler. Pearl snaps on his shirts and everything."

"Sounds like a match made in heaven."

"Did I tell you about his hair?"

"So you're just seeing him because he's attractive." See how I tone down my own redneck roots when I'm in professional mode? Yee-haw.

"Well…" He shrugged. "That and his dogs."

"He has dogs?"

"A couple," he said, but his tone almost sounded defensive.

"Two dogs is a lot of responsibility," I said, thinking of Harlequin. But maybe a Great Dane counted as one hundred and two dogs.

"Actually there are six of them."

“Six.” That was a lot of dogs.

He looked as if he rather wished he hadn’t started down this road. “Six greyhounds.”

“Oh?” Now we were getting somewhere, I thought, but I kept my tone level. I can be sneaky if I want to. “Does he race them?”

He stared at me for several seconds, mouth tilted slightly as he contemplated my question. “You know he doesn’t race them,” he said finally.

I raised my hands, palms up. “He’s a messy Southerner with no positive attributes other than the physical. I naturally assumed…” I let my voice trail off.

He glanced out the window, hands tense on the arms of the chair, before he turned back. “He fosters them.”

“Oh? From the Grey Save organization?”

“Maybe.” He was being evasive. That meant I had touched a nerve. Go, me.

“I’ve heard good things,” I said, keeping my voice level.

He shrugged. “It doesn’t mean he should be canonized or anything.”

“Six big foster dogs in one apartment.”

“It’s a two-bedroom.”

I almost laughed out loud, but that would have been unprofessional. “Maybe just listed as a lesser saint, then.”

“I know what you’re thinking,” he said. “But you’re way off-base. I don’t have a thing for him because of his sensitive soul.”

"Okay."

He scowled. Clearly I had not sold the "okay."

"Love is just a figment of Hollywood's overdeveloped—"

"McMullen!"

I snapped my attention to the left. Lieutenant Jack Rivera stood there, right hand on the doorknob, left on the jamb. A half dozen unexpected expletives tried to escape my mouth, but I held them at bay like a real live grownup. "I'm sorry," I said, and gave him the benefit of a prissy smile. "But you'll have to wait for an appointment like all my other clients."

"We need to talk," hc growled.

I upped the wattage of my smile. "I'm sure your returning psychosis seems particularly disturbing, Lieutenant. But you'll have to speak to my secretary about my next available—"

"Listen—" he snarled, but Shirley, my super-secretary, interrupted him.

"I'm sorry, Ms McMullen." She spoke from the hallway, sounding professional and harried and more than a little pissed. "I told him you were with someone."

Rivera's gaze, dark and hard and brooding, snapped to Phillip's. "I need to talk to her," he said.

Phillip raised a brow, first at Rivera then at me. For a petite, self-proclaimed pacifistic, he seemed pretty unfazed.

"LAPD, lieutenant," Rivera said, and flipped open his badge. I was impressed by his self-control.

With Rivera, the flashing of the badge generally takes place before the salutations.

"Actor's Guild, plebe," Phillip countered.

"Listen…" Rivera said, and stepped into the room. He was looking pretty caveman himself by the time I stood up and leapt into the fray.

"Surely this can wait until after Mr. Murray—" I began, but Rivera interrupted me.

"No!" he said. "It can't."

Phillip stood, too, but he kept his gaze on Rivera though he spoke to me. "I'm friends with Chief Haskell," he said. "Do you want me to give him a call?"

I snapped my gaze to his. Turns out little Phillip was no slacker in the balls department. "No. Thank you, Phillip. I'm very sorry for the interruption, but do you mind giving us a minute?"

He stared at me for a second, eyes asking a dozen questions at once. "No," he said finally, seeming to find answers I wasn't sure I had provided. "Of course not. I'll be outside if you need me."

"Thank you." I tried to keep my professional tone, but the surprises were coming at me rough and ready: Phillip was kind of a champion. Rivera was kind of a prick. Some things were more surprising than others.

A moment later, the room was empty except for Rivera and myself. I stood beside my desk, pissed and stiff.

"Perhaps you weren't aware that this is actually my place of business," I said.

"Listen—" he began, but by then I had worked up a pretty good head of steam.

"Perhaps you didn't realize that this is actually my chosen career and that that"—I pointed toward the reception area, to where Phillip had just retreated and from which my front bell chimed—"is my client."

Rivera's jaw ticked, but he didn't glance toward the entrance. Instead, he kept his gaze as steady as a wolf's on my face. "What did you do after I left your house last night?" His voice was little more than a growl.

Surprise took me by surprise, but I didn't let it show on my face. "It's none of your business what I do in my spare time," I hissed, and hoped rather frantically that he didn't know about my date with Francois.

"That's bullshit!"

"That's not—"

"Dammit!" he snarled, then visibly pulled himself together and drew a deep breath. "Andrews was shot last night. A single bullet to the head."

"Jackson Andrews?" Just the sound of the name put a little tremor in my fingertips. I placed them carefully on the edge of my desk.

Voices murmured from the reception area. Rivera glanced in that direction now, but only for an instant before turning back to me.

"Is he…dead?" My voice was fraught with something that might have been hopefulness in a less charitable person.

"No."

Outside my office, the voices were getting louder. Two male tenors plus Shirley's bossy alto. Hers almost drowned them out. "I said she's busy at the moment."

"We understand that, ma'am." Male One's voice was low and reasonable.

Shirley's was neither. "If you understood that, sir, you'd already have your butts in the chairs like good little boys."

"We're here on official business. We have a—"

"Sit your asses down!" she ordered, but I barely heard her. The world around me was sinking slowly inward, caving in under my feet. Rivera's haunting eyes were all I could see.

"You think I did it," I said.

He watched me, face expressionless, hiding a thousand secrets. "You knew he was free."

I shook my head.

"He hurt Elaine," he added. "You're a vengeful person."

"But how would I even…" I ran out of words. He filled in the blanks.

"You have a lot of friends."

"No, I—"

"Friends who don't mind breaking a few laws."

"That's crazy."

"D," he said.

I winced. D is a gangster from Chicago. An actual gangster who was said to have removed people's livers if they displeased him. If there was anyone in the world who would know how to make someone dead, it would be D. But I hadn't spoken to him in months.

"Solberg," Rivera suggested.

J.D. Solberg might be a geek of extraterrestrial proportions, but he loved Brainy Laney with every fiber in his scrawny, disgusting little body and might, in fact, shoot Andrews to avenge her. The thought fired through my mind like a torpedo. Rivera must have seen my uncertainty. He stepped forward, strides long and aggressive.

"You told Solberg that Andrews was free, didn't you?" he asked.

I wanted to back away, but I don't like being a wienie in my own office so I raised my chin and gave him my best Scarface impression. "You know I won't talk to Solberg without a Hazmat and a—"

"You can't go in there!" Shirley shouted. Her voice was stretched tight with terror. Shirley, I knew, had premonitions. "You leave her alone."

My gaze had melded with Rivera's. I was barely able to draw a breath. "They're coming to arrest me, aren't they?" I asked. My voice sounded hollow to my own ears.

"No," he said, and as my door flew open, he turned toward it, held out his arms behind his back and pressed his wrists together.

Chapter 6

There's a surprisingly fine line between interesting and stark raving mad.
—Chrissy McMullen, who's found stark raving mad quite interesting on more than one occasion

I stumbled back a step as two officers rushed into the room.

"Jack Rivera…" One was Hollywood handsome, medium height and sandy haired. He was already pulling handcuffs from his belt. "You have the right to remain silent."

I stared at Rivera, at Hollywood, at Rivera. "What's going on?" My voice was flat, my extremities numb.

"Anything you say or do—"

"Jack!" I moved toward him, but the second officer stepped into my path, blocking my way. He was short and squat with a bulldog body and a face that made his body irresistible by comparison. "What's happening?"

"Stay back, ma'am," said Bulldog.

"I am back!" I snapped, then softened my tone. This was my office. I try not to be the queen of the bitches in my office. "I just want an explanation," I said. I sounded reasonable, but Rivera was already being pivoted away and nudged toward the door.

Something ripped inside of me, sending a thousand shards of terror shrieking through me. "Jack!"

He turned his head and glanced over his shoulder at me. His eyes were hooded, his back hunched, his soul shuttered. "Don't worry about it," he said.

"Don't worry about it? Don't worry about it!" I was still attempting to remain professional, but remaining human was becoming more difficult by the second. I shouldered past the squat cop. He reached for my arm but I jerked away. "Let him go!"

"It's all right," Rivera said, but something in me screamed that it was a lie. It wasn't all right at all. Who was going to drag me out of my next stupid mistake? Who was going to save me from the next psychiatrist or octogenarian or CEO who wanted to kill me for reasons I couldn't even guess? Who was going to save me from myself?

"Ma'am—"

"He saved my life!" A dozen frantic memories streamed through my mind. "He saved Laney's life!" I said, but he was still being prodded toward the door.

"Stop it!" Things were happening too fast. "Just wait a minute!" I demanded, reaching frantically for the officer guiding him out.

"Ma'am!" said the one behind me. He grabbed my arm.

And here's where things get kind of fuzzy. I mean, I know better than to strike an officer of the law. It's not as if I regularly go around punching them out. I'm not crazy. People go to jail for that sort of offense. People get decked for that sort of offense. But my Irish was up. One minute I was following Rivera like a lost lamb and the next I was swinging my elbow to the rear. I followed it with the weight of my body like Casey at the bat.

As luck would have it, my olecranon struck Bulldog square in the nose. He stumbled backward, bent at the waist, blood seeping between his Vienna-sausage fingers, but I had already swung back toward the door.

"Rivera." My voice was breathy with uncertainty. "Talk to me." But his attention was glued on the officer who had just been accosted by an Irish elbow.

"Tell me what's happening," I tried again, but in that instant, Rivera leapt forward. The cop behind him tried to hold him, but his prisoner burst free, shoving me aside with his shoulder as he made a beeline for Bulldog.

The two faced off. Bulldog's hand was on his weapon.

"Don't be stupid." Rivera's voice was nothing more than a feral growl.

"Get the fuck out of the way."

"Albertson!" Rivera snapped, half turning his head toward the cop behind him. "Control your hound."

"Listen, you goddamn wetback—"

"Coggins!" Albertson's voice was clipped. "Stand down."

"The bitch—"

"Joel!" he barked, and this time the squat officer backed away, hands held shoulder high, gaze still hard on Rivera.

Coggins tightened his anvil jaw, grin twisted and ugly. "I've been waiting for this day," he said.

Rivera narrowed his eyes. "Then keep your fucking hands to yourself and you just might live through it," he suggested.

"Threatening an officer of the law?" Coggins asked.

"I'll write it into the report myself."

Coggins' eyes were small and mean and full of venom. "Anytime you wanna—" he began, but Albertson stepped into the breach, effectively stopping the pissing contest.

"Shut up, Coggins. Rivera! You're in enough trouble already." He jerked his head toward the door. "Get in the car."

Rivera remained where he was, body taut as he shifted his attention toward me. Our gazes met and clashed and melded. In the flash of an instant, I thought of half a dozen dumb-ass things to do, but he narrowed his eyes, breaking my line of thought. "Don't make trouble," he said.

I shook my head, even though that had been exactly what my skittering subconscious had been planning to do.

He nodded once and walked toward the door. I moved along in tandem. "Where are they taking you?"

He didn't answer. His jaw was tense. A dark copse of hair fell forward across his brow. "Just…" His teeth were gritted. "Please! Don't do anything stupid," he said, and then he left the building with his fellow officers close behind.

I watched them walk away. In a matter of moments, they were gone, Rivera locked into the back seat of the squad car, eyes angry until he disappeared from sight.

"Holy cats!" Shirley said from behind me.

"Shit," Phillip said. "Your cop's got good hair too."

Chapter 7

Ice cream—sweet goodness wrapped in guilt.
—*Suzie Ernst, Chrissy's rather chubby middle-school friend*

"What do you mean you can't divulge that information?"

I'd been on the phone for most of the day and knew just a little less about the situation than I had when Rivera had burst into my office eight hours earlier. My first call had been to the lieutenant's captain, but Kindred was said to be unavailable. He would, however, call me at the first possible opportunity. It was now nine o'clock in the evening. Apparently opportunity had not yet come knocking, so I'd moved on, trying every avenue I could think of to gain information.

"Are you unfamiliar with the meaning of divulge, or is information the term you're uncertain of?" The bimbo at Central Community Police Station was so saccharine sweet that it was difficult to believe she was mocking me. But I was pretty sure she was.

"Listen, you little…" I caught myself, forced a smile into the receiver and matched her sugary tone with my own. "I just need to know where Lieutenant Jack Rivera is being held. Surely even you know that much." It was fast approaching my bedtime and my patience, usually so stellar, seemed to be at a low ebb.

"Perhaps it would help if I used smaller words," she said. "Maybe English isn't your first language. I could transfer you to—"

My patience snapped like a chicken bone. "I'll transfer your—"

"Hey, Mac."

I turned with a start. Laney was standing in the doorway of my kitchen. I stared, mouth open. Matamata was hell and gone from Sunland, California. She raised a brow at me. "Using your innate charisma to charm and influence people again?"

"Laney." I said her name like a prayer. I mean, I'm not gay or anything, but if I were, Brainy Laney would be the one I had wet dreams about. Normally, she's curvy and gorgeous with a mess of strawberry blond hair and a smile that makes men from nine to ninety willing to sell major organs just to get a chance to drool over her. Tonight, however, her hair was short and black, her eyes heavily lined with dark mascara smeared beneath uneven bangs. Since her rise to fame, Laney had become pretty creative with disguises.

"How's it going?"

"Laney," I said again, and bumbled to my feet. The receiver dropped from my hand as I took a couple steps toward her.

She met me halfway, catching me in her arms and hugging me as if I were an unsteady toddler.

And suddenly I was crying. I don’t know why. There has been more than one person in my life who was so impressed with my hard-ass demeanor that they swore I was born without tear ducts.

“It’s all right.” Laney was rocking me a little, crooning. Rocking. “It’s all right.”

I shook my head, smearing snot across the ugliest jacket I had ever seen. It smelled a little like sheep droppings. Apparently she was in deep disguise.

“It is,” she repeated.

“No, it isn’t.”

“Ma’am.” The voice on the other end of the line sounded mildly peeved and ultimately tinny. “Another nut job,” she muttered, then the phone went dead.

We ignored it.

“How’s Rivera?” Laney asked.

“I don’t know. I don’t even know where he’s being held.” I winced before I delivered the next piece of news. “Andrews is out of prison.”

“I know.”

“He was shot.”

“I heard he's expected to recover."

I felt frenetic and shocky. “Doesn’t anybody take pride in their marksmanship anymore?”

She grinned. Even her teeth looked different, but I was too distracted to wonder why. “I’m just glad you weren’t implicated.”

“I thought I would be. But then…” I shook my head. “How’d you find out?” I was still blubbering, but I'd gained enough control to formulate moderately articulate sentences.

"Don't worry about that," she said, and easing back, took my hands in hers. "You okay?"

"No, I'm not okay," I said, and wiped my nose with the back of my hand. "I'm obviously deranged."

She smiled. "That's never bothered you before."

"Well, before....before..." I was kind of hiccupy. "Shit."

She squeezed my hand, then turned slightly to set the receiver back in its cradle.

"Before you had Rivera to blame for the crazies," she said.

I winced. I've never been a huge fan of honesty, but it was an integral part of Laney. Even in disguise. "I don't even like him."

"I know."

"I don't!"

"I know."

"But he's..." I shrugged.

She eased me into a kitchen chair. "Hot?"

I gave her a scowl, as if to ask how she could be so shallow at a time like this. "He's an ass sometimes, but he doesn't deserve this. I mean..." I watched her pull off her wig. Her hair swung to her shoulders in red-gold waves as she pulled a carton of Rocky Road ice cream from the freezer. "That's the only reason I care. Because of the blatant unfairness of the situation."

“So you’re over him.”

“I’d be stupid to care about a guy who cheated on me,” I said.

“Or crazy.” She was already dishing up enough rocky goodness to feed a battalion. Or me.

She caught my gaze. “You’re sure he didn’t shoot Andrews?”

I was honestly surprised. “Of course I’m sure. He’s an overbearing pain in the ass. But he’s cop clean through to his blue-tinted clavicle. He might cheat on me but not on his department.”

"Who accused him of the crime?"

"I don't know. No one will tell me anything."

“But Andrews was shot after Rivera left here, right?”

“Maybe.” I was hedging.

She gave me a look.

“How would I know?” I asked.

“The lieutenant left here at approximately 11:02. Andrews didn’t show up at the hospital until nearly three o’clock in the morning.” I never knew how Laney obtained the information she did. Maybe she magically divined it, but perhaps it was attributable to the fact that men were willing to sell their kidneys to give her whatever she wanted…information not withstanding.

"Which hospital?" I asked.

She narrowed her eyes at me. "If I tell you will you promise not to go there?"

"I promise not to go tonight."

She stared at me a second then sighed. "Cedars-Sinai."

I nodded. The choice seemed likely. Cedars was a top notch facility.

“What’s the department’s official line?” She asked and scowled at the ice cream. I would never do anything so heinous. In a world of unsavory acts, ice cream is ever the innocent.

“Some bullshit about their total faith in their officers.”

“Isn’t that good news?”

“If they have faith in him why’s he in jail?” I felt the crying hiccups advancing again.

“Are you even sure he is in jail?”

“I’m not sure of anything.” My voice was rising a little, which isn’t like me. I’m usually more careful not to upset the ice cream. “He could be dead for all I know.”

“I’m sure he’s fine,” she said. “Captain Kindred believes in him.”

“And you don’t?” My tone was kind of whiny, kind of pissy, kind of watery.

She glanced sideways at me, eyes expressive enough to make granite weep. “He hasn’t always been the most traditional police officer on the planet.”

I stared at her. “I know that.”

She returned the stare, eyes questioning.

“He accused me of murdering Bomstad! You think I’ll forget that?” Bomstad had been a tight end for the L.A. Lions and my most illustrious client, until he overdosed on Viagra and started chasing me around my desk like a thoroughbred on crack. I'd screamed. He'd laughed. Ninety seconds later he had dropped dead as a shoehorn on my ivory carpet, and Rivera had shown up to blame me. No one ever said life was fair. At least not if they had a drop of Celtic blood in their overly dramatic veins.

Laney set the ice cream in front of me, then armed me with a spoon.

"He took my shirt to test the cherry stain for blood," I added, remembering a night from years ago. "There wasn't even any blood to be tested."

She didn't say anything.

"And he handcuffed me to his dad's kitchen cupboard once. You remember that?"

"I do."

"And oh…here's a good one. He tried to make me move back in with my parents."

"To keep you safe."

"No. Just to drive me crazy."

Laney smiled. "Eat," she said.

"He's always ordering me around."

"It's going to melt."

I fiddled with a rocky part of my dessert. "Always acting like my head is full of air." I swiped away a tear with the back of my hand. "My head's not full of air."

"Your head is full of your cerebellum and four rather important lobes, just like everyone else's."

"I'm actually very intelligent."

"Thirty-two on the ACTs."

"People always underestimate me."

She nodded toward the bowl, then nudged it toward me. "It's one of your fifteen favorite flavors."

"Rivera always underestimates me."

"Maybe."

"He treats me like I'm some dumb bitch."

"You've never been dumb."

"Damn straight." I sniffled a little, trying to buck up, but the truth was beating down on me like the L.A. sun. I gave a little shrug. "Maybe I was kind of a bitch sometimes, though."

"Could be."

"But he was an ass!" I looked up at her through blurry eyes.

She had retrieved a spoon of her own, dipped it into my ice cream and offered it to me.

I ate it out of a sense of loyalty. "He's still an ass…but…"

"He's your ass," she said.

"He's my ass," I warbled, and then I was crying again.

By midnight I was worn out. I hadn't felt so tired since I was thirteen and had filled Michael's condoms with super glue. He'd come home looking pale and frazzled, took one glance at me and chased me into the next burb. After that, I had hidden in the attic for a week until he quit twitching when he walked. My self-imposed exile had been totally worth it.

“That’s a nice memory,” I murmured. I was almost asleep. My head was resting on Laney’s ridiculously firm thigh. She'd changed out of her butt-ugly cargo pants into blue jeans. Every once in a while she’d stroke my hair away from my face.

“The one where you put super glue in your brother’s condoms?”

I smiled. I didn’t know if she was reading my mind or if I had recounted the scene out loud. The options had equal probability.

“He’s an ass, too,” I said.

“But you’re not in love with him.”

“No.” I sighed, then snapped my eyes open and rolled my head sideways. Our faces were less than twenty-four inches apart. “I’m not in love with Rivera either. Not anymore at least.”

She raised her brows at me. Our gazes met. “Need I remind you of the ice cream, Mac?”

I scowled up at her. Gilded curls framed her angelic face. It’s not easy scowling at a celestial being. It takes some practice. “I don’t know what you’re talking about.”

“The Rocky Road.” Her voice was soothing and patient. “You didn’t finish it off for a good twenty minutes. For a while I thought I was going to lose you.”

“I’ve turned down ice cream before.”

“Yes.” She squinted into the near distance and brushed a lock of misplaced hair behind my ear. “I believe you were eleven years old and you had the stomach flu.”

I tried to remain sober, but the grin peeked out. "I've never been so sick in my life."

"So you threw up in Peter's face."

I giggled and rolled onto my back. "Ahhh, good times."

The room went quiet. "What are you going to do, Mac?"

"About what?"

"About Rivera," she said, and yanked the hair she had just brushed behind my ear.

"Ow!"

"Somehow they've kept the media out of this. But the press is going to have a field day when it gets wind of this. That alone is going to be a pain for his department."

It was also going to be a pain for her if they discovered she was back in the country, but she didn't mention that.

"What are you going to do about Rivera?" she asked again. Her tone was a little tougher.

Mine was whiny. "Nothing."

She yanked again.

"Quit that. What can I do?"

"You can forget about it," she said. "Just let it go."

"Okay."

"I mean it, Mac. You can leave this up to the authorities to handle. This isn't your battle."

"I know."

"He's gotten out of worse jams without your help."

"Of course he has."

"He'll be fine."

I shifted my eyes away.

"Mac!" She tapped my forehead with one sensible fingernail. "Don't mess with this."

"But—"

"No buts!" she said, and rising abruptly, dumped my head onto the lumpy sofa cushion. "No buts. He's a big boy."

"How do you know?" I asked and narrowed my eyes at her.

She gave me a how-nuts-are-you glance but managed to ignore the worst of the insanity. "He's a big cop."

"But he—"

She swung toward me, hands on perfectly proportioned hips. "What? What? He needs help from a civilian? Needs help from you? Mac, his dad's a senator."

"An ex-senator."

"A wealthy ex-senator with a tremendous amount of clout."

"An ex-senator who will hardly even talk to him."

"And whose fault is that, Mac? It's not as if Rivera is Mr. Cotton Candy. I mean, for all we know he might have shot Andrews."

"He did not!" I said, and suddenly I was on my feet. "You take that back!"

She stared at me, both eyebrows lost in her hairline.

I faced her for an instant longer, then collapsed back onto the couch, deflated, head in my hands, eyes closed.

"So it's official," I said, and nodded dismally at the obvious truth. "I'm certifiable."

Chapter 8

A fool and his money are soon elected.
—*Senator Rivera's political opponent, who actually stole the quote from someone older and wiser…and consequently not in politics*

"Christina." Senator Rivera drew me into his arms with warmth, caring and a good deal of drama. I could feel heads turn toward us as every eye in the room was brought to bear. Maybe it was the fact that he had been California's senator for umpteen years. Maybe it was because he had once been a presidential hopeful, but perhaps it was simply his phenotype that made men growl and women purr.

Miguel Rivera was an extremely attractive man. He was tall, dark and exotic, with a honey-edged Spanish accent and the politically advantageous ability to make an individual feel as if she were the center of the universe.

He pushed me to arms' length and stared into my eyes, making me grateful that I had taken special care with my makeup that morning. Usually it's a dab of this and a smidgen of that, but today it was more like a boatload of this and a couple tons of that. Plus my hair, usually as lank as an anemic mule's tail, had been curled and tortured and lacquered into submission.

"Christina." He said my name again, crooning it like a Latin lover. The sound made me miss

Francois something fierce. "How are you faring, my dear?"

"I'm…" I cleared my throat and managed to refrain from glancing at the onlookers. Their attention made me fidgety. It's possible that the senator no longer noticed when he was the epicenter of attention, but I rather suspected he was not entirely oblivious. "I'm well," I said, using my best diction. It always came out when my hair was curled. "How are you?"

He shook his head, looking somber and wise and paternal. It was an impressive performance, considering his history involving young women and old scotch. "Let us not speak of me. It is you with whom I am concerned." That's how he spoke. Not like an everyday, on-the-street kind of guy, but with an old-world charm that left the great unwashed masses, of which I was just one mass, hanging onto every word. Sometimes I wondered if he had to spend extra time slumped in his easy chair at home, wearing nothing but his whitey-tighties and cursing the TV just to offset his public demeanor. "I know this is not easy for you."

"Senator." The maitre d' appeared with shining obsequiousness. "Might you wish for your usual seat?"

"Ahh, Antoine. Si, gracias." And touching a hand to my back, the senator ushered me toward the inner sanctum of one of L.A.'s snootiest restaurants. If I were paying for the meal we would have been throwing down French fries at Micky D's by then, but the senator had picked the spot and therefore, I assumed, also planned on making the payments.

The maitre d' pulled out my chair. I eased into it, remembering, before I sat down, to tuck my skirt against my thighs like an honest-to-goodness lady. The ensemble I wore was one of my favorites. The skirt was a cute little silky number, popsicle green with a ruffle around the hem just for fun. My blouse was just as adorable. It was strappy and form fitting and topped off with a funky beaded necklace that my sister-in-law had made while pregnant. She and my brother's ensuing offspring was proof positive that it doesn't take a shitload of brain cells to create motile sperm.

"Antoine," the senator said, "we shall have a bottle of your '95 Chateau Margaux, please, and a few minutes alone." The maitre d' left with a slight bow. The senator turned toward me. "Christina…" he said, and reaching across the table, took my right hand in his. His fingernails were prettier than mine. "You look more lovely than ever."

I refrained from clearing my throat but couldn't quite resist fiddling with the silverware with my free hand. Each piece weighed half a ton and if hocked, could probably pay my second mortgage. "Thank you."

His expression sobered even further, which was quite a miraculous feat. "I cannot tell you how it pained me to hear that you and my son had gone your separate ways. I have, for so long, thought of you as my daughter," he said, and stroked my knuckles. A little shiver of something less than familial raced up my spine. It was difficult to identify. In fact, maybe it was best not to try. After all, it wasn't that long ago that the senator had become engaged to one of his son's ex-girlfriends. Even more recently, said girlfriend had been found toes up on the senator's well-polished hardwood floor.

The Rivera family closets come fully stocked…skeletons being liberally scattered amongst the Armani suits.

"Thank you," I said again, and coyly dropped my gaze to the tablecloth. "But that's not what I wished to speak to you about."

"Of course not." He drew a deep breath, making his nostrils flare dramatically. "Of course it is not, Christina, for you are a wonderful, caring woman."

I stared at him. I've been called a bunch of things. Wonderful, caring…not so often.

He shrugged, eyes sparking a little at my obvious uncertainty. "Even though you and my son are no longer lovers, you still care for his well-being, si?"

I wasn't sure how to answer that one. I mean, I had no intention of saying that I retained any sort of feelings for Rivera. He was an ass, remember? Then again, it seemed kind of wrong to tell the senator that his only son was a cheating piece of dog poop and I didn't care if he burned in hell for all eternity.

I hedged carefully. “Do you know where he’s being held?”

He stared at me for a second, saying nothing, then, “Christina…” His paternal voice was one of his best, but my knuckles hadn’t forgotten the stroking. “I know you only wish to help, but this wound…” He shook his head gently. “…it is not yours to heal.”

“I know, but Rivera…” I paused and adjusted my phraseology to fit the audience. “Gerald and I were…” What were we exactly? “We were friends, and it only seems right that I help him.” I leaned forward, hands fisted on the table, emotions circling like angry buzzards inside me. “I need answers, Senator. Why was he arrested? What kind of evidence do they have that he was involved? Where is he?”

“Ahhh…” He shook his head and stroked my hand again. “Such is your kindness even though he broke your heart.”

“He didn’t break my heart,” I said, even though he had kind of broken my heart. “We simply decided it would be best if we went our separate ways. I mean, we’re too different. But that’s not the point. The point is, he’s been unjustly accused.”

He smiled with kindly understanding. “You are a generous woman,” he said. “And I am certain you are right. I am certain that the other woman meant nothing to him.”

Who was talking about the other woman? I certainly hadn't. I hadn’t even been thinking of the other woman…mostly. Still, I felt my face heat up, felt my anger flare like an acetylene torch. “You know about her?”

His smile lifted a little more. “I have been planted in the City of Angels for a long while, Christina. My roots go deep. There is little I do not know, especially if it concerns those for whom I care.”

“I care for him, too,” I said, but if Rivera had been standing right in front of me at that precise moment, I would have been hard pressed not to smack him in the eye with the just-arrived bottle of whatever the hell it was. “Not in a romantic way,” I hurried to add, “but more like a…” I was going to say brother, but I detest my own brothers. Besides, the idea of doing the things with a brother that I had done with Rivera made me want to heave up my ovaries. “Senator…,” I said, changing tact. Leaning back slightly, I carefully withdrew my hand from his grasp. “Do you know where your son is being held?”

He stared at me with doleful earnestness. “I am afraid I do not.”

Like most politicians, Senator Rivera was an exemplary liar. I mean, I’m good, but I may never have the opportunity to hone my skills to the razor-sharp edge he had achieved. Practice, you know, is everything.

“As you said, your roots go deep,” I reminded him. “Therefore, I find it somewhat difficult to believe—” He held up a perfectly manicured hand.

"Perhaps I should have said that I do not wish to know where he is."

"Senator, please," I began, ready to plead in earnest, but in that instant I realized what he had just said and canted my head in his direction. "You don't want to know?"

He shrugged, a ridiculously graceful lift of his ridiculously expensive shoulder pads. "I am certain that seems harsh, Christina, but the truth is this…" Another deep sigh of paternal patience. "I believe now that I was wrong to fight my son's battles for so long. I did him no favors, I think, by disallowing him to pay his debt to society." It was said that Rivera Junior had spent some time in juvie…but only until Rivera Senior could pull the necessary strings to get him out. How he had, later, been accepted into cop class with no questions asked was not much of a mystery. "I fear it is time for Gerald to pay his own debts."

"His own debts?" Something bubbled in my innards, but I calmed the digestive juices. "You're not saying you think he's guilty."

"Ahh, Christina…" He stared at me with tender understanding. "How it warms the cockles of my heart to realize your loyalty even after all he has done."

I scowled at him. I didn't really care what it did to his cockles. The man's son was in trouble. And a father was supposed to care about that sort of thing. Wasn't he?

"This isn't about what he's done to me," I said. "This has to do with the fact that he's innocent."

He leaned toward me, and though he didn't glance right or left, I got the impression that he was sensing those around him, making sure none were listening…or perhaps making sure they were. "And are you so certain he is innocent, Christina? Are you really?"

I stared at him, dumbfounded. "He's not a murderer."

The senator watched me in silence for a moment, then shook his head. "I do not wish to degrade your faith in him, Christina, but perhaps you do not know him as well as you think. My son, though I care a great deal for him, can be a very difficult man."

I stared at him, keeping my expression bland and managing to refrain from reminding him that his son had been the bane of my existence for more than five years. He'd accused me of murdering my would-be rapist, for God's sake. "All right," I said carefully. "I'll grant that he can be difficult. But being a police officer is extremely important to him. He would never sabotage his career."

"Christina, my dear…" He sighed heavily and shook his head once.

I gritted my teeth. Patience is not my first virtue. I can name a couple dozen other qualities that aren't right up there at the top of the list as well. I considered telling the good senator, before things got out of hand, that self control was amongst them. But he blissfully continued in his increasingly irritating patient tone.

"I know it may seem, at times, that Gerald does not care for you as you deserve, but I believe, in my heart"—he curled his long fingers against the left side of his chest–"that he does."

I shook my head, unsure what that had to do with the price of tortillas. But he went on to explain.

"Think on it, Christina. My son is a good man in his own way. But he is, sometimes, impulsive. Rash, even. Does it not seem that he might well be capable of doing something…" He shrugged again. "…illegal, if he felt it would accomplish his goals?"

"Goals?"

A flicker of sympathy zipped across his fatherly expression. "He has, for a long while, been extremely concerned with your safety, my dear."

"What?"

"Surely you have considered the possibility that he has done this to make certain that this Jackson Andrews does not harm you."

I blinked. I honestly had not considered that. And I really didn't care to consider it now. I shook my head. "That's ridiculous."

"Perhaps you do not realize how very much he cares for you."

"I…" I shook my head again. It still didn't do much good.

"We Latinos," he said, "It is a problem of ours, but …sometimes we love too much."

One of my eyebrows rose of its own volition. "What's that?"

"The fact that he was with another…" He shrugged. "It does not mean that he cares any the less for you."

I blinked. "So you're saying your son doesn't care enough about me to keep his pants zipped, but he cares enough to spend the rest of his life in prison?"

The senator lifted his hands, palms up, as if to say he had finally found a woman who understood his kind. I stared at him.

"This actually makes sense to you?" I asked.

"Well, my dear, I care a great deal for Rosita."

"Your ex-wife."

"Si. She is the light of my life." He placed both weirdly expressive hands over the place where his heart might have been if he hadn't thrown his hat into the political ring. "The flame that ever burns in my—"

"Do you always cheat on the light of your life?"

"I did not cheat…so much as…" He lifted his shoulders, letting his hands drop to the table. "Stray."

"You—" I stopped myself before my head began spinning like Linda Blair's and icky things came spewing out of my mouth. Although I'm a firm believer that cursing is our God-given right and an excellent stress reliever, I have yet to see documentation that it improves inter-personal relationships. I cleared my throat, smoothed a wrinkle from the pristine white napkin in front of me, and gave him a prim smile. "I'm afraid I don't understand what this has to do with your son."

"He…strayed from you."

"Okay."

"The culture of our people…the passion of our people makes us…" He wobbled his head back and forth as if searching for the perfect word. The term assholes popped into my mind but I held it captive pending later release. "There are times when it makes us wander."

I waited.

"But the Amcrican culture…" He shrugged. "It suggests we should confine our passions to but one woman forever."

I remained spectacularly silent.

"This…what is the word? This dichotomy…it tears at us," he said, and made a ripping motion with his hands. "There is the passion we feel in our hearts that must be quenched. But once our ardor is sated, then there is the guilt."

I settled back in my seat, took a deep breath and wondered if it would be wrong to stab him in the nuts with my sterling silver fork.

"Let me get this straight." I narrowed my eyes at him. He watched me steadily. More cowardly men, I have to admit, have dived under the table at less provocation. "You believe your son cheated on me, then felt so guilty about it that he attempted to murder a man in an attempt to save me from him."

He shrugged. “As I have said, Christina, we are a passionate people.”

I opened my mouth to spew forth the aforementioned venom, then closed it judiciously and smiled a little. “All right. Well…” I spread my hands and did not consider how it would feel to tighten them around his throat. “Wouldn't that same passion guarantee that you would try to exonerate your only son?”

His sigh was heavy and long suffering. “I would so love to, Christina. Truly I would, but as I’ve said, I feel it is time for Gerald to fight his own battles, to—”

“Senator?”

I turned my head at the sound of a female voice. The woman standing beside our table was in her late thirties. She was round on top, small on the bottom, and disappeared to practically nothing in between.

“I’m so sorry to interrupt.” She sounded a little breathless. Maybe I would too if I had no in-between. “But could I bother you for a photograph?”

The senator delayed just a moment, as if debating whether it would be better to insult a potential constituent or to interrupt a conversation concerning the continued well-being of his only son. In a fraction of a second, he graced her with his million-watt smile. “Certainly,” he said.

She gushed. They stood. Someone took about forty-seven pictures.

“Thank you so much,” she crooned.

“My pleasure.”

“And I hope the rumors are true.”

“Rumors?” he asked.

She leaned in close. “A little birdie told me you might yet run for president.”

“Well…” He smiled. “Let us keep that between us and the sparrows, shall we?”

“Of course,” she said, and giggled as she made a motion to zip her lips.

He smoothed a hand down the front of his thousand-dollar suit coat, sat down and sighed. “How I long for a simple life,” he said.

I still didn’t stab him. “You could move to Nelson, Nebraska,” I said.

“What?”

“Population four hundred and twenty-seven. I hear it’s very picturesque.”

He stared at me a moment, as if trying to ascertain if I was kidding, but I kept my expression deadpan, and he sighed again. “There are times when I would like nothing better than to return to my agrarian roots, Christina, but I feel that this great country of ours…this wonderful, sprawling land”—he waved one benevolent hand at the world at large as if blessing it with his presence—“it is not finished with me yet. And I cannot in good conscience leave—”

“You’re selling him out.” The idea struck me like a thunderclap.

“What?” He looked both shocked and appalled. “Christina—” he began, but I huffed a laugh.

“You’re hoping for another public office and you want your constituents to believe you’re so honest, so unbiased, that you won’t even pull any strings to save your own son.”

“Christina, you cut me to the quick!”

I jerked to my feet, finding, with some surprise, that my fork had come with me. But he was still talking.

“You wound me to the core.”

“I might,” I snarled and tightened my grip on the sterling silver handle, “if you don’t even try to the learn the truth!”

He held my gaze with steely steadiness. “Is it the truth you want, Christina? Is it really?”

I blinked. “Of course it is.”

He nodded once, as serious as death. “Sit down, my dear.”

I felt an odd premonition tingle the soles of my feet, but remained as I was, bent at the waist, leaning into his face like a slavering hound. “I prefer to stand,” I said.

“Very well then,” he said. “The truth is this; Gerald was at Andrews’ house the night he was shot."

“What?” I felt myself weaken at the knees.

“Sit down, Christina.”

“You’re lying,” I said. My tone sounded fuzzy.

“Sadly, I am not.”

I searched his eyes, his expression, his body language. He looked old suddenly and hopelessly honest. “How do you know?” My voice was barely a whisper.

“I know because Gerald told Captain Kindred that it is so,” he said.

I blinked, nodded, took a deep breath and drifted back into my just-abandoned chair. "What else did Kindred tell you?"

"He said it would do my son no good if I got involved."

Chapter 9

Reality is for guys who don't know how to make shit up.
—Michael McMullen, who made up quite a bit of shit

"So Rivera was seen hanging around Andrews's house on the night of the shooting?" Elaine was sitting in my kitchen, nibbling on an organic lettuce leaf like an environmentally friendly French Lop.

"That's what the senator said?"

"You don't believe him?"

"I don't know what to believe. I don't even know where Andrews's house is."

She looked pale but resolute even though talk of Jackson Andrews must have stirred up the same shit-storm in her gut that it did in mine. Said shit-storm had caused me to call Cedars-Sinai three times since breakfast just to make sure Andrews was still confined to their critical care unit. So far so good. "Not in Glendale anymore?"

I tamped down the memories that tried to engulf me and shook my head. "A family bought his place there half a year after he was incarcerated."

"You know that for sure?"

"Yeah." During a particularly serious bout of anxiety a few months earlier, I had stopped in at Andrews' old address. It was now home to the all-

American family. A dad, a mom, 1.8 kids, and four thousand plastic toys strewn about the living room like confetti on New Year's eve.

She nodded, thinking. "If the senator knew Rivera had been at Andrews' home he must know where that home is."

"If he did he didn't share the information with me."

"How about Captain Kindred? What did he say?"

"He hasn't returned my calls."

"Then how are you going to question Andrews's neighbors?"

"I'm not."

She snorted.

"I'm not!" I said. "I can't. I don't know anything." Frustration was bubbling like an unstable volcano inside me. "No one will talk to me. I think there might be some kind of gag order. I think they're making him the fall guy."

"That's ridiculous."

"It's not ridiculous, Laney. He's innocent."

"It's not your job to prove that."

"Then whose job is it?"

"I'm sure he has an attorney."

I opened my mouth to interject, but she spoke over me.

"An excellent attorney."

"On a cop's wages?"

"His father is one of the most powerful men in California."

"His father thinks he's guilty."

She paused, almost winced. "He didn't say that."

"He barely said anything. He didn't even want to discuss it. All he wanted to talk about was…" I shook my head. "Skank Girl."

"What did he say exactly?"

"He said…" I paused to remember. "His are a passionate people and they sometimes can't help themselves. They have to cheat on the women they love."

"And you let him live?"

I slathered some Skippy's on a freshly toasted piece of white bread. From what I had read, it actually had negative nutritional value. "The restaurant was pretty busy."

Laney nodded her understanding, then scowled a little. If I ate as many lettuce leaves as she did, I'd scowl a whole lot more. "You know, Mac, just because the senator cheated on his wife, doesn't mean Rivera cheated on you."

"Hmmm." I made a ruminative noise and narrowed my eyes as I chewed. "Does that translate into just because his dad's a dick, it doesn't mean he's a dick?"

"Something like that."

I gave that some judicious consideration as I polished off my peanut butter toast. I am nothing like an environmentally friendly French Lop. "I'd believe you, Laney. Really I would. But it just so happens I know a little something about human psychology."

"And?"

"And…" I pulled a pencil out from under the oven mitt atop the table and doodled fretfully on a frayed napkin. "It's been scientifically proven that if one's father is a dick, one has an eighty-seven-point-three percent chance of becoming a dick oneself."

"Eighty-seven-point-three."

"I might be point-seven percent off."

"Well, if it's scientifically proven…"

"One can't argue with mathematical equations," I said, but I knew she would anyway.

"Mac—"

"Listen." I stood abruptly. "I don't even know why we're discussing this. The point is not whether Rivera cheated on me or not. I don't even care. I'm over it. Moved on. There's a new man in my life. A wonderful man. Why, just the other day…" I paused, searching frantically for his name in a mind that had suddenly turned to mush.

"Marc," she supplied.

"Marc!" Fuck it. "Anyway, the point is whether Rivera is guilty or not."

"And if he's not?"

"Then he deserves to be exonerated."

"Even if he slept with Skank Girl?"

I was cool. I was calm, and sophisticated, and grown up. Besides, I had never been with a man as wonderfully sensitive as… Dammit! Marc! Still, thinking about Skank Girl made it a little more personal. I felt the pencil snap in my hand, hid it against my appropriately sized thigh and raised my chin a little. "I'm a big enough person to look beyond that to make certain justice is served."

She stared at me for a couple seconds, then, "No, you're not."

"What?"

"You're not big at all." She stood and faced me. "Remember Maynard Carlson?"

"No." It wasn't even a plausible lie. Maynard had been my main squeeze throughout my freshman year of college.

"The guy with the Mazda and the teeth," she reminded me. "I believe you threatened to castrate him with a spoon if he took Liz Geddy to the formal."

"I did no such thing."

She scowled. "You're right. It wasn't a spoon." She paused, thinking, face scrunched up in a manner that would make a lesser woman look like a garden gnome. "It was a cantaloupe—"

"A melon baller!" I snapped, then drew a steadying breath and gave her a who cares kind of look. "That was a long time ago." There was no point denying the castration threat. Have I mentioned Laney and her freakishly accurate memory? "And I think you'll agree that since then I have grown up considerably."

She ignored my last statement and nodded. "A melon baller. That was it. You were going to castrate the man with a melon baller."

"I wouldn't have really done it, of course," I said, although teenage Chrissy had been even crazier than thirty-something Chrissy. "Probably."

"But you threatened to do it. You threatened him and you didn't even like him."

"I did too like him. He had really nice…fingernails."

She narrowed her eyes as if thinking hard. The expression scared the hell out of me. Sometimes when Laney thinks hard, things spontaneously combust.

"What?" I asked cautiously.

"You lied to me," she said. Her voice was level and thoughtful, her gaze elsewhere, as if she were carefully picking her way through a minefield.

"What are you talking about? No, I didn't. He had exceptional fingernails. Exemplary fingernails. He kept them nicely trimmed and hardly ever chewed them. In fact…" I was prepared to pontificate further and the state of his nails, but she gasped softly.

I started and jerked my eyes expectantly toward the front door, but was pleasantly surprised to see that no marauding bandits were attacking just yet.

"You never believed Rivera cheated on you," Laney said.

I yanked my gaze back toward her, but her attention remained elsewhere, as if she were divining the truth from some unseen force.

"What?" I rasped. "That's crazy. Of course I did. I saw them together in his car. They were—" I began, but she barely even noticed I existed.

"I was wondering why you were so calm. Why there were no death threats or cherry bombs or—"

"That cherry bomb incident was years ago."

"For a while I thought you must not care about him as much as I thought you did, but now I realize the truth." She turned slowly toward me, expression placid, eyes eerie. "You just wanted a way out."

"What are you talking about? A way out of what?"

"Out of love."

I stared at her for a second, then threw my head back like a hyena on a hot scent and cackled. "That's insane."

She didn't argue, but I wasn't done raving.

"Being a star has made you delusional."

"Living alone has made you a coward."

I was honestly stricken. Laney doesn't say mean things. Not unless they are absolutely true and might somehow be helpful. But I was far beyond caring about that kind of ridiculous detail. "I am not a coward."

"Then why didn't you make Rivera explain himself?"

"He did explain."

"Once. He explained it once. After which, you failed to demand a hundred replays of the situation. Instead, you simply decided not to believe him."

"Because he's male."

She gave me a WTF look.

"He's male," I explained. "And therefore he lies."

"That's the dumbest…" She paused, took a deep breath. "What exactly did you see?"

"What?" I felt a little skittish suddenly, though I couldn't have said why. I mean, I had the moral high ground.

"When you saw them in his car, what were they doing?"

"She was sitting on his lap."

"On his lap. In the car."

"It can be done. Trust me." In fact, if one was truly motivated it could be done while wearing a tuba. Go, teenage Chrissy!

"All right. What were they wearing?"

I swallowed and steadied my hands. "He was naked."

"Naked."

"Yes."

"You could see that even though she was sitting on his lap?"

I gritted my teeth. "Listen, Laney, I know Rivera. He's not the Dalai Lama or anything."

"So you know he had his pants off. Somehow divined it."

"Yes."

"So when he saw you…when he came running after you, did he put on his pants first?"

My lips twitched.

"He didn't follow you buck naked, did he?"

I glanced toward the door.

"Did he?"

"Of course not. We were in the middle of Highland Avenue."

"But he had his pants on by the time he caught up to you."

"He's very fast," I said.

She remained silent, watching me.

"He's had a lot of practice. The man's a—"

"He didn't have his pants off, did he, Mac?" she asked.

"It doesn't matter what he had off. I knew his intent."

"So you were ready to take a melon baller to Maynard, who, for the record, did not have particularly dazzling fingernails, but you weren't willing to even hang around to find out what Rivera was doing?"

"I knew what he was doing."

"Really? Then Skank Girl must have been naked."

I pursed my lips. "For your information, people don't have to be entirely unclothed to have sex."

She looked puzzled. "Are you sure? That's not what I've been told."

I sputtered something nonsensical at her, but before I was even done, she interrupted.

"Nobody wants to be hurt, Mac."

"That's exactly—"

"But you can't bail just because you're afraid it might happen."

"He propositioned—"

"I don't lie to you," she said, and there was something about her expression that sucked all the air out of my lungs.

I stood there frozen for several seconds, then closed my eyes and pressed the heels of my hands into my eye sockets. "I just…" I drew a careful breath. "When I saw them together, I... I couldn't stand to have my heart…" I stopped myself before the words spilled out, but it was already too late.

"Oh, Mac…" She slipped out of her chair and hugged me. "You don't know he'll break your heart."

I laughed. "I didn't…I wasn't going to say that. You know my heart's made of shoe leather. I just didn't want to be…" I managed a shrug even though she had a death grip on my shoulders. "Disappointed."

She drew away a couple of inches. "You don't know he'll disappoint you, either."

I found myself swallowed up by Laney's caring. "Why would it be different this time?" My voice was very small.

"Sometimes things change," she said. "Sometimes things get better."

I looked at her, trying for a cynical expression, trying to ignore the fact that my eyes were stinging and it probably wasn't allergies.

"Sometimes there are happy endings," she said. "You know that. Just think of—"

"Don't mention Solberg," I warned, but the threat might have been a little offset by a sniffle.

"Solberg and I are—"

"Don't say you're blissfully happy."

"—blissfully happy."

"Shit," I said, and wiped my nose with the back of one hand.

"Before him I didn't know sex—"

"Dear God," I said, and tried to pull away, but Laney has a grip like a grizzly.

"—could be so great."

"Ohh…" I rolled my eyes. "I'm in hell."

"He's so gentle and—"

I covered my ears with my hands and started singing God Bless America. It's been said that I couldn't carry a tune if you shoved it in an alligator tote, but I didn't care. I sang it at the top of my lungs, blurting out lyrics I hadn't even known when I was in elementary school.

"I know where he is."

I stopped singing, tilted my head at her, removed my hands. "What?"

"Rivera," she said, expression solemn, eyes steady. "He's being held at Men's Central."

Chapter 10

I'd like to apologize…but I'm Irish.
—Shamus McMullen, Chrissy's great grandfather, shortly before beginning the Grand Brawl o' London in 1889

The gray block building that makes up the largest jail in the world was only slightly more depressing than I expected it to be. I arrived there at eight in the morning, presented my picture I.D., got searched, surrendered my cell phone and waited until I was ushered into the visiting area with fourteen other guests.

The previous evening with Laney had been enlightening and terrifying; despite myself, I had to reluctantly admit that I had no real proof that Rivera had cheated on me. Maybe Laney was right. Perhaps fear and latent Irish stubbornness had made me jump to conclusions. I owed him the chance to explain himself. And perhaps…just maybe, I owed him an apology.

I waited impatiently in front of the glass partition. Rivera arrived in a few minutes. He looked lean and hard and tired. His gaze settled on me for just an instant before he sat down and picked up the phone that connected our worlds. I did the same. "What's wrong?" His voice was taut and gravelly.

I stared at him. I had had no way of knowing how seeing him dressed in cheap blue prison garb would affect me. But suddenly I felt weak and watery. My lips moved. Nothing came out.

"God damn it, McMullen! What's going on?"

"Nothing." I tried to buck up. I mean, he was the one in jail, and he wasn't crying. In fact, he just looked kind of pissed about the whole thing. His gaze swept the part of me he could see above the counter. "You're okay?"

"Yes. Of course. It's you—" Had there not been a guard, a glass wall, fourteen other visitors, and a million unresolved problems between us, I would have gladly thrown myself into his arms and reenacted a jungle scene from Animal Kingdom.

"What happened?" he asked. "What'd you do?"

I shook my head. "What do you mean?"

He drew a deep breath, flaring his nostrils. The gesture reminded me a little of his father and a little of Spirit, stallion of the Cimarron. Both were sexy. "You didn't call D, did you?"

"D?" Dagwood Dean Daley, better known as D, if you recall, was the Chicago gangster who had come to my aid on more than one occasion. He and Rivera might still have some unresolved issues, even though they had duked it out on one auspicious occasion. "No. Why would I?"

"Don't get him involved," he warned.

It was said that if D's loans weren't returned in a timely fashion the borrower would sometimes turn up missing internal organs. I didn't believe a word of it. Usually.

"Chrissy!"

"I didn't call him," I said.

He scowled at me. "How about Angler?"

"Vinny?" Vincent Angler was a defensive lineman for the L.A. Lions. He had helped me once, too, and even though I hardly knew him, I liked to throw his name around whenever an opportunity presented itself. "No."

Rivera lowered his brows even farther. "Are your brothers somehow involved in this?"

"Of course not."

He pursed his lips. "Then, who'd you piss off?"

Anger washed the tears right out of my eyes. "I didn't piss anyone—" I began but he laughed. The sound was low and rumbly.

I fortified my resolve and drew a deep breath, determined to start over, to think clearly, maybe even to apologize for my past transgressions. My lips and my sphincter tightened against the idea. Turns out I'd rather eat Spirit's wild horse dung than admit a mistake, and I was pretty damn sure Rivera wasn't going to make it easy.

"Listen," I said, "I'm…" I shook my head. It wasn't as if I had never apologized in the past. I'd just never done it without someone holding my head over a toilet bowl. I swallowed. "I'm glad you're okay."

His brows rose a fraction of an inch and maybe his body relaxed a little, but he said nothing.

I cleared my throat. “You look good.” He looked, in fact, good enough to put on top of a cake and devour whole. Or put in a cake. Don’t get me wrong, I’m not one of those women who’s attracted to criminals. Except for Nicolas Cage in Con Air and Sean Connery in anything.

“Say something,” I said.

“I’m waiting for you to get around to your reason for coming.”

“I just stopped by to make sure you were all right.”

The left corner of his mouth quirked.

“And to tell you that I’m…” The word was stuck in my throat like an orange in a whisky bottle. “I’m concerned about your well-being.”

“My well-being.”

“And I… I’m…” For the life of me, I couldn’t cough up the word. “What happened? I mean…” I shook my head. “Why are you here?”

“I think you know that one.”

“I know you didn’t shoot Andrews.”

He shrugged. Only one shoulder lifted. “Turns out there was an eyewitness.”

My breath stopped in my throat. “A witness! Who? Where?”

“That’s not something you need to worry about.”

My lips moved of their own accord, fueled by outrage and terror and a dozen other emotions I wasn’t quite ready to own up to. “You’re being framed,” I barely breathed the words. “Set up. Who says they saw you? Why are you here? Why aren't you at least out on bail?"

"Don't get all riled up," he warned.

"Riled up?" I choked a laugh. "What the hell are you talking about? Have you spoken to the senator? Maybe if you apologize for…" I shrugged spasmodically. "…whatever, he can get you out."

"Bail's set pretty high."

"How much? I can get some money together, and if I ask Laney, she'll-"

"Forget it," he said and sat perfectly motionless, eyes steady, body still as granite as he watched me.

Wild emotions sluiced through me. I leaned closer to the glass. "Some people think you did it to save me," I said.

"Some people?"

"But I know better." Fear was cascading through me like water over a ledge. What if I was wrong and his father was right? What if he was here because of me? The senator seemed to intend to do nothing about Rivera's incarceration. Was that because he had already determined there was nothing he could do? Was he simply cutting his losses? "You're not that dumb."

His eyes were steaming, and through the smoke I envisioned two people going at it on a kitchen table that looked a lot like mine. "You sure?"

I swallowed, pulled into his eyes, drawn under the memories. But I yanked myself off the slippery slope and shook my head.

"You're a pain in the ass, Rivera, but you're not particularly stupid."

He leaned back in his chair and stretched out his right leg. His lips remained immobile, but there was a light of something in his dark devil eyes. "Gee, I'm so glad you stopped by," he said. "We'll have to do this again sometime."

I drew a fortifying breath, feeling better, but then I noticed the bruise on his left temple. I winced against my will. "Tell me what happened."

"Go home, McMullen," he said. "This isn't your problem."

"Not my problem? Are you kidding me?" The emotions were pouring in again though I tried to keep them wrangled up. "You're rotting in here while—"

"Take it easy."

I drew a deep breath, trying to do just that. "While the real perpetrator goes free." I leaned forward, employing my very best self-control. "Who was it, Rivera? Another cop? Was it someone you know?"

He jerked forward, all semblance of congeniality gone. "Don't do this."

"I can help," I said. My brain was storming through a half-dozen other cases in which I had been involved. "Let me help. I know you didn't—"

"I fucked her!"

I blinked. "What?"

"The woman you saw me with. It wasn't the first time."

I sat absolutely still, mouth agape.

"I've known her for years."

I could feel my heart beating a slow dirge in my chest, could feel the air passing into and out of my lungs. The world spun slowly on its axis.

Maybe I was vaguely aware of the fact that Rivera rose and left. And eventually, I'm pretty sure, I did, too.

"Mac?" Laney's voice rang through the house as she slammed the front door. I intended to answer, but I had just thrust my head into the refrigerator for the eighty-ninth time that evening. "Mac!" There was already worry in her tone and fear in her eyes as she charged into the kitchen.

"What?" I sounded unsteady even to myself as I straightened from the bowels of the fridge.

She stopped in the doorway, brows furrowed then rising. "Have you been drinking?"

"Drinking? No," I said and stumbled toward the kitchen table. Atop its modest expanse was a gallon-sized Häagen Dazs tub, a crushed bag of chocolate chips and four empty cartons of Chinese leftovers.

"Oh, no. Mac, tell me you didn't eat all that."

"Me? No." I made a generous swipe in the general direction of the detritus on the table. "Don't be ridiculous. The ice cream was already half-gone."

She lifted the empty bucket, then set it gingerly aside. I had licked the rim. "What happened?"

I would have answered immediately, but I was busy shoving potato chips into my mouth while simultaneously searching the cupboards. "Have you seen the salsa? I thought I bought—"

"Mac!" she said. Grabbing my arm, she pulled me over to the table and nudged me none too gently into the nearest chair. "What's wrong?"

"Nothing's wrong. I'm celebrating."

"With potato chips and salsa?"

"Potatoes in honor of my Irish antecedents. And salsa in deference to Lieutenant Jack Rivera." I made a saluting motion with my right hand, which still held a soggy trio of chips.

She blanched. "You went to see him?"

"I did."

The room filled with quiet. My eyes filled with tears. I wiped my nose with the back of my hand. "Hot sauce always makes my eyes water," I said.

Apparently the lie wasn't even good enough to be offensive. Possibly because I hadn't located the hot sauce yet. She ignored my ludicrous explanation.

"He told you he slept with her," she said. Her tone was flat and sure. I wasn't even a little surprised at her knowledge.

"Yeah, he did." I grinned, then shoved the three chips into my mouth and washed them down with a swig of milk. Beer would have probably been a more appropriate option, but I hate beer.

"Well…" She watched my face like another might study a hungry cougar, sensitive to any change. "I guess he's on his own then, huh?"

"Damn straight." I shoved in another couple of chips. "He can become Bubba's bitch for all I care."

"Bubba's…" She gave me an uncertain look. "Oh, because he'll go to prison."

"That's right."

"And you don't care."

"I'd have to be an idiot," I said, and filled the silence with more verbiage, lest she take that particular moment to jump into the fray. "And I guess you're not always right after all."

She said nothing.

"He did sleep with her," I explained.

"Oh. Yeah," she said finally, and shifted her gaze toward the hallway. "I'm sorry."

I drew a deep breath, took another handful of chips and soldiered on. "It's all right. You can't know everything. I mean—"

Our gazes met. A figment of truth slithered into my poly-saturated brain.

"Yes, you can," I said.

She stared at me in silence, body tense.

"And you are always right," I said.

"Mac—"

"Fuck it." I breathed the words.

"Mac, don't do this."

"He lied." The truth came at me pretty hard.

She winced. "You don't know that for sure."

"But you do."

"No. Like you said, I don't know everything." She skittered her gaze away for a moment, then rushed it back, eyes pleading. "And think about it, why would he admit to cheating on you if it wasn't true? You're a scary person. You're—"

"For the same reason you would."

Her face looked pale and strained. "I don't lie."

I took a deep breath. "But you would," I said. "You would to keep me safe. He was framed."

"You don't know that."

"He lied about sleeping with her so I wouldn't investigate."

"That's ridiculous." She laughed. I knew it was an act, but it wasn't too badly done, not compared to the performances of her early years on film. "He's not that brave. I mean, the chances of you killing him for having an affair are extremely high. Astronomically high. He must know that. He wouldn't—" But I had quit listening. In fact, I was pacing.

"Do you think he has an idea who did it?" I asked. "Do you think he's protecting someone?"

"Listen…"

"I bet he does. He's a good cop. A dumb ass and a liar." I scowled at her. "But a good cop."

"Please…"

"Coggins!" I stopped short. "The bullodog-faced cop. He said he's been waiting for Rivera to screw up. He said—"

"I'm pregnant!"

I froze, numb to the core as her words seeped slowly into my fat-saturated system. “What?” I drew the word out, lest she answer too quickly and throw my life into a tailspin. “What’d you say?”

She squeezed her hand into a fist near her heart, as if her emotions were a little too much to contain. “It’s a girl.”

I shook my head, perhaps to deny the fact that a guy as nerdy as the Geek God could reproduce. “You’re just saying that so I don’t do anything stupid,” I said, but she shook her head. There were tears in her eyes, but I was still in denial. “Solberg wouldn’t have shifted two millimeters from your side if he knew you were—” But the truth came home to me in one fell swoop. I sank into the closest chair. “He doesn’t know.”

She looked pale and beautiful and so happy it almost made me cry. “You’re the first person I’ve told.”

“Which means…” I reasoned, mind spinning slowly. “You really did sleep with him.”

She laughed. The noise sounded a little more like crying, and suddenly I saw it…that glow they talk about. It radiated from her eyes and shone from her freakishly perfect skin. I'd always assumed 'the glow' was a myth concocted by husbands who were trying to calm the fractious beast we know as gestating women.

“Mac,” she said, settling into the chair beside me. “I want you to be a part of her life. I want you to teach her to be obdurate and irritating and wonderfully perverse. Please, please don't get yourself killed."

Chapter 11

The presence of a well-endowed woman can often make men butt heads even if they've previously been on the most congenial terms.
—Dr. Candon, Chrissy's psych professor

The presence of a well-endowed woman can make men buttheads.
—Chrissy

"Officer Coggins?" I was dressed to maim in an eye-popping yellow blouse, a multi-tiered black skirt that just cleared my ass, and high-heeled sandals. Screw classy. I was going straight for mind-boggling skank. "Joel, isn't it?" The ensemble would have been good for dancing, but far better for fornicating.

The bulldog-faced cop seemed to notice. He turned toward me, nose misshapen and discolored from an overly aggressive elbow. It didn't take a genius to realize he was three sheets to the wind. He stared at me, recognition dawning slowly behind his half-mast eyelids.

"Christina McMullen," I reminded him, and leaned in to shake his hand. My boobs, relatively unimpressive under their own steam, were improved by sixteen-gauge under-wire, a half a peck of padding and mankind's best engineering feats. They loomed into view, as amicable as two bald-headed guys on a bender.

I didn't want to make the good officer think too hard.

"Thanks for the dance," Eddie said from behind me. His voice was low and manly, and he touched my arm lightly like men do when they're infatuated. Eddie Friar was big and buff and beautiful. We had dated shortly after my arrival in California. It was something of a disappointment…perhaps for both of us, when he was discovered to be as gay as a tulip. But he wasn't averse to doing me a favor now and then. And he was aces at taking directions; he remembered his predetermined lines down to the letter. "Call me later?"

"Sure," I said, and dismissed him with faux confidence as I turned back toward Coggins. "What are you doing here?" I asked. As if I didn't know he came to the Pain Reliever every Saturday and Wednesday without fail.

He didn't answer me right off. Instead, he watched me with beady canine eyes and a slight twist of his lips. "Rivera know you're stepping out on him already?"

"What?" I eased up beside him at the bar and nodded to the guy behind the rows of inverted glasses. He was as busy as a two-dollar hooker, but my boobs were on display and he took notice.

"I'll have a seven and seven," I said.

Coggins was still staring at me. "Rivera," he said, "he ain't the kind to share."

"Share what?" I asked, and taking a handful of nuts from the bowl on the counter, popped them into my mouth, casual as Fridays.

"Women," he said.

I turned toward him, eyes wide, freshly glossed lips parted provocatively…in case the boobs weren't in working order. "You think Rivera and I are a thing?"

He snorted. "Shit! You about tore me a new one when we went to pick him up."

I shrugged and gave the bartender a ten as I took my drink. "It's my job."

"What? Being a bitch?"

I gave him a laugh and a coy over-the-shoulder smile, as if I was just discovering his sterling wit. Refraining from giving him a black eye wasn't quite as simple. "Some people might call it that."

He watched me as if thinking really hard. I hoped the process wouldn't be fatal, at least until I learned what I had come for. "You saying you're his shrink?"

I bobbled my head in a noncommittal gesture. "Client confidentiality. You understand," I said.

His grin cranked up a little higher. "Rivera's seeing a shrink?"

I raised a haughty brow at him. "Turns out he needed more help than I could offer."

"Fuck," he said, and laughed out loud before slamming down the rest of his whisky sour and staring at me. "If you ain't into him, why'd you 'bout break my fucking nose?"

I shrugged. “I’m Irish,” I said. “That’s how we say good morning.”

He looked at me askance for an instant, then shook his head. “You got a thing for him,” he said. There was something like a snarl in his voice. My heart beat a little faster. “Damn wetback, I don’t know what women see in him.”

The statement smacked of anger well blended with jealousy and a spritz of admiration. I threw back my drink. It was almost palatable.

“A shithead?” I suggested.

He gave me a puzzled look. I could see by the hazy cast to his eyes that I was going to have to speak slower.

“They see a shithead,” I explained.

He made a noise that was something between a snort and a grunt. “That’s not how you acted on Wednesday.”

“Let’s just assume I’m better educated now,” I said.

He watched me, then took his new drink from the bartender.

“Let me guess,” he said. “You found out he was screwing your best friend.”

I curled up my lip a little and propped my boobs onto my left arm where it rested on the bar. I’d practiced the move at home and could now almost do it while chewing gum. “Do I look like the kind of woman that men cheat on?”

“You look like the kind of woman men cheat with.”

"Damn straight," I said, imbuing my tone with pride that some might call misplaced.

"So the pretty boy…," Coggins said, nodding toward Eddie. "Is he here to help you get over Rivera?"

I didn't bother to glance in my friend's direction. Instead, I silently hoped he wasn't hitting on some guy with boobs bigger than my own. I motioned toward Coggins' empty glass. "Looks like it's time to reload."

"I probably had enough," he said, which, in this particular situation, was a sure sign to the contrary.

"It's the least I can do," I said, and nodding toward his bruised nose, signaled the bartender for a refill.

In a minute, a fresh whisky sour was perspiring freely near Coggins' Ballpark Franks fingers.

"Rivera would get steamed if I even looked at another guy," I said as he took his first sip. I let a little vitriol seep into my voice and took a swig myself. "And all along, he was sleeping with every skank from here to Albuquerque."

"The guy's a prick from the ground up."

"You don't have to tell me."

"What?"

"I was his shrink, remember?"

"I bet you got some shit on him, huh?"

I shrugged. "Client privileges," I said again. "But I wasn't surprised to see that his behavior had caught up with him."

"Bout fuckin' time," he said, and finished his drink with impressive speed.

I watched him with a crafty eye. "So what was her name?" I asked finally.

"What the hell you talking about?" he asked, and I laughed.

"The girl he stole from you."

"There wasn't no girl."

I chuckled again, jolly as Saturday-morning cartoons. "Well, I wouldn't worry about it. He'll drop her fast enough."

"Like he did you?"

I eyed him as if I was about to revisit his nose job, but then I drew a deep breath and snorted. "I'm lucky to be rid of him."

"Didn't seem like you were feeling real fortunate Wednesday night."

"Like I said, I've been educated since then."

He thought about that for a second. I let him ruminate. It looked as if it was getting to be more painful by the second.

"So you don't mind pissing him off," he reasoned.

"I wouldn't even mind pissing on him."

He chuckled. The sound wasn't pretty. "You're in luck then. 'Cause he's going to be away for a long time."

I shook my head. "You must have forgotten who his father is."

"It don't matter," he said. "There's enough evidence to lock him up 'til someone's gotta chew his food for him."

"He'll find a way around it."

"I'll make sure he doesn't."

I smiled at him, heart thumping with excitement. "You can do that?"

He turned, hooked his elbows behind him on the bar and watched me with the kind of growing confidence that only guys like Jim Beam can inspire.

"You know what would really piss him off?" he asked.

I caught his gaze in a cunning half nelson. "If I slept with the man who set him up?"

He straightened, sobering with alarming speed. "I didn't say nothing about setting him up."

I nodded knowingly and took a casual sip of my drink, but my pulse was still racing. "Kudos to you for not having to brag."

He narrowed his eyes again. "I take it you wouldn't cry too hard to learn he'd been framed."

"I think I'd manage to carry on."

"That's—"

"Coggins," someone called.

I cursed in silence and turned to my left. A man was sifting through the crowd toward the bar.

He was tall and blond and too good looking to be 3D. It took me a moment to recognize him as the other cop who had invaded my office just a few days before. Maybe the mental delay was caused by the ingestion of alcohol. My tolerance for intoxicating beverages is just below that of a flea's. Nevertheless, his name popped unexpectedly into my head: Eric Albertson. Was he somehow involved in this? Maybe Coggins wasn't the culprit at all.

"Hey." He nodded toward the bartender before clapping a friendly hand on his partner's shoulder.

"I'm kind of busy right now," Coggins said.

Albertson grinned before turning to the bartender. "I'll have the same as him," he said, then, "What's up?" he asked. "You make some kind of pact with the devil or something?"

Coggins scowled.

Albertson nodded with faux surreptitiousness toward me, and the other grudgingly caught on.

"Oh, this is…" He paused, searching for my name.

"Christina McMullen," I said, and reached for Albertson's hand. I showed him the bald headed twins, but he just nodded, manfully keeping his gaze above my clavicle.

"Nice to meet you."

We all waited a beat.

"She's the shrink," Coggins explained finally. He didn't seem all that thrilled to see his buddy. Boobs can do that to fellas.

"What?"

"We met in my office a couple days ago," I reminded him.

Albertson scowled, then opened his eyes wide and leaned back from the bar a little. “Jesus! When we picked up Lieutenant Rivera. Christ!” He canted his head a little, studying me. “That was you, wasn’t it?”

“It was.”

“I’m sorry." He almost managed to cover his wince, but both embarrassment and regret were just visible in his sea foam eyes. "That was a bad deal. I hate to do that to a fellow officer. It's especially hard with someone from my own shop. Rivera is hard working and conscienscious. Not everyone is." He shook his head once as if deep in thought before shifting his eyes back to me. "You two must be pretty tight?”

“She’s his ex,” Coggins said.

Albertson raised his brows and lifted his freshly arrived drink from the bar. “No.”

I drank simultaneously, resentful to think I could have purchased two peanut buster parfaits for less cash. “It’s true.”

“His ex.”

“Yup.”

“Christ, I’d hate to see you if you were in love.”

I canted my head at him.

“You throw a pretty mean elbow for an ex.”

“It’s Irish,” I said, and when he scowled a question, I explained. “My elbow.”

He laughed. Go, me.

“Well, I have to get to bed. It was very nice seeing you again, Officer Albertson." I nodded in his direction, but kept my boobage to myself this time. I couldn't think of any reason to cozy up to him. "And you, Mr. Coggins… I'm always up for a lively…debate." I glanced up through my lashes, granting him my craftiest smile and hoping he was still coherent enough to sniff out the pheromones I was shoveling toward him with the subtlety of a backstreet brawler. "Maybe we could continue our discussion some other time." I shrugged one shoulder, showcasing Leftie and feeling his gaze slip into my cleavage like marbles down a drain. "I'll debate anything from picture frames to politics," I said and pivoting on one sassy heel, hoped to hell that he'd feel the need to brag about how he'd set up the dark lieutenant while simultaneously outwitting his politically savvy sire.

Chapter 12

I don't suffer from stress, but recent circumstances suggest that I may be a carrier.
—Chrissy McMullen, after one of her more harrowing conversations with Lieutenant Jack Rivera

"Captain Kindred?" I unfolded from my Saturn and speed-walked after Rivera's superior officer. The asphalt burned beneath my feet like a dry heat sauna. I was wearing three-inch heels, a form-fitting silk blouse and a black pencil skirt. Speed walking is a relative term.

The captain glanced over his shoulder. His face was made of leftover hound dog and yesterday's woes. I thought I saw him curse silently, but I must have been wrong; he didn't know me well enough to hate me yet.

"Captain, do you have a minute?"

"I'm extremely busy," he said, and emphasized his point by continuing to walk away. But I've been put off by more determined men.

I grabbed his sleeve. He swung toward me, looking dark, peeved and intimidatingly large.

"He didn't do it," I said.

There was a momentary pause during which he seemed to resign himself to a certain amount of annoyance. "I assume you're talking about Lieutenant Rivera?" He sounded tired and annoyed but managed not to roll his eyes. Maybe I should have been impressed by his self-restraint but I was pretty tired myself. After my visit to the Pain Reliever on the previous evening, I had spent most of the night searching the internet for information about Coggins. Cops, it seems, are fairly public characters.

On the other hand, I still hadn't heard a word on the news about the attempt on Andrews's life. I had no idea who was keeping that under wraps or how they were doing it.

"You know he's innocent," I said.

"The department is reserving judgment until—"

I made a pssting noise, like a hissing air hose or a dog relieving himself on hot asphalt. I was fairly familiar with that sound. "Listen, I spoke to Officer Coggins."

"You what?" His tone suggested he was fully awake now. Awake and listening.

"I think he set Rivera up." Maybe I should have waited to see if Coggins came around to offer more information but I was already beginning to doubt my own sex appeal and his ability to understand my heavy-handed invitation while under the influence. So here I was.

Captain Kindred stared at me for several more seconds then pulled out of my grip and strode with determined haste toward the building.

"I have reason to believe they had a dispute over a woman," I said, and caught up in five strides. I was pacing along beside him in a matter of moments. “Stacy Marquet. She and Coggins were engaged. But then she met Rivera.” I shrugged, willing to let him believe it was water under the bridge so far as I was concerned. “I think Officer Coggins is carrying a grudge and…”

“Ms. McMullen!” Kindred stopped so abruptly that I almost torpedoed past him on my pretty, but hopelessly impractical shoes. “The department is fully capable of handling this situation.”

I stared up at him, heart pumping adrenaline into my system at a rate which should have alarmed me…or him. “Then why is he still incarcerated?”

“The legal system is a long, involved—”

“He’s innocent,” I said. “You and I both know—”

“It takes a good deal of time and manpower to—”

“Coggins has means, motive and—”

“Don’t do it!” he warned, and shoved a dark, blunt index finger toward my face. “Don’t you get involved in this or I’ll make sure you never interfere with so much as a traffic ticket—”

“He deeply resents Rivera’s—”

“Good God,” he said, and now he did roll his eyes. “He told me you would be a pain in the ass.”

“What do you mean would be?” I snorted. “Coggins doesn’t know me well enough to understand just how much of a pain I can—”

“Rivera!” he snapped. “That was Lieutenant Rivera's assessment."

"Well..." I gave him a pissy expression. "Rivera and I have had our share of disagreements, but that doesn't mean I can allow him to languish in jail while the true culprit lives his life with impunity."

The captain stared at me as if I'd grown a second head, then, "Go home," he said.

"I wish I could, but justice-"

"If you want justice why don't you leave me alone and let me do my job?" he asked, and pivoted away.

"Because you suck at your job!" I snapped.

He turned toward me like an angry bull, burly head lowered. "What'd you say?"

I swallowed, realized a bit belatedly that while I was not a small woman, small was a relative term. I tried a smile. "I said, I would suck at your job." The smile wobbled on my face. "If I... If I had your job." He was still glaring. "If I had your job, I would suck at it."

The furrows in his forehead were deep enough to lose small pets in. His scowl was like a black holc. "Go home," he repeated, and turned away again, but I dashed around him, then spun about, dancing backward while I speed-talked.

"I feel quite strongly that Coggins is somehow involved."

He shook his head once, like a grizzly trying to rid himself of gnats. "You can feel whatever you like."

"He deeply resents Lieutenant Rivera."

"You worry about everyone who doesn't like your boyfriend, you're not going to get much sleep at night."

"The lieutenant is no longer my boyfriend, Captain, but that fact is not pertinent in this particular situation. Officer Coggins said he's been waiting for the day Rivera was arrested."

Kindred stopped. So I had finally gotten his attention, I thought, but then he snorted and continued belligerently on toward the cop shop.

"You've been watching too much Matlock," he said.

I do love Matlock, but I didn't think that statement was necessarily a testament to my clear-headed deductions. "Can you think of anyone else who might bear the lieutenant ill will?"

"Besides you?" he asked.

I tripped in my backward journey, then righted myself and stared at him in shock. I'm a little ashamed to admit that I may have clasped my hand to my heart in weak-assed surprise.

"I'm a mental health practitioner," I said, though in all honesty I have no idea why I thought that made a difference. After all, Dr. David Hawkins, one of L.A.'s most noted mental health practitioners, had once tried to fillet me with a stainless steel kitchen knife.

Apparently it didn't make much of an impact on the captain, because he chuckled a little as he strode past me.

Nevertheless, I shouted, “I can help you," at his retreating back.

“Don’t,” he said, and disappeared into his chosen sanctuary.

“I’m a psychologist,” I said again, but I wasn’t panting it to an oversized black man with a hound dog face this time. Now I sat with regal aplomb in my office. A young woman I still referred to as Emily occupied my client couch. There were scars on her right wrist. The ones on her soul were less visible but more deadly. “And I can honestly tell you that you’re not as screwed up as you think you are.”

“Really?” She crossed her disgustingly slim legs at the ankle and settled back against the cushion behind her. She still dressed as prim as a church lady, but since she’d begun coming a year of so before, she’d unwound a little. Eventually, she’d even admitted her real name. “Give me a for instance.”

“You know I can’t discuss my other clients.”

“Don’t use their names,” she said. “Just the situations.”

I thought about that for a second. This might very well be a game I shouldn’t play, but the girl was too serious for her age. In fact, she was too serious for any age. “On three separate instances, clients have shown me their genitalia.”

She made a face. “Ohhhh, please tell me they weren’t sitting on this couch.”

I laughed, shrugged. “You can’t imagine how grateful I am that you remain fully dressed at all times.”

“My pleasure,” she said, and uncrossing her legs, toed off her practical little pumps to tuck her feet under her bottom. The relaxed gesture was unprecedented, but I refrained from breaking out the champagne. “The thing is…” She pulled another face, and a fraction of her old angst stole in. “The thing is…”

“What’s the thing?” I asked.

“It’s the people one cares for the most who disappoint to the greatest degree.” Her gaze found mine. I remembered her showing up for the first time. She’d talked about her over-zealous but proud parents, who gave her the best of everything in an effort to make her as spectacular as themselves. It had been a lie from the word go. “Those are the ones who do the most profound job of messing with your mind.”

“What happened?” I asked.

She shrugged. The movement should have been casual. It was not.

“Aggie Christian called me an ice queen. Mr. Marshall gave me an A when I clearly deserved an A plus, and Will…”

I waited.

She sighed. “Will dumped me.”

“I’m sorry,” I said, and maybe I kind of was, but I wasn’t the least bit surprised. Will was never going to be right for her. Never smart enough or driven enough or understanding enough. Emily demanded a lot of energy, emotional and otherwise, and always would. Maybe that's why I liked her so well.

"He didn't even have a reason."

"How was your weekend away together?" I asked.

"I didn't go." She shook her head. "I had to prepare for Introduction to Drama."

I raised a brow.

"Literature," she said. "It's my most challenging subject. I mean, there's no right or wrong. Not really. You can't get a straight answer."

"I thought you didn't start college until the middle of September."

She gave me a pinched nosed expression. "That's the kind of attitude that'll get you an A minus," she said.

I opened my mouth to object, but she raised a prim hand and hurried on. "That's not the point anyway. It's…" She shook her head. "We're too young to get serious. But it just proves that it's the people who are supposed to care about you that…" She paused, glanced out the window toward the coffee shop that housed my favorite frosted scones.

"That what?" I asked.

"That screw you the worst," she said.

From the mouths of babes… I sighed. "That is, sometimes, unfortunately true."

"I think it's always true."

I took a deep mental breath and jumped in. “Have you seen your mother lately?”

She smoothed out a wrinkle in her skirt. It would have been invisible to the average eye, but Emily wasn’t average. “I’ve been so busy. Studying for the ACTs, checking into medical schools. Mom knows how important it is that I have exemplary grades in order to succeed.” She shifted her eyes to mine and held my gaze, daring me to object. “She told me not to bother visiting her until I had time.”

The room went quiet.

“In other words,” I said. “You don’t know where she is.”

“Of course I—” she began, then clenched her jaw and stared out the window again. I had the feeling she wasn’t thinking about frosted scones. “Damn her,” she whispered, and we were off and running.

Four hours and two clients later, I was home.

After three days of begging me to be careful, Laney had returned to Matamata. The emptiness of the house filled me like a dark cloud. Thoughts and worries and fears chased themselves around in my brain like half-starved piranhas.

Emily was right. It was the people you care about the most who can do the most harm. My parents, for instance, had done a fairly stellar job of making me into the nut-case I could sometimes be. Dr. David Hawkins had been something of a personal hero before he'd tried to kill me with that filet knife, and Lieutenant Rivera…

I sighed as my mind rambled on. It didn't really matter any longer how I had felt about the lieutenant. The question was who had hated him enough to frame him. Or maybe… I scrunched up my face as I settled onto the couch and stroked Harlequin's floppy ears. Maybe the question wasn't who hated him, but who cared about him.

I was just about ready to fetch a pad of paper to begin listing his old flames when the phone blurted from the kitchen, startling me from my musings. I picked up on the fifth ring, voice a little breathless.

"Christina?"

"Yes?"

"This is Joel."

I remained silent, thinking, my heart beating a dull tattoo in my chest.

"Joel Coggins," he said. "I was wondering if you'd like to get together for a drink sometime."

Chapter 13

When a man talks dirty to a woman, it's sexual harassment. When a woman talks dirty to a man, it's $3.95 a minute.
—One of Chrissy's illustrious clients, who was certain he was not a sex addict but would just as soon remain anonymous anyway

I told myself once again that it didn't matter whether Rivera had been as faithful as a Labrador or as loose as a goose; I was absolutely certain he was innocent. And if he wasn't innocent, there was a high likelihood that he had acted as he did in an effort to keep me safe.

Okay, maybe I wasn't as absolutely certain as I would like to believe. And maybe that's why I placed a call to Officer Tavis.

"Christina McMullen," he said in that slow, small-town way he has. Tavis is a cop in a little village a couple lifetimes west of L.A. where jaywalking is considered a heinous crime punishable by thirty lashes or the rack. "You must have finally had your fill of those big-time cops and small-time dicks, huh?"

Tavis had a dirty mouth but a quick mind. If I were going to be completely honest, which I generally am not, I would have to admit that I kind of appreciate both.

"How's life in Smallville?" I asked.

"Oh…" I could hear the shrug in his voice as he settled back in his springy chair. "The county fair's coming up soon, so everybody's pretty hepped about that. And Opie Taylor got busted for spitting on Main Street last Tuesday."

I adjusted my skirt a little. It was a bit tight around the waist. I tend to eat when I'm nervous. And sometimes when I'm scared. Always when I'm bored, and usually when I'm frustrated. Eating—the emotional catch-all. "There's actually a kid named Opie in town?"

There was a pause. "What's wrong?" he asked finally.

"Nothing. Why?"

"You're usually a little quicker to recognize sarcasm than that. It's one of my favorite things about you. That and your ass. Although your—"

"A simple no would have been sufficient," I said.

"Oh. Okay. No, Christina. There's no Opie Taylor in Edmond Park. This isn't Mayberry.

"So, what's up?"

"Not much," I lied, nervous now about calling. "What's up with you?"

"You really have to ask, knowing the dearth of datable women in this little burg?"

I rolled my eyes. "I had almost forgotten how perverted you are."

"Want a refresher course?"

"Maybe later."

"Really? Damn. That's the best offer I've had in months. So…on to your concerns; my advice is that you forget the whole thing."

"What are you talking about?"

"Whatever you have in mind. Forget it. Stay home. Get a good bottle of wine. Call an old boyfriend. Hell, call me. I'm free, available and hard up."

I was silent for a moment then, "You heard about Rivera."

"I did."

"He's not guilty."

He inhaled audibly. "He's a big boy, Christina."

People kept saying things like that. It made me wonder if everyone was familiar with his size.

"Not as big as me, I'm sure," he rushed to add. "But big enough. He can take care of himself."

"I'm not calling about that."

"Really?"

"Yes." I was lying again, but without my usual panache.

"So you just wanted to talk dirty?"

"I wanted you to check someone out for me."

"Someone…."

"A cop," I said, and paused to chew my lip.

He waited in silence for a while then, "Some particular cop, or will any old cop do?"

"His name's Joel Coggins."

"So this has nothing to do with Rivera?"

"No."

"Then why—"

"He asked me out on a date."

"Seriously?"

"Yes, seriously."

"I can't believe you're going to date another cop and you haven't even slept with me yet."

"Well, believe it."

"You know, despite the rumors, I'm not that bad in bed."

"Well, you do know how to sell yourself. So I'll certainly keep you in mind."

"Do. Please. I mean—"

"Tavis…" I interrupted him rather abruptly. Maybe there was a little bit of panic in my voice. "Just check him out, will you?"

"When's your date?" His tone was almost serious.

"Tomorrow night."

"I'll call you back," he said, and hung up.

It was a long day. I saw two depressed CEOs, a kleptomaniac and a cross-dresser. None of them was as screwy as I was.

After work, I stopped at a big box electronics store and bought a very small battery-run recorder. I was fiddling with it when Tavis called at 7:42.

"Are you a masochist?" he asked.

"What are you talking about?"

"Joel Coggins. I saw a picture of him."

“Oh.” I shrugged, trying to relieve the tension in my shoulders. “I don’t base my relationships on a person’s physical appearance.”

There was a pause, then, “Why the hell not?”

“Because—” I began, then remembered not to play his ridiculous games and stopped myself.

“What did you find out?”

“That you must be severely myopic.”

“Can you get beyond looks, please?”

“I never have so far.”

“Tavis—”

He sighed. I kind of wondered how he ever got anything done in Edmond Park, but apparently he was a pretty good cop. “It looks as if Officer Coggins graduated at the middle of his class. Been with the L.A.P.D. for four years. No commendations, but no reports of misconduct, either.”

“Is he…” I didn’t know what questions to ask. I really wanted to know what the chances were of me getting dead, but I wasn’t sure how to frame that particular query. “…single?”

“You’re killing me.”

“Is he?”

“Used to be married. Divorced two years ago.”

“Any sign of trouble there?”

“What do you think, Christina, that divorces are made of dewdrops and funnel cakes?”

“Did she file any complaints?”

He paused a moment. I could almost hear his scowl. “Not that were recorded.”

I thought about that for a second. “Are you saying the department might have hushed up something like that?”

“I hate to burst your illusions about cops and their god-like moral standards.”

I ignored his sarcasm as best I could, though it was pretty impressive. “So he’s single now.”

“Are you kidding me? With a face like that, it’s amazing he’s not on a leash.”

“Is he seeing anyone?” I asked again.

He issued a long-suffering sigh. “Looks like he used to be.”

“How long ago?”

“Five months, maybe. There’s a picture with him and a Stacy Marquet at the Policeman’s Ball. That name mean anything to you?”

She was the woman Rivera had supposedly stolen from Coggins, but I didn’t say that. “No.” Another lie. A little better this time. “Why should it?”

“Because you’re lying through your teeth.”

“I don’t know what you’re talking about.”

“Of course you don’t.”

“What’s this um….what was her name?” I asked. My voice retained a sweetness that made me a little sick to my stomach. And I have a great tolerance for sugar.

“Sally?” he said.

I made a face, wondering if he was playing me. “I don’t think that was it.”

"Probably because you know everything about her but her shoe size."

Seven, I thought, but I didn't say that either. "Stacy? Was that her name?"

He didn't bother to comment.

"What's she doing now?" I asked.

"How the hell would I know?"

"You're a cop," I reminded him.

"Oh right, and in Christina's I-only-date-cops-who-aren't-named-Tavis world that's tantamount to Superman."

"Tantamount?"

"I ran out of jigsaw puzzles at the station. Been reading the dictionary. Let me guess," he said, rudely eschewing all segues. "You think this ugly-ass Joel Coggins is somehow responsible for your lieutenant's current predicament."

"Why would you think that?"

"When I get tired of the dictionary, I sometimes read sleuth novels."

"I'm not a sleuth."

"That's good, because in the books those sleuths usually get themselves in a shitload of trouble."

I swallowed.

"But that's just fiction."

"Good to know."

"In real life, I'm pretty sure those dumb-ass sleuths would end up decomposing in a dumpster somewhere."

Something banged in the kitchen. I jumped as if shot, then froze as Harlequin pranced into the living room wearing an aluminum can on his nose. Harley loves the recyclables. Which is only one of the reasons I spend half my income at the emergency veterinary clinic. The other reason generally has something to do with the ingestion of copious amounts of chocolate.

"Chrissy?"

I tugged the can off Harley's nose and checked the front door. It was locked. The security system was on. It's not as if I can't learn.

"I'm not sleuthing," I reminded him.

"How about prying?" he asked. "You doing any of that?"

"Just going out for drinks."

"With dog-face boy?"

"Apparently I'm not as shallow as you are."

"Who is?"

"Yet to be determined. So he has no priors, right?"

"Good God, you even sound like a cop."

"Does he or doesn't he?"

"There are rumors about domestic abuse."

"Shit." The word escaped on its own.

"Listen…" He sounded serious for an unprecedented second time. "Just because he's as ugly as a small-town whore, doesn't mean he's a nice guy."

"It doesn't mean he's not."

"Maybe, but you might as well date a cop with a decent face and a really gigantic—"

"Thanks for the advice," I hurried to say.

He chuckled. "There's more where that came from."

"Anything helpful?"

"Yeah." He paused, exuding quiet reflection. "Don't do it."

"Do what?"

"Whatever you're planning. Forget it."

"We're just going to have a couple of drinks. Maybe a little conversation. That's it."

He swore. It was neither as inventive nor as passionate as Rivera's used to be, but there was a nice rhythm to it.

"He's not coming to your house, is he?"

"Do you think I'm crazy?"

"More often than not. Where are you meeting him?"

I paused.

"Chrissy, unless you're driving a hundred miles west for this little rendezvous tonight, I can't interfere. But if you're found hacked to pieces in a mail box on Pico Boulevard, I'd like to know where to locate the rest of your body parts."

I swallowed the bile that had somehow worked its way into my esophagus. "You always sweet talk a girl like this?"

"My own brand of foreplay. Where you meeting him?"

"The Wheel, in Glendale."

"Well, that's a decent part of town anyway."

"I'm not a complete idiot."

"Good to know. Call me when you get home."

"Okay."

"And Christina…"

"What?"

"Don't waste your money on one of those cheap recorders."

"What?" I stopped fiddling with my brand-new device. "Recorders? I don't know what you're talking about."

He sighed.

"I don't know what you're talking about," I repeated, voice a little higher pitched.

"Those cheap pieces of shit are as tinny as hell," he said. "If you can't understand anything Coggins says, it's not going to do you a damn bit of good in court."

Chapter14

Whoever said that all we have to fear is fear itself wasn't married for more than thirty-two seconds.
—Mr. Howard Lepinski, who was married for an eternity

I was as jumpy as the mythical virgin bride on the following day. After barely hearing a word my clients spoke and nearly causing an accident on the eternally gridlocked 5, I deliberately slowed down and focused on thinking clearly. Tonight I would be logical and smart and sophisticated. I would exude class and confidence, I promised myself.

In an attempt to reach those lofty goals, I emptied my front seat of burger wrappers and pastry bags, wrangled my hair into an upswept do, and slipped into an ivory skirt and navy blue blouse. My brand new recorder, a slim, high-end (aka, expensive) unit, fit neatly into my bra. I was the very picture of sophistication…and I was nervous enough to pee in my pants.

Hence, I stopped at a Shell station to use a restroom. Even before exiting my car, however, I realized the ladies' was one of those terrifying outside units. I sat there in cystic agony for a while. But in the end, history won out. I'd had too many nasty experiences to warrant venturing out into the dark alone like a brain-damaged sorority girl in a horror flick. I'd rather wear a diaper for the remainder of the evening.

Luckily, an Arco station saved me from investing in Depends. After driving an additional five blocks I discovered that that esteemed establishment housed the doors of its restrooms inside. Ahh, the beauty of modern conveniences that will prevent you from getting mugged.

Still, I was as jittery as hell as I crossed the parking lot and subsequently dropped my keys on the asphalt twice. The second time I bent to retrieve them, someone whistled from a waiting van, but I was too harried to appreciate being subjugated. Hurrying into the well-lit interior, I waited outside the bathroom for a miserable thirty seconds, then hustled inside to relieve myself at the earliest possible moment.

While in the privacy of the restroom, I slipped the tiny recorder out of my bra and switched it on. Its brochure had promised sixteen hours of high quality audio so the time frame was the least of my worries. The fact that it was finally wedged between my boobs like a miniature cinder block again was both comforting and disconcerting.

Still, all was well when I paid for gas and a car wash and folded myself back into my Saturn. With a happy bladder, I felt confident and strong once again. I was in control.

The car wash was one of those fully automated units that sucks you through like a dark, weirdly animated tunnel of love. I put the car in neutral and shut off the engine. The whooshing sound of the washers was oddly soothing, giving me a few needed seconds to get in touch with my thoughts. Maybe, like my Saturn, I had been in neutral. But no more. Now I was being proactive but not foolhardy. Thoughtful but not obsessed. I'd wash my car, meet Coggins, learn what I could and go home to ponder—

I heard a noise from the backseat a fraction of a second before a hand slapped over my mouth. Terror ripped through me like a hurricane. I tried to scream, to twist away, but I couldn't.

"Don't do anything stupid, McMullen." The voice was low and guttural. I froze, cranking my eyes backward, but I couldn't see a thing.

My mind was buzzing, trying to think. Trying to figure out what to do. At that particular juncture, I was utterly willing to give him anything—my purse, my car, my firstborn—but I had no way to verbalize my stupendous generosity.

It wasn't until that moment that my mind slammed into the realization that he'd used my name. But not my given name. My surname. My Irish name. McMullen. Who called me—

Rivera!

I knew it…knew that he had gotten out of jail and was trying to teach me a lesson…again. Rage pumped through me like molten lava. I twisted wildly toward the rear. He tried to hold me still, but I was pissed. I bit down, drawing blood between his thumb and pointer finger.

He cursed and tried to pull away, but I was already clambering over the seat toward him, skirt bunching around my scrambling legs.

"Turn around! Stay back!" he warned, but I've never been one for taking orders.

"What the hell is wrong with you?" I was hissing with fury, snarling with a dangerous mix of rage and relief to learn that Rivera was not only safe but free.

That's when he hit me in the face!

I flattened back against the front seat, head spinning, cheek throbbing, thoughts scrambling like broken eggs in my cranium. The lieutenant may be a cheat and a liar. But he wouldn't hit me. Raking my thoughts haphazardly together, I lunged for the door, but he yanked me back inside.

I screamed but the noise was washed away by the soggy arms that struck the Saturn. He hit me again, clubbing me on the side of the head. My ears exploded, spurring up a new batch of rage and terror. I slammed my elbow backward and heard cartilage crunch, but it didn't do me any good.

He was already pushing me face down into the seat, compressing my lungs, straddling my thigh. I felt his erection against my backside and almost gagged, but that was before I realized there was a cord around my neck. And suddenly I couldn't breathe. My chest ached. I bucked against him, sobbing and rasping for breath.

He growled something, a curse or a threat.

But at that second one of the washer arms must have hit my trunk just right. It popped open. The asshole atop me jerked his attention to the left, and in that moment I jabbed backward with my elbow. He slammed toward the door. I yanked my right knee over the edge of the seat, then kicked with all the force my screaming muscles could muster. I felt my heel strike his jaw, heard his teeth clack. I rolled onto my back and kicked with both feet. My heels caught him mid body. He fell against the door, hands flying up. I realized for the first time that he was wearing something over his head. But the sheer fabric didn't hide the rage in his eyes. For an abbreviated moment, I could see they were bright with hatred, and then he was gone, toppling backward into the swooshing arms of the car wash.

One arm struck the open door, banging it closed. It took all my strength to reach up and punch the locks closed. Then I lay on the seat like a beached trout, crying and trembling.

I have no way of knowing how much time passed, maybe it was several minutes before my car rolled to a halt.

But finally a face appeared at my window. I gasped and jerked to a seated position at the sight of an acne-riddled boy staring into the car. He scanned the front seat, then saw me in the back and adjusted his position, making a rolling down motion as he did so. My hands shook like leaflets in a windstorm as I tried to open the window, but the car was shut off. I was almost entirely incapable of opening the door. The boy scanned the backseat as if searching for a covert lover. His voice was quizzical.

"You gotta clear the area," he said. "We got another customer wants a wash."

I filed a police report at the nearest station that night, sat in a snot-green plastic chair while they dusted for fingerprints and checked for DNA, then refused an escort and drove home like someone in a functional coma. Once there, I turned on every light in the house and crawled into bed, fully dressed. Harlequin heaved himself up beside me and let me cry onto his velvety ear until I fell asleep.

I woke up sometime before dawn. The house was as bright as a shooting nova and utterly silent. Harley's right ear was still wet from my tears, I was sweating like an ox, and my chest ached. For a second I thought I might be experiencing a well-deserved heart attack, but then I remembered the diminutive tape recorder I had shoved between my boobs.

Harley gave me a jaundiced glance as I sat up and retrieved the tiny device. It took me a few minutes to remember how to play back the recording. A series of hisses and scrapes issued from the machine. The noises were totally unidentifiable and did nothing but make my hands shake and my stomach heave.

The rest of the night was pretty much of a bust.

The following morning wasn't much better, but I applied makeup to the worst of the bruises, assured myself I looked somewhat better than road-kill and drove to the office. Once there, I told my clients a not-too-far-fetched story about being dragged down the sidewalk by Harlequin, and tried to carry on as if my face didn't look as though it had mauled by a grizzly.

In the afternoon, I drove to Rivera's station to talk to Captain Kindred. He came in through the back door finally, hound-dog face haggard, but when he saw mine he winced.

"Holy shit," he rumbled, and motioned me irritably toward his office.

I followed him into a room the size of my thumb. Dcspitc the fact that my face looked like an impressionist's angry pallet, I was doing a pretty fair job of controlling my tears if I do say so myself. But by then I had spent the past sixteen hours blubbering like a spanked infant, so maybe my stoicism had more to do with a lack of body fluids than with fortitude.

"Sit down," he ordered, and motioned toward a chair beside the door.

I considered refusing, but my legs were as weak as my bladder. The chair felt hard and solid against my thighs.

"What happened?" His voice was as hard as the chair.

"Last night…" I took a deep breath and wondered if the proverbial dam would hold. "At approximately 7:15 I stopped at an Arco station on Foothill and Cullen." I'd been through enough of these situations to know how to give a detailed report. It wasn't a good sign. "I paid for thirty dollars worth of gas and a car wash. When I returned to my vehicle there was someone in the backseat."

He clenched his teeth and moved to the far side of his desk for a pad of paper. "You filled out a full report?"

I swallowed hard and managed a nod.

"I'm sure they've checked the video cam, but I'll look into it."

"Thank you." I still didn't cry. Miracles do happen. I took a deep breath and dove in. "I believe the perpetrator was Officer Coggins."

The pad dropped out of his hand. He didn't seem to notice. "What the hell are you talking about?"

I tightened my fists and wished I had fortified myself with a couple dozen cupcakes. Or at least a glass of wine.

"I was supposed to meet him at the Wheel at 7:30. I was attacked at 7:17. When I called the restaurant at 7:42, he still hadn't shown—"

"Why?" His body was very still, his voice low.

"What?"

"Why the hell were you supposed to meet him?"

"I just…" I considered telling him I was irresistibly attracted to the man, but my face hurt too much to formulate a decent lie. My Emerald Isle antecedents, a list of prostitutes and con artists as long as my arm, were probably rolling over in their graves like loose dice at my lack of ability. "I believe I told you about my suspicions regarding his connection with Rivera's incarceration."

"God damn it." He said the words very softly.

I straightened my spine. "He knew my name." My hands were shaking again. I put them against my thighs and raised my chin like a martyr at a lynching. "I believe he was going to warn me not to interfere with the…" My voice failed me. I cleared my throat. "With the investigation."

The captain's hang-dog gaze didn't leave my face for several seconds, but finally he strode to the door, yanked it open and growled at some poor gopher on the far side.

In a second he was back. He turned away from me, gazing out his dusty window. He had a dynamite view of the parking lot and the northwest corner of the city library.

"Did I or did I not warn you against getting involved in this?" His back was as broad as a Ping-Pong table. His button-down shirt was wrinkled except where it was stretched tight across his shoulders.

I felt my eyes tear up and swiped the back of my hand beneath my nose lest it join the drippy brigade.

"Miss McMullen," he snarled, and pivoted toward me just as the first traitorous tear fell.

"Ahh, hell," he said, and dipped his head as if trying to disavow my tears, but they were the real deal…the stuff that makes grown men run screaming into the night.

He reached for a squashed box of tissues just as the door swung open.

Coggins stood in the opening, gaze sharp on the captain's. His squinty eyes were narrowed. His nose was an odd hue of purple and his left cheekbone harbored a superficial laceration about two inches long. "You wanted to see me?"

"Come in here," the captain ordered.

He stepped inside. I felt my guts shake.

"Shut the door."

He did so. And in that second his porcine eyes swung toward me.

"Holy fuck!" He breathed the words, narrow eyes going wide. "What are you doing here?"

I tried to speak, but it was impossible to open my mouth.

"Where were you at 7:15 last night?" Captain Kindred asked.

"What? I…" Coggins's mouth remained open as he stared at me. No more words came.

"Coggins!"

"What the fuck is this about?" he rasped.

"Just answer the damn question."

"This is a fucking set-up."

The captain took a step toward him. "Where were you?"

Coggins scowled. His eyes darted from side to side, but he finally conquered the worst of his terror and steadied his gaze. "I was supposed to meet her."

The captain fisted mallet-sized hands beside his thighs and lowered his head.

"But you already know that, don't you?" Coggins asked.

"So why didn't you?" The captain's voice was low, laced with suspicion and anger. "Why didn't you meet her?"

"I don't think it matters," Coggins said, and flattened me with his glare. "Not when Rivera's bitch is here telling stories about-"

"I'm going to ask you once more," the captain said. His tone had gone from dangerous to deadly. "Where were you?"

For a moment I thought Coggins would refuse to answer, but he wasn't suicidal. "I got a flat."

Silence filled the room like toxic smog.

"A flat tire?"

"Yeah."

"Where?"

"What the hell difference—"

"Where?" the captain asked, but I was already speaking despite my smarter instincts.

"What happened to your face?" I asked. I meant to sound accusatory and self-assured. I may have sounded more like a quivering castrato.

He tightened his hands to fists and took half a step forward. "You hit me in the nose, you—"

"Coggins!"

He straightened immediately at the captain's reprimand. "She hit me," he said. "When we went to pick up Rivera."

"I didn't hit you in the cheek. What happened to your cheek?"

"That's from the tire iron. Not that it's any of your business, you fucking little-"

“Watch your language!” Kindred snarled, then turned to me. “Is that true?”

“I—”

“What the hell is this?” Coggins snapped. “You sucking up to her, too, just because she’s Rivera’s—”

Kindred took a step toward him. Coggins dropped his head and went immediately silent. The room echoed with tension.

“Tell me what happened last night,” Kindred ordered.

“Just because—”

“Tell me!” he growled.

Coggins snorted a laugh. “You’re not going to believe me anyway. The whole fucking department knows you’re kissing up to Rivera’s old man. We all know who the real problem is in this—”

“Coggins!” the captain barked.

The man seemed to visibly shrink. “My tire blew on the 710.”

Their gazes met and smoldered. “Any witnesses?”

“Sure. Sure there are. About a thousand fucking commuters flying by at a hundred miles an hour over the speed—” He stopped, frowned, seemed to try to think. “Yeah,” he said, relief lightening his tone. "Yeah, I have a witness. A guy from some towing company stopped."

"You called a tow truck?"

"On my god damn salary?" The words were a sneer. "He wanted fifty bucks just to drag the piece of shit off the interstate."

"Who was he?"

"How the hell should I know? You thinking we were pen pals or something?"

"I'm not a patient man," the captain warned.

Coggins stuck out his jaw, but there was caution in his eyes now. Caution and enough fear to make him seem sane. "Hey," he said. "He gave me his card."

Chapter 15

You're only given a drop of madness. Don't piss it away.
—Dagwood Dean Daly, who may have been granted more than his fair share

It took forever for the captain to contact Sure-Fire Towing. Longer still to get connected with the right man. But finally he did. And that right man collaborated Coggins's story.

Ten minutes later, I stumbled out of the station like a chimpanzee on opium, mind buzzing with possibilities. Maybe the 'right man' was lying. Maybe Coggins had hired someone to attack me. Maybe I was on the wrong track entirely and Andrews had been released from the hospital. It was entirely possible, if not probable, that he still held a grudge and was-

"Ms. McMullen?"

I jumped at the sound of my name and spun toward the speaker in a kind of pseudo-kung fu stance.

Officer Eric Albertson stepped back a pace at my weird-ass reaction, then straightened and sobered at the sight of my face.

"Who did that?" he asked, voice low.

I stared at him.

"I mean…Jesus!" He said the word on a harsh exhalation.

I shook my head. “I doubt it was him.”

He gave me a look that suggested he thought I might be two scoops short of a banana split. For a licensed psychologist, I get that more than one would think probable. “Are you all right?”

“Never better,” I said, and turned toward my car.

He followed. “What happened?”

I didn’t answer.

“Hey, that’s okay if you don’t want to talk about it. Just…” He lengthened his strides to catch up. “Just let me buy you a drink.”

“I don’t need a drink,” I said. My voice was petulant, but he didn’t seem to notice.

“Then buy me a drink.”

I snorted. It was better than crying.

“Dinner. Let me buy you dinner.”

He’d followed me to my car. I gazed into the tiny backseat, hunting for perverts, thieves and guys who like to jump defenseless psychologists in car washes. All I saw was fingerprint dust sticking to every possible surface. They'd left enough of the stuff to build sandcastles but had come up empty. The perpetrator, they said, had probably worn gloves.

“Ms. McMullen?”

“It’s three o’clock in the afternoon,” I said, and turned fuzzily back toward him. My backseat seemed to be empty, but one can’t be too cautious. Rivera had once suggested that I check my trunk. I believe that at the time I had maligned his mental capacity. The idea didn't seem quite so ludicrous now. In fact, I found myself contemplating checking the inside of the Saturn's tires.

"Pie, then? A scone? A cup of coffee?" he offered.

"It's a million degrees out here." I tried to scoff the words but they came out a little wobbly.

"Ice cream. How about a hot-fudge sundae?"

Maybe he knew I was about to cry. But to my credit, the thought of ice cream often makes me cry. It may have had nothing to do with the fact that I'd been attacked in a car wash. I mean, for Pete's sake, who gets attacked in a car wash?

I wiped my knuckles roughly beneath my nose.

"Would you prefer butterscotch?" he asked, leaning around me a little as if to catch a glimpse of my reaction.

I shook my head. "Listen, I really appreciate your concern, Officer…"

"Call me, Eric. Please. And we'll go all out. Hot fudge with cashews or something. Just wait here one minute," he said, and left me alone in the parking lot. To his credit, his mission really did take sixty seconds or less. He was back before I got up enough nerve to enter my traitorous vehicle and leave without further conversation, which was just as well because I would have hated myself in the morning if I had missed out on the free-ice-cream offer.

"Want to take my car?" he asked.

I shrugged. He touched his hand to my back in that protective way that men sometimes have and ushered me toward a late-model Toyota. It was still cool inside. Air conditioning, I knew, was contributing to the global-warming problem, but just then the irony failed to either horrify or amuse me.

"Where to?" he asked.

I wanted to simply shrug again, but that seemed infantile and a little bit dumb. "It doesn't matter," I said. "I should be getting back to work anyway."

"When's your next appointment?"

"Four thirty." It was a decent lie. I didn't have any clients for the rest of the day, but it's often a dynamite idea to have an end time to a date. Mostly because if you sit around too long sometimes men will attack you. Not that I was still obsessing about the car wash incident or anything.

He glanced at the digital clock on his dash. It was three twenty-seven. "How about Dairy Queen?"

I may have made a childish face. He grinned.

"Okay. No," he said, and listed off a couple other mediocre suggestions before coming up with Cold Stone. Maybe he recognized the adulation gleaming in my puffy eyes, because we were walking through the door of that esteemed establishment in less than fifteen minutes.

I considered getting something modest like a small vanilla cone, remembered the car wash, and ordered two scoops of cake-batter ice cream with caramel, chocolate and almonds. At the last second, I added bananas, in case I was low on potassium.

The very first bite made the world a better place. The second made it almost bearable.

Eric stared at me from across the table. He was a good-looking man with cleanly etched features, heavily lashed eyes and a dimple in the exact center of his chin.

"Aren't you going to get anything?" I asked, which was a small miracle, because generally when I'm communing with ice cream there's no time for chitchat.

"I don't really care for dessert." To his credit, he did look a little chagrined, but I didn't cut him any slack.

"Were you dropped on your head as a child or something?"

He grinned and shook the aforementioned head, still watching my eyes. I licked the edge of my waffle cone.

"Did you suffer from some sort of frozen food trauma?"

He smiled at me. It was a pretty good smile. "What happened?" he asked.

I considered not telling him, but I really couldn't think of any reason reticence would improve the situation.

"When I returned to my car after getting gas…" My hand shook a little and I resented the hell out of that. If I lost a droplet of ice cream, someone was going to pay in blood. "…a man was in the backseat of the Saturn."

"Fuck it," he said.

"Yeah."

His eyes sparked with anger. His mouth was pursed into a hard line. "Did you get a description?"

I took a deep breath and held it. I didn't want to tell him about my suspicions, but it wasn't as though he wouldn't find out.

"I thought it was your partner."

"What?"

I winced. "Do you want to confiscate the rest of my cone?"

"Coggins? You thought it was Coggins?" He sounded incredulous.

I scowled at the ice cream, though it had done nothing wrong. "I know Rivera is innocent."

He shook his head. "That doesn't make Joel guilty."

I exhaled carefully, keeping all the tension inside like I tell my clients never to do. "Tell me about Stacy."

"Stacy?" he began, then scowled. "Oh yeah." He gave me a guilty glance.

So it was true. There had been something between her and Rivera. I shouldn't have been surprised. But I was. Surprised and wounded. Still, I told myself I had bigger fish to fry.

Eric sighed and glanced toward the table. "Yeah, Coggins was pissed about that, but sometimes he's just a loose…" He paused, shot his attention back toward me and shook his head. "It wasn't him."

"He called me by name."

"The bastard in the car wash?"

My throat was freezing up. Not from the ice cream. It was innocent of all crimes. "He called me McMullen." I tried to relax the muscles around my larynx and slanted a glance in his direction, going for casual, almost achieving better-than-totally-freaked. "Any idea why that makes it worse?"

"That he knew you?"

I nodded.

"Maybe he didn't. Maybe he just knew of you. I mean…" He shrugged. "Considering your profession, I have to assume some of the people you know aren't the most stellar examples of sanity."

I gave that a moment of consideration, then, "I hardly ever associate with my brothers anymore."

He stared at me, then laughed, relaxing a little. "You've got an amazing attitude."

I licked the edge of the cone again. It was getting a little soft, which was okay. I like soft for ice-cream cones and porn. "And a pretty good vocabulary," I added.

"Rivera is one lucky son of a bitch."

"Probably true," I said, then pursed my lips and refused to cry while I was holding ice cream. It was my one incontrovertible rule. "We broke up. Months ago."

He studied me. "For real?"

"Why would I lie?"

"Jesus. I mean…" He glanced out the window. On the far side of the street, a lone man in what looked to be a Jedi costume was holding up a sign that read 'Don't be a douche.' L.A. has its moments. "If you're that aggressive for old flames, what are you like with current lovers?"

I cleared my throat.

"I didn't mean it quite like that," he said, but he didn't retract the question. In fact, he reached across the table and took my hand. "I'm so sorry this happened."

His palms felt good encasing my fingers…not so rough it was scratchy, but not girly either, and God knows I was in need of some well-meaning attention. But really, eating ice cream is a two-handed job for me. I pulled from his grip. "I'm seeing someone else."

"Shit," he said, and grinned a little as he leaned back against the booth. "Another lucky bastard."

"The city is full of them."

"I bet he's ready to kill someone."

I scowled, unsure of his meaning.

His gaze never moved from mine. "That's an awfully good-looking face to mess up."

"Oh," I said, and almost forgot about the ice cream for a moment. "He hasn't seen it yet."

"What? You're kidding."

"He's out of town."

"Well, if it was me, I'd get my ass back in town," he said, and leaned forward again, still holding my gaze.

I fidgeted and pulled back a little. Ice cream dripped onto the table.

Dammit. First the car wash attack and now this.

"I'm sorry," he said, and lifting his hands palms forward, shifted away again. "Really. It's just that you're so…" He shrugged, seeming to be laughing at himself. "I've always been a sucker for a damsel in distress."

"Wish you had been there last night."

"Me, too," he said, and there was something in his eyes that suggested he wasn't kidding. I have to say just about then that something was almost preferable to ice cream, but I cleansed my head with the memory of my boyfriend's IQ.

"Is that why you became a police officer?" I asked. "For damsels?"

"Maybe," he said. "There's not much money in it. But my old man was a cop and he always made it sound so damn romantic…fighting crime, saving—" He chuckled and shook his head. "Listen to me. You really are a therapist, aren't you. Here I am yapping away about myself when your poor face…" He paused, seeming to need a second to collect himself. "Tell me what you know about the asshole. Tell me everything you can remember."

I kind of wanted to play it cool and ask what asshole he was referring to. I mean this was L.A. But I didn't think I could pull it off. Besides, I had been through this routine enough times with Rivera to realize it could really help me remember things I didn't realize were in my gray matter.

The half-catatonic attitude of the woman who had taken my statement on the previous evening had left me little hope that the cops would find the perpetrator. She'd asked for his height and weight: A hundred eighty pounds. Approximately five ten. He could be any one of about ten million people. In fact, there were more than a few house pets who would fit that same description. Harley included if he stood on his hind legs to take hamburger off the counter. But I was pretty sure he was innocent.

"Did you get a look at his face?"

"It…" I tried to remember, but the memories came at me pretty hard and I winced. "No. I think he was wearing…" I shook my head. "I think he had pantyhose or something over his face."

"Okay. Well…just think back, Christina. Was he white or black?""I can't say. His features were obscured."

"How old was he?"

"I don't know."

"Think about the voice. He said something."

My hands were shaking on the ice-cream cone. "He told me not to do anything stupid."

Eric nodded encouragingly. "Deep voice, quiet, hissy, prissy, accented?"

The memories were visceral. "Deep. Guttural."

He nodded encouragement. "Any smells that you can remember? Body odor? Shaving cream?"

I gave it a moment while trying not to hyperventilate. "No. Nothing."

"Are you sure?"

I nodded.

He sat back, seeming to relax. “Okay.”

“But I kicked him.”

He leaned forward and clenched his right hand into a fist atop the table. “Good girl.”

It was sad really how much I needed an atta girl, but I tried not to press my head against his palm and pant for more attention. “I think I caught him in the face with my elbow. And maybe…maybe in the crotch with my heel.”

“Jesus, I’m almost orgasmic,” he said. “Was there any blood left at the scene?”

I shook my head. “Not that they found. The door popped open a second later. He fell out of the car and then he was gone.”

“I suppose it’s too much to ask that the fucker might have drowned.”

I swallowed my bile and looked sadly at my ice cream. I’d lost my appetite.

“Well…if I see a guy with a black eye and a limp, I’ll kill him myself,” he said.

My face twisted into what might have been a grin. “Shouldn’t you question him first?”

“I can’t see why.”

“Seems fair. I’m sure there’s only one person in L.A. with a bruised face,” I said, and refrained from touching my own wounded cheek.

His eyes gleamed a little, but he went on. “Who do you think it could have been?”

I opened my mouth. He raised a hand.

“Other than Joel.”

I shut my mouth.

"Have you pissed anybody else off lately?"

"Not since I arrived here," I said, and dropped my gaze to the table. "I try to be on my best behavior when there's ice cream involved."

"Oh, come on, a girl like you can't have many enemies."

I raised my brows at him. "I just about broke Coggins's nose. And he's a police officer."

"Well…" He shrugged. "It wouldn't look any worse broken."

I felt my shoulders slump. "The funny thing is, I don't even like Rivera."

"Are you sure?" he asked, and stared deep into my eyes.

I exhaled noisily and licked the perimeter of the cone, but I had lost my gusto. "We gave it a shot, but he's not…" I let the words trail off.

"What?"

I shrugged and cleared my throat. "It would never work out," I admitted, and ignored the sting of tears behind my eyes. "Still…he's the father of my Great Dane."

He stared at me a second. "Brindle or merle?"

"Harlequin. Black and white."

"Well…" He shook his head. "A harlequin like that's well worth throwing a few elbows for."

I gave him an appreciative if watery grin. "I'm sorry I did it."

"I'm sorry we had to haul Rivera in."

"Are you?" I asked. It was my turn to watch him.

"Sure," he said, then glanced at the table and fiddled with a napkin. "I mean…we're never going to be BFFs or anything. Rivera's a…" He shrugged. "Sometimes he's kind of a…"

"An ass."

"Yeah."

"I've noticed."

"But he's a good cop, and I never want to see a fellow officer go down. Neither does Joel. Not really. Believe me," he said. "It wasn't him. He's a little rough around the edges, maybe. Has a grudge against women sometimes. But the allegations that he…" He stopped himself, tensed, tried to relax.

"What allegations?" I asked but he shook his head and grinned a little, leaving me with nothing more than suspicions.

"He's a good guy at heart."

"If you say so," I said. I was too drained to pry. And that's saying something.

"I do. So who else might have a grudge against you?"

"I've give that some thought," I promised, and left the Cold Stone sanctuary a few minutes later

.

Chapter 16

Men, they have the two emotions: Hungry and Horny. If you see him without an erection, you fix him the burrito.
—*Rosita Rivera, who was well acquainted with politicians and men*

I was true to my word. I gave it some thought…a lot of thought. Okay, the fact is, I was obsessed with the thought. Who, I wondered, had I pissed off? The answer was a little depressing; there were enough of them to turn an intimate gathering into a nice-sized orgy. I mean, let's face it, I rub elbows with an awful lot of weird-ass people. And then there are my clients. Still, I couldn't think of anybody who would want to do me bodily harm. Except, of course, for the people who had tried to do me bodily harm in the past. It was also depressing to realize how many of those there were.

I ran through the list as I ate breakfast. Peanut butter on bagels—breakfast of pale, flabby Americans with more girth than stamina.

But I didn't care about girth or stamina just then, since staying alive seemed more important than being svelte. To emphasize that point, I put another bagel in the toaster, then found a notepad in my junk drawer and started a list with the name Emery Black at the top.

Mr. Black had once been J.D. Solberg's boss. He was guilty of some pretty-big-money blue-collar crimes and had spent a good deal of time in jail because of that. It was possible, I supposed, that he blamed me. I did, after all, have a little something to do with his incarceration. And he was a free man now, so it was conceivable that he might have sent someone to avenge him, but even in the pen he'd kept his head down and played nice. This just didn't feel like something he would do. Especially since he was back to making a sizable income again and probably would rather enjoy it than spend the rest of his life back in a box the size of his money safe.

There were others, of course, who hadn't fared so well financially or physically after their interaction with me.

Gordon Adams, for instant, the man who had attacked me while gunning for my fucktard brother, Pete, was dead. Rivera had killed him with a single bullet to the temple when he'd threatened to do the same to me. And son of a bitch that Adams had been, I doubted he had come back from the grave to haunt me. Neither did it seem likely that there would be anyone else who was fond enough of him to make trouble for themselves.

I over-peanut buttered another half a bagel and let my mind move on.

Robert Peachtree was another person who had felt compelled to try to kill me. He was a wealthy octogenarian who had become embroiled in Rivera's weird-ass family circumstances. Suffice it to say, there had been a shitload of things Peachtree had tried to keep quiet. In fact, he had been more than willing to brain me with a poker to achieve that goal. But it was extremely doubtful that he was the culprit, since he had eventually succumbed to age-related complications while in Folsom.

A shiver ran through me. Maybe it's a good sign that it's still a little disconcerting when someone tries to kill me. And let me tell you, somehow it's even worse when cute little old men take offense to your existence. Still, my current problems probably didn't stem from that front, considering his wife had also since passed and none of his extremely wealthy heirs had surfaced to complain about their benefactor's demise.

I moved on. Theodore Altove had been a truly disturbed man with a legitimate beef. Unfortunately, I had been the discoverer of that beef: Apparently he had been humming his way through life, helping Senator Rivera with his various and sundry campaigns, cohabitating with his beautiful wife and daughter, when one unhappy morning he realized that the daughter resembled the senator a bit more than she resembled him. A rather bloody escapade followed. After which, he had made a serious attempt on the senator's life. Failing to succeed in murdering the one man he hated above all others, he had killed himself with a bullet to the brainpan.

I sighed as I wiped a droplet of chocolate milk off my notepad. Theodore Altove was gone, but he did have a daughter, or…at least he had a young woman who had believed she was his daughter, a young woman whose life had surely been turned upside down at the advent of his death.

I followed his little epilogue with a dash and the name Thea.

That led to David Hawkins. My hand shook a little as I wrote his name. He had been a colleague of mine. A friend, in fact. A respected member of the community. Unfortunately, he had tried to murder me when I figured out he'd not only killed his wife but the man I was accused of murdering. I had subsequently proven his guilt, and he'd gotten life imprisonment. Signs were good that he was still holding a grudge. He had money, brains, and motive. The evil trifecta. Still, I wasn't sure how much damage he could do from a prison cell the size of my molar.

So who did that leave? I drew a deep breath and let my mind sweep back a few months to when Laney had been kidnapped by the crazed, just-released-from-prison drug dealer man named Jackson Andrews. In an attempt to retrieve his brainchild, a drug called Intensity, from her misbegotten jacket, he'd stripped her naked, tied her to a chair and threatened her life before we were able to set her free. If a man was willing to do that to the nicest woman in the universe, what would he be willing to do to me…the most irritating woman on the planet? The woman who had foiled his plans and sent him to jail.

Facts and fears jostled around in my head like well-oiled popcorn. I tried sorting them out, but it was tough. Memories of near-death experiences tend to make me a little jittery, and the thought of Rivera in jail seemed to throw the whole world off kilter. Although he was, more often than not, a royal pain in the ass, he was also the epitome of law and order, the very standard by which such things were set.

I dialed the phone without further thought.

“Hola.” The woman’s voice was young and smooth and a little accusatory. I scowled.

“Hello? Is Senator Rivera available?”

“Who is this, please?”

I could hear someone murmur something in the background. The woman’s voice was slightly louder as they discussed the situation.

“Why do you not wish for me to know who—” she began, but then the receiver was muffled. It took several seconds before the senator was on the line.

“Hello?”

“Hello. Senator?”

There was only a momentary pause as he sorted my voice from the surely thousands he knew. “Christina, it is so good of you to call, but I’m afraid I am quite busy. My political advisor is here to discuss some future possibilities. But I cannot tell you how it gladdens my heart to hear your lovely voice.”

He sounded flirty and effusive. I could imagine his current political advisor grinding her teeth in the background. But perhaps she would have to take the pacifier out of her mouth to do so. To say the senator liked younger women would be an understatement of statutory proportions.

I put that thought out of my mind and jumped into the fray. “I was wondering if you’ve heard anything about your son’s situation.”

“My dearest Christina, as I have stated before, I do not believe it is in his best interest for me to interfere with his life at this point.”

“His best interest or yours?”

“Qué?”

I clenched my teeth to prevent more vitriol from seeping out. Vitriol, while lovely, poisonous stuff, often does little to improve interpersonal relationships.

“You know he didn’t do it,” I said.

His breathy sigh seemed longsuffering. “I am always heartened by your faith in him, Christina. He is indeed lucky to have you.”

“He doesn’t have me.” I felt irritable and itchy and frustrated. I also kind of wished I had a political advisor of my own. “We broke up months ago, remember?”

“And yet you call to inquire about his well-being, si?”

“I had other things to talk about, too,” I said, but for a moment I couldn’t remember what they were.

"He cares deeply for you as well, Christina. You must know that in your heart of hearts."

"That's not why I…" I paused, conflicted. "Do you really think—" I caught myself before I stumbled further into stupidity enabled by hope and enhanced by loneliness. "I just called to ask about Thea."

The phone went quiet. "Thea Altove?"

"Yes."

"My…daughter?"

To his credit, he still had a bit of trouble saying the words. Maybe that was because he had cuckolded an old friend to create that daughter. Maybe because he had been kind of attracted to said daughter before he realized the kinship they shared. It's hard to say exactly. All I know is that the McMullens are not the only family that puts the fun in dysfunctional.

"Yes," I said simply, though I was thinking of a butt-load of sarcastic addendums with which to follow up that statement. "Your daughter."

"What is it you wish to know about her?" He sounded a little leery, a little protective. Apparently, he didn't mind throwing his son under the bus, but messing with his daughter was verboten.

"How's she doing?" I asked.

He drew a deep breath. I could hear him thinking. Senator Rivera is not a stupid man. Which is funny. Most men either have brains or looks or money. Ten years ago, I would have given my spleen for any guy who possessed one of the three.

Now I realized, I might want to keep my spleen. "Christina…" His voice was soft. "Thea is not responsible for Gerald's incarceration."

"I know," I said. And I really did. From what I had seen, Thea Altove, long-legged beauty that she was, adored her half brother. It was one of the many things I resented about her. Her long-legged beauty being the first.

"Honey Bear…" I could hear his political advisor's voice in the background. It had gone from angry to silky in less than sixty seconds. I envied that speed. When I'm mad I stay mad for approximately…well…there seems to be no statute of limitations on my anger. "I am tired."

He covered the phone with his hand, but it was pretty ineffective.

"… just be a minute. Why don't you—"

"And I am hot." Her voice might have been a little louder than it needed to be to be heard by the senator. But just about loud enough to be heard by me.

"Turn up the air, then, and I shall…" He stopped. I wasn't sure if I imagined it or if I really could hear silk sliding against well-moisturized skin, but I was sure about his raspy intake of breath.

I rolled my eyes and waited for some of his blood to flow back up to his brain cells.

"Christina," he said after a few sparse droplets had, apparently, rejuvenated his cranium. "I'm afraid I must run."

"Someone tried to kill me," I said, and noticed with some satisfaction that the end of the phone went absolutely silent. Apparently murder attempts got his attention irregardless how much well-moisturized skin his political advisor had exposed.

"Dear God, no," he whispered. "Not again."

"Again." My voice was miraculously steady. In fact, my hands were hardly shaking at all.

"And you think my daughter is somehow implicated."

"The possibility has crossed my mind."

"Because you were involved in her father's death."

"Not technically," I said, reminding him with my tone that he, in fact, was her father. I wondered vaguely if it was difficult for him to justify his chronic womanizing when his current conquests made his daughter look like an aged spinster by numerical comparison.

"I hope you do not think less of me since learning of her existence, Christina."

I would have liked to have said that there was no way I could think less of him. I mean, he was a sleazy old narcissist with visions of grandeur, the kind of father that made my own rather dubious sire look like something out of a Rockwell painting. But the truth was, Senator Rivera was a difficult man to dislike. I'm sure it had nothing to do with his sexy voice, his still-toned body, or his mountains of money.

“I would just like to cross her off the list,” I said.

He was silent for a moment longer, then, “Thea is currently visiting relatives in Mexico.”

“That doesn’t mean she couldn’t have hired someone to kill me.” I mean, it wasn’t as if I thought she had attacked me herself. I’m no wilting flower, but whoever had been waiting for me in my backseat had had a penis and the musculature to go along with it.

“Christina, think on it,” he said. “Why would she bear you ill will?”

I stared blankly at my window for a second, then, “Because I caused the death of the man she thought of as her father for the first twenty years of her life?” Which left her with a father who dated woman barely out of the womb, I thought, but I didn’t say that out loud.

“Theodore was disturbed. She is fully aware that his death was not of your doing.”

“You can’t be sure of that, Senator. Many people feel the need to place guilt where it is not necessarily due. She may very well be one of those—”

“She blames me, Christina,” he said. I sat utterly silent. “Me and me alone.”

“Really?” I didn’t want to say it, but I was incredibly relieved. I mean, it’s really nice to pass the blame around sometimes. “What makes you think that?”

There was a lengthy pause, then, "She accused me of being a…how did she say it?" He drew a deep breath. "A pathetic old man who defies his age by sleeping with…"

He hissed a breath. I heard a giggle in the near background and then murmured voices.

"Senator?" I said cautiously.

"I really must go, Christina," he said. "I have important matters to discuss with my advisors."

"I just…" I paused. "There's more than one advisor?"

"Of course," he said. "A presidential hopeful must garner as much advice as he can. It will take a great deal of dedication and stamina—" Another sharp inhalation, but he rallied. "To become the chosen one. It is a heavy burden, but one that I would gladly bear if I could but put this great nation back on track to emotional health and fiscal well-being. Indeed, I do not look forward to the hardships ahead, but as an American I feel it is my duty to—"

"Senator…" I had heard enough.

"Yes, Christina?"

"Be sure to wear a condom to your meetings."

Chapter 17

I'm not crazy. Crazy is when you paint yourself orange and go around thinking you're a kumquat. I hardly ever paint myself orange.
—*Dagwood Dean Daly*

"Hey, Miss Chris." Apparently Dagwood Dean Daly, better known as D to the underbelly of Chicago, Illinois, had caller ID. He answered on the first ring. It was 9:52 L.A. time, which meant it was almost noon by Midwestern standards. "You ready to sleep with me yet?"

"I'm not very tired," I said, but it was a lie. My conversation with the senator the previous night had worn me out. Apparently the thought of orgies is exhausting to a person who rarely even has onesies.

"Well, we wouldn't have to sleep," he said, then spoke to someone nearby. "Uh huh. I'll be with you in a minute, Sandy.

"Not till later, anyway," he added to me.

"And I have to get to work."

"Hmm." He sounded like he was debating hard. "Hey, I know. I could come to your office. I mean, you're a therapist, right? What's more therapeutic than sex?"

"Sex can as easily cause severe emotional damage as…" I began, then realized a little belatedly that I may have gotten off on the wrong foot…again. I took a deep breath. “I need your help.”

“With sexual tension?”

“With remaining alive.”

I could almost hear him nod. “One of your fucktard brothers being threatened again?

“Just put it there, Sandy. Thanks,” he said.

Doesn’t anyone just carry on one conversation at a time anymore?

“No. It’s me this time,” I said, and almost laughed at the improbability of it all.

“Someone’s trying to kill you?”

“Hard to believe, isn't it?” I tried to sound amused. I was not.

“In the city of angels?”

“I think the demons have a pretty good grip on things.”

“Tell me,” he said, and I launched into the tale. When it came right down to it, there wasn’t all that much to tell. Still, I felt even more exhausted by the time I was done.

“And this all happened while you were in the car wash.”

“Yes.”

There was a momentary silence. “Genius,” he said.

I scowled. “I didn’t really tell you so you could admire his methods.”

“You’re sure it was a man?”

“He had a penis.” It wasn’t until that moment that I remembered D’s propensity for hiring women with abilities like Hercules and bodies like Wonder Woman. "Even your employees don't have penises." I paused a second, thinking. "Do they?"

"I'm not sure. Just a minute.

"Sandy, do any of the girls have penises?"

I heard a murmur in the background.

"Uh huh. Alright. Thanks. Hey, why don't you take the rest of the day off." Another murmur. "I'll be fine," he said, and in a moment he was back on the phone.

"Sandy said they don't, to the best of her knowledge. So…other than the opportunity to talk about penises, why call me, Miss Chris?"

"I was hoping you could help me figure out who might be wanting me dead."

"Well…" He sounded thoughtful. "We know he has a penis, so that narrows it down to fifty percent of the population."

"I was hoping for more."

"I suppose that's the price I pay for being a giant in the collection business." D didn't like the term gangster. "My uncle, Leslie, told me to be a cobbler. I guess I sort of followed his advice."

"Really?" I'd once traveled to his office to repay a debt one of my aforementioned fucktard brother owed. It was a high-rise unit on Chicago's illustrious Gold Coast. There hadn't been a single shoe jack in sight.

"I make cement boots," he said, and felt free to laugh at his own joke. It's probably one of the many advantages of being a gangster/collection engineer.

"Who do you think might have been visiting you in the car wash?"

I took a deep breath. "Originally, I thought it was a police officer. But his alibi was pretty solid."

"What's his name?" D was not shy about his love for causing trouble for the police force…any police force.

"Joel Coggins."

"I'll check into it. Anybody else?"

"There's a man named Jackson Andrews who—"

"Jackson Andrews the drug designer? I thought he was in prison."

"Not anymore."

"Huh, my intel must be slow."

"Don't beat yourself up too much; he just got out a few days ago."

"I wasn't planning on beating myself," he said.

"Oh." I cleared my throat.

He laughed. "Listen, Chris, Andrews is a pretty clever guy, and he makes me look all warm and fuzzy. Tell me you're not involved with him."

I cut my eyes toward the window. They were tearing up a little. "I wish I could."

"All right." He drew a heavy breath. "Tell me about it."

So I told him the whole sordid story about Andrews and drugs and mixed-up jackets that had led to Laney's kidnapping a few months earlier.

When I was finished, there was a long silence, followed by, "You're not making this up?"

"My imagination's not that…creepy."

He laughed. "So you think Andrews is out of jail now?"

"Yeah."

"Do you want him back in?"

I sighed. "So much."

"Okay, but it'd be easier to just kill him."

I paused for a moment, taking that opportunity to worry at my lower lip. "But wouldn't that be morally wrong?"

He was silent for a second. "Maybe you need someone else on your Friends and Family plan to answer that one, honey."

I scowled, came to a quick decision and spoke before I changed my mind. "I don't want him dead, D. I just want to know if it was him…you know…in the car wash."

"And then you want him dead, right."

"No," I said, but I knew it was a lie even before the words left my lips.

At 10:30 I had shellacked my hair into a back-combed do to keep it off my neck, dragged on the coolest clothes I could find that wouldn't get me arrested, and left for work. The 5 was more like an automotive battle ground than an interstate, but forty-seven minutes later I arrived at L.A. Counseling, where I tried to look chill and chic. My orange-popsicle sheath, however, seemed determined to stick to the back of my legs no matter how high we cranked up the AC, and it was hard to focus on Mr. Wilson's water-balloon fetish when my own problems seemed so much more immediate.

By the time my last client rolled out the door, I was ready to tear out my well-coifed hair.

"You okay?" Shirley asked. "You look kind of…" She gave me an analytical eye. "…like one of them TV evangelists."

"Big-haired?" I asked.

"Crazy," she said.

I had given her the short version of my latest trauma earlier in the week. It wasn't much more fun than the long version. "Yeah, I'm all right. Just a little…" I peeked out the door into the parking lot. It was almost dark. Sometimes I work late on Mondays and Fridays. Mondays because some of my clients have just spent the weekend with their families. Fridays because some of them are just about to. "Nervous."

"You look about ready to fly. It's time you go home and lay on the couch in front of a fan."

"I agree."

"Then that's what you're going to do, right?"

I slung the strap of my purse over my shoulder. It was a Coach knock-off. Twenty-seven ninety-nine brand new. "It sounds like a great plan."

She stuck out her jaw. She's got a good, firm jaw. The rest of her was good too, but not necessarily firm. "So that's what you're going to do, right?" she asked again.

I considered lying, but I wasn't brave enough. "Right after I meet with a friend."

"What friend?"

More hedging didn't seem prudent.

"Micky," I said, and turned toward the door.

"Micky Goldenstone?" Her voice suggested trouble might be brewing. Shirley had given birth to, and subsequently survived the teenage years of, seven kids. I figured she could, therefore, shoot death rays out of her eyeballs if she wanted to, but I defended myself as best I could.

"He's not a client anymore," I said. But I had been his therapist when he'd shot Jackson Andrews, subsequently tying me to that unsavory character for all time.

"That doesn't mean the board of psychology isn't going to fry your skinny behind if they find out you're fraternizing with him."

"I'm not fraternizing with him."

"He's got connections to all manner of hell," she said.

"I'm not fraternizing with him," I repeated, and put my hand on the door latch.

"Ms. McMullen!" she barked.

I turned like a spanked cadet… and froze. She was pointing a handgun directly at my left eyeball. I felt the blood rush to my extremities.

"Take this with you," she said.

I managed to pull a little air into my lungs. "What?"

"The Glock," she said, letting it droop in her fingers before handing it over. "Dion gave it to me a couple months ago."

"Is it…" I swallowed, not even sure how to frame a question. "Where did Dion get it?"

"I don't know," she said. "But I figure it's better off with you than where it's been."

Chapter 18

Kids…you spend a couple years teaching them to walk and talk, then spend the rest of your life wishing they'd just sit their butts down and shut the hell up.
—*Shirley Templeton, mother of many*

Micky Goldenstone was a beautiful man with a beautiful soul and a not-so-beautiful past. He was waiting for me in a booth at the Grill and Chill when I slid in beside him.

"How you doing?" he asked. He had a beer the size of a water cooler in front of him. It looked fantastic in all its amber glory. Unfortunately, I've actually sampled beer and know it tastes like cat pee; I have brothers who were always graciously willing to introduce me to the taste of the urine of several species.

"I'm doing well," I said, and thought I must be doing okay because he hadn't shrunk away when he saw my face and I'd only applied half a quart of concealer, followed by a bushel basket of foundation. I'll admit, I wanted to unload on him, but hard as it is to believe, Micky's issues are generally more serious than my own. And because I had once been his therapist, I felt it was my moral obligation to be professional. Well, that and the fact that the board of psychology would fricassee me and serve me with Hollandaise sauce if they found one more infraction on my record. "How are you?"

He gave me a jaundiced glance over the edge of his mug. "You know how some people say parenthood is hell?"

I did, in fact. My own parents had generally looked as if they needed a shot of whisky and an exorcist. But I'm quite sure that had nothing to do with me. Remember the brothers of urinary fame? "Yeah?"

"Turns out they lied." He took a deep quaff from the cooler in front of him. "It's worse."

I laughed. "Jamel giving you a little trouble?" Jamel was the son he'd only realized he had after the boy's mother had died of an overdose. A shitstorm of problems had followed in the wake of her death. A shitstorm which I had foolishly galloped into.

He gave me the evil eye over the top of his mug. "A little trouble I could handle. Hell, I'd welcome a little trouble. But the boy questions everything I say. Challenges every order, has a smart remark for every possible situation."

"Have you tried tying him to the banister and reading him Bible verses yet?"

He stared at me a second, then chuckled and put his beer down. "Who would have thought Grams's methods were the only ones that actually work?"

I'd met his grandmother on more than one occasion. She was a hundred and eighty if she was a day and she'd still scared the bejeezus out of me. "How's she doing?" I asked.

He was watching me with those gorgeous devilish eyes, dark skin shining beneath the overhead lights. "Better than you."

"What are you talking about?" I asked, but at that moment our waitress appeared. I ignored her horrified expression as best I could, ordered a glass of water with a lemon twist, accepted a menu, and stared at the choices, hoping to look nonchalant, but I could feel Micky watching me.

"What's going on?" he asked.

"I don't know." I tried a shrug, casual as hell, but to tell the truth, even that caused pain to radiate from my cheek to my neck and lower. "The lasagna looks good. But I've heard the chef's salad is excellent, too, and I can't ever decide between making my stomach happy and keeping my heart pumping for another—"

"Doc," he said, "is this about Andrews?"

I didn't answer right away. Hell, I didn't have an answer.

"I heard he was out of jail," he said. "Truth is, a cop the size of a fucking minivan showed up at my door to question me about my whereabouts that night."

"And?"

"You asking if I shot him, too?" he asked.

I gave him a half shrug, too tired to give him the full version. "I wish I could say I'd resent it if you had."

He snorted. "I had conferences on last Tuesday. Saw and was seen by about a hundred fifty clueless parents. After that Jamel and I spent the night at Grandma's. Even the minivan cop didn't dare doubt her word."

“I never doubted you either," I said. Maybe it was odd that that was the truth.

"Well you should have," he said. His expression was placid but his eyes were a little eerie. "Because if that son of a bitch touches a hair on my boy’s head, I’ll cut off his balls with a hacksaw.”

This was the Micky I had rarely seen. The Micky that simmered quietly beneath the surface of the Micky who taught elementary school and played Scrabble with his son.

“Is Lavonn still with him?” I asked. Back before Laney had been kidnapped by Andrews, Lavonn had been Andrews’s live-in girlfriend.

“Swear to God I will,” he said quietly. “Fuck the—”

“Micky!” I said, voice sharpening without my consent.

He scowled at me. Generally Micky looks pleasant and witty. This wasn’t generally, but I didn’t back down.

“I need to talk to Lavonn. Maybe she can shed some light on things.”

He drew a deep breath and studied me. “I’m not exactly on her speed dial,” he said.

“But you must know where she is.”

“Last time I saw her, she tried to shoot me, remember?”

I did. It had been the same night he had shot Andrews. In fact, she had used the same gun. If I had it to do over again, which I sincerely hoped I would not, I would have tried to keep the damn thing out of her possession. But maybe that's just me.

He wrinkled his brow. “Tell me what happened.”

“Listen, Micky, I know you have troubles of your own. I don’t want to add to—”

“Tell me.”

So I gave him the shortened short version.

He looked sober and angry when I was done. “You think this has something to do with Lavonn?”

I shrugged. “I checked into her house.”

“The big-ass one in Glendale?”

“Yeah.” The one where Micky had shot her boyfriend. The one where I’d shown up, peeing-in-my-pants scared and trying to talk Micky out of putting a bullet in his own ear. “Someone else lives there now.”

He exhaled carefully. “It was in Andrews’s name. She lost it when he went to prison.”

I nodded.

He watched me. “Lost her shiny car and buckets of bling, too.”

I waited, breath held. Micky was not a stupid man.

"You think she might be blaming you," he guessed.

"I just wanted to make sure…" I cleared my throat, trying to be strong. I felt about as powerful as a petunia. "She hasn't given you any trouble?"

"She called me a couple months ago. Said I didn't deserve to have her sister's baby. Said she loved Jamel, wanted him back. Said just because I was well-educated and sexy as hell didn't mean I was a better parent than her."

"She said that?"

His eyes crinkled a little, but the rest of his face remained sober. "I may have improvised a little."

I didn't bother agreeing with her assessment regarding his looks. Handsome men are rarely surprised to learn of their appeal. "And?"

He stared at his beer as if it had lost its taste. "Nothing since."

"And you're not worried?"

He leaned back against the padded booth cushion. "The woman's got her hands full with her own kids. And I hear there's a new brother in her life." He scowled. "Didn't take her long to find someone after Andrews got put away."

Goose flesh crawled across my arms. "A brother?"

His eyes narrowed a little more. "You said you didn't get a description."

"I don't know what—"

"So you just assume the guy in the car wash was black." There was sudden anger in his voice, sudden aggression in the bunched muscles of his bare arms as he leaned toward me.

My heart rate skittered up a little. But I forced my extremities to remain relaxed. Hell, I'd fixed my hair and worn my popsicle sheath. Now was not the time to panic. "Do I look like the enemy to you, Micky?"

His nostrils flared as he inhaled. I held his gaze like a cobra, afraid to look away.

"Shit," he said finally, and pushed his beer toward the middle of the table. "Every time I think I can relax a little, you wind me back up."

"I'm sorry," I said, and I meant it. I half stood, ready to scoot out from behind the table. "You don't owe me anything."

He grabbed my arm, making me reconsider the panic idea. Now might be the perfect time. "Fuck that," he said.

Our eyes met. Mine felt a little leaky.

"Sit down," he ordered.

I remained where I was.

"Please," he added, and jerked a nod toward our fellow patrons.

The couple next to us was staring as if we were on stage. For a moment I thought Micky might confront them, but he released my arm and grinned instead.

I sat back down and tried to force myself to relax. The process was about as effective as thinking away your acne. We stared across the table at each other.

"Where do you think I'd be if it wasn't for you?" he asked.

"You're a smart guy, Micky. You'd be—"

"Dead," he said. "Dead or in jail. And the boy…" He swallowed. "My son." There were tears in his eyes. "He's a pain in the ass." He glanced toward the front door and pursed his lips. "But I'd give my soul for him."

"I know," I said.

"And you…" He shook his head. "What was it? About midnight when I called you?"

I shrugged.

"Said I'd shot someone."

"You said he was dead," I remembered. He had been wrong. Jackson Andrews had still been very much alive. Why the hell was he still so alive? I was beginning to believe that the news regarding the deadliness of firearms was no more than hype.

"So what do you do?" he asked and chuckled at the memories. "You march in there like some damn…" He made a face. If he started crying, that was it for me. There was something about seeing a bad-ass brother break down that was a little disconcerting. He cleared his throat. "What do you want me to do?"

"You don't owe me," I said again, and I meant it. Micky had done me a few favors in the past.

"Fuck that, too." He drew a deep breath through his nostrils. "I'll find Lavonn for you."

"I don't want you to get in any kind of—"

“I’ll find her,” he said, and we ordered our meals.

By the time I left, I was full to the gills and so focused on our past conversation that I forgot to look in the backseat of my car.

Micky didn’t though. He stared through the little back window, then glanced around the parking lot. “What? You think shit only happens in car washes?” he asked, and taking my keys, opened the driver’s door. After that, he glanced around inside.

“Looks like I’m good,” I said. He turned toward me. We were standing pretty close.

“Yeah, you are,” he agreed, and took a step closer. “You still have a thing for that cop?”

“We broke up.”

“Yeah?”

I swallowed. We were way close now. He slipped a hand around my waist. My mind did a nosedive for my ovaries. He leaned toward me, and suddenly I felt the chemistry like a hot wire to my gooey parts, but there was something I was forgetting. Something…

His lips met mine.

“I have a boyfriend!” I rasped.

He paused, eyes glowing in the dim parking lot. “A new one?”

“Yeah.” I practically breathed the word into his mouth.

“Damn, you’re quick. What’s his name?” I could feel his breath on my cheek.

I opened my mouth. Nothing came out. "Shit," I said.

One corner of his lips cranked up, revealing an incredibly white smile. "That his last name or his given name?"

I shook my head once. "I knew that one when I got here."

His smile twisted up a little higher. He pushed a few stray hairs behind my ear. "In all those months of therapy, I never once saw you flustered, Doc."

"You never kissed me."

"This Shit fellow…," he said, and crowded me a little between the door and the car seat. "You and him serious?"

I licked my lips. "Isn't it obvious?"

He chuckled, then moved closer still.

I scrunched back half an inch.

We watched each other. He nodded.

"Sometime," he said, "when you're no longer obsessed with Mr. Shit and no one's trying to kill you, you give me a call, okay?"

"Like that's ever going to happen," I breathed. Then he was gone, melting into the night like a chocolate-flavored shadow.

Chapter 19

If I could train Francois to change a tire, I'd never date again.
—Chrissy McMullen, waxing philosophical on the shortcomings of men and the wonders of 'personal appliances'

Marc!

My boyfriend's name popped into my head as soon as Micky was out of sight and my hormones had simmered down to a soft boil. I muttered it out loud like a mantra as I drove, then on a spurt of guilt or something like it, dialed his number.

His voice mail picked up on the third ring.

"Thank you for calling Dr. Marcus Jefferson Carlton's cellular phone. I'm sorry I'm not available right now. If this is an emergency, please hang up and dial 911."

I considered doing just that, but wasn't sure exactly what I would say. Yes, my ovaries are on fire. What can you do for me?

Dammit. I snapped my phone shut and dropped it onto my lap, where it nestled cozily between my legs.

"Shit," I said, then giggled a little. "Mr. Shit," I corrected. But I knew in my questionable soul that he wasn't the one who had made me back away from Micky Goldenstone.

Jack Rivera's eyes burned in my memory. I swore again and gunned it for home. But even though I was exhausted, I didn't sleep well that night.

Dreams of rogue car washes haunted me. At 8 A.M. I decided to get out of bed. It was too early for a Saturday morning, but I didn't need any more of those dreams. So I went for a run. Which is almost as bad as a nightmare.

Three miles later I was feeling fit, and angry about being so. I showered, did a cursory cleaning of my little house and tried to figure out who had made this last attempt on my life…if that's what it was. And why? I was a nice person. Well, I was a relatively nice person. So maybe that simply meant that I associated with the wrong sector of society.

Maybe the ridiculously numerous attempts on my life didn't have anything to do with me at all. I mean, when Elaine was kidnapped it had nothing to do with her. It was my fault. Which probably meant that she associated with the wrong kind of people. Namely me. Therefore, it stood to reason that my association with Rivera had probably caused the problem. After all, the Backseat Bastard, as I had dubbed him in an attempt to make light of the situation, had called me McMullen, which was the name Rivera usually used.

I made a few phone calls, did seven circuits around my tiny living space, then gave up checked Men's Central website. Visiting hours were over at three.

If I hurried, I could still get in a few minutes with Rivera. Luckily, it didn't matter how I looked. I was only going there to see if he could shed some light on my current predicament.

After pulling on a pair of jeans and a T-shirt androgynous enough to suit anyone in the homo sapiens species, I stared at myself in the mirror and grimaced. The color of the shirt, I decided, highlighted my fading bruises, and I certainly didn't want to draw attention to my recent attack. It wasn't as if I was looking for sympathy or hoping to have some proof of Rivera's continuing feelings for me. It didn't matter if he still cared for me or not. I just wanted information.

So after digging through my closet for a hue that would somehow magically hide my battle wounds, I changed my jeans three times, my shirt twice, and somehow ended up in a pink-and-white sundress that boasted a flowery halter top. I bottomed it off with strappy high-heeled sandals and dangled a pair of flashy earrings from my lobes. Screw conservative. If I showed enough cleavage, Rivera was unlikely to notice the discoloration on my cheek. And that was all I wanted.

I reached the station at 2:32. Only twenty-eight minutes remaining and I still hadn't been frisked or promised security my firstborn.

By the time I walked into the visiting area, Rivera was already seated on the far side of the glass. His expression didn't change as he skimmed me from sandal to sundress. But there was something feral in his eyes that made my pituitary gland fire up. Something that sizzled along my twittering nerve endings and blazed into my viscera.

"How are you doing?" My hand was steady on the receiver that connected our worlds. I kept my voice casual, as if men torched me with their eyes every day of my life.

His gaze slipped down the open neck of my dress. "You looking to seduce somebody, McMullen?"

I cleared my throat. "My T-shirts were all in the wash."

The right corner of his mouth twitched a little, and though he didn't turn his eyes away for a second, he nodded to the left, indicating the other men on his side of the glass. "There are a couple dozen guys here who'd like to thank your washing machine."

I actually felt myself blush. Holy crap. I mean, it's not as if I'd never been flirted with before. It's just that flirting doesn't usually make my endocrine system throb like a horny bass drum. I cleared my throat and worried the telephone cord with my free hand.

"Are you doing okay?" I asked and struggled for the über practical tone I had learned in shrink school.

"I was until you got here. It's hard enough to sleep without your damn legs showing up in my dreams."

"Oh." I blushed again, like a pimply faced teenager. All that was missing was the tuba from my high school years. But I searched for my professional demeanor and charged on. "As I said, I was out of clean shirts."

He didn't argue. In fact, he almost smiled. "And that little dress just needed an outing?"

I shrugged one bare shoulder. "It's hot."

"God bless global warming.

"So what's wrong?" he asked.

I began to shake my head, then realized it wouldn't be a terrible idea to defuse whatever situation might be brewing in his mind. Add a little small talk. Maybe reduce the tension. "Laney's pregnant."

"Really." For a moment, honest happiness shone in his eyes. "That's nice."

"What are you talking about?" My horrified expression wasn't entirely fake. "Do you know who the father is?"

"I'm going to have to assume it's her husband."

"That's right, Solberg," I said. "The ickiest guy on the face of the earth."

He almost smiled. The sight made my heart feel strangely warm. "He's not so bad."

"What are you talking about? He tried to proposition me."

One eyebrow rose a fraction of a millimeter. "Recently?"

"Well, no. It was before he even knew Laney existed in his universe. But it's still disgusting."

He shrugged, letting his gaze skim me again. "The man's not a complete idiot."

His eyes were about to burn right through my solar plexus. I managed not to squirm, but it was physically impossible to hold his gaze. "Listen, I just came by to ask you a few questions about—"

"No."

I glanced up. His tone was still dark and deep, but the flirty edge was gone, replaced by that hard-ass implacability that had made my teeth grind from the first day we'd met.

I drew a deep breath, watched him with what I hoped was casual affability and changed my verbal attack. "—the cactus you gave me," I said.

He narrowed his eyes and sat absolutely still.

I refused to look away. "Should I fertilize it or do you think it'll be okay fighting its own battles?"

He remained silent for a moment longer, then shook his head slowly, gaze never leaving mine. "Stay out of this," he said.

My hackles were beginning to rise like a damn Rhodesian Ridgeback's, but I put on my patient face and capped it with a raised eyebrow of surprise. "Why are you getting all wound up? I'm just asking about fertilizer."

"No," he said, voice just above a rumble. "You're asking for trouble."

"You don't know what you're talking—"

"Listen," he said, and leaned forward suddenly. I was almost tempted to tilt backward even though there was glass between us. "Things are shitty enough without having to spend every waking second worrying about—" He stopped abruptly, gaze glued to my throat. I froze. Swear to God, I could feel the blood pulsing through the very spot at which he stared. "What happened to your neck?" His body had gone rock still again, his eyes dark and steady and as angry as hell.

I didn't know if I should play stupid or play dead. It took me a minute to decide I was better at stupid, and although I wanted desperately to cover the bruise with my hand, I kept my fingers tightly tangled in my skirt. "What are you talking about?" "Damn it, McMullen." The words were a low growl, barely audible in the quiet room. But his eyes shouted volumes. "Don't fuck with me."

"I'm not. I just don't—"

"Was it Carlton?"

"What?"

"Your fucking boyfriend!" The words were an animalistic snarl from between clenched teeth. "Carlton. Was it him?"
I blinked in honest-to-God surprise. "Marcus? I thought you didn't even believe I had a—"

"Was it fucking him?"

"Rivera," the guard warned quietly from behind.

"Answer me, God damn it or—"

"Rivera!" Louder now. A little more aggressive.

Rivera pulled back and drew a hard breath through his nostrils, though his gaze never shifted from mine. "Everything's fine," he said.

"All right." The guard was as big as a boulder but not quite as cuddly. "See that it stays that way."

Rivera stared at me, opened his fist with an obvious effort and let his fingers curl softly against the worn counter, but his knuckles looked suspiciously pale.

"If you want to keep the asshole alive, you'll tell me the truth." His tone was almost civil now, but his eyes were predatory.

"It wasn't him," I said.

He smiled. I knew it was for the guard's benefit. But if that esteemed individual thought the expression looked friendly, he needed to be reintroduced to the human race.

"You're lying," Rivera said.

"I'm not."

"It's always the boyfriend."

"Not this time. He's out of town."

He snorted, incredulous, head jerking back just a little so that the tendons in his neck jerked tight. "Don't tell me he's still in Belarus?"

"How did you know he was—"

"You're shitting me!" He leaned forward again, hand fisting. "He's still flitting around Europe while you're getting—"

The guard stepped toward us. Rivera raised a placating hand and pulled his gaze from me as if it were being dragged through sledge. "Just…" He unlocked his teeth. "Give me a damn minute."

Boulder widened his stance. "Listen—"

"Just one minute," Rivera said, then turned his head and lowered his voice. "Please."

Boulder scowled but backed away.

Rivera returned his attention to me. "Just tell me who did it."

I raised my chin, ready to deny everything, but murder flared in his eyes like summer lightning and the truth seemed like a refreshing alternative.

"I don't know," I said.

A muscle jumped in his jaw. "Swear to God it wasn't Carlton?"

"Yes."

He inhaled, nostrils flaring. I squirmed. "Tell me what happened."

"It doesn't matter. I—"

"Tell me now or Carlton will wish he'd never seen your fucking legs." His eyes dipped, and although he couldn't see past the counter above my lap, his eyes fired up again. "And if that asshole has any balls at all, that's going to take a hell of a lot."

I was holding my breath. His gravelly tone and enraged expression vowed vengeance.

It was barbaric. It was disgusting. I had never in my life wanted to jump him more.

"Tell me," he repeated.

I cleared my throat. The memories burned like acid, but I tried to ignore the fear and push through to the facts. "I bought gas and a car wash."

A muscle bulged like an angry python in his jaw. I watched it and swallowed.

"When I returned to my car, someone was in the backseat."

Except for the slightest tremor, he sat perfectly still. "Tell me you killed the son of a bitch."

"I—"

"Tell me you killed him, McMullen." His voice was low and steady, evenly modulated, devoid of emotion, but somehow that only made the tension more palpable.

"No. I…" I shook my head, struggling. "I kicked him, though…in the face, I think." I paused to clear my throat, to breathe, to gather my courage. "The door popped open. He fell out." I managed a shrug. It wasn't easy. "I never saw him after that."

He drew a deep breath as if pulling in calmness, as if sorting through his lists of questions to find the most pertinent ones. "Had you locked your car?"

I scowled, barely noticing that the other men had begun to file out of the room. "When I got—"

"Before you went to pay…" He paused momentarily as if gathering patience. "Did you have the Saturn locked?"

"Yes. I mean…" This was the hard part. If Rivera had told me once, he'd told me half a trillion times to lock everything. If he had his way, chastity belts would be the new look for fall. "I was sure I had. I—"

“You were sure?” His fingers twitched with tension. “Or you think you were sure?”

“It doesn’t matter.” The memories were overwhelming me, drowning me. “The fact—”

“It does matter.” His voice broke. "It matters to me." His calm shattered for a second, but he drew a steadying breath and slowly lifted his hand to the glass between us.

I couldn’t help but do the same. Our fingers almost met, almost touched.

“Jack…” My voice was no more than a murmur of emotion, but he drove me back to practicality,

“It matters,” he said. “Think back. What were you wearing?”

“What difference—”

“Recreate it, McMullen. Think it through.”

I sunk into his eyes.

“A dress? Slacks?”

I swallowed, remembering my skirt twisted around my thighs. “An ivory skirt. Navy blue blouse.”

Emotion flared in his eyes but he nodded, holding himself in tight restraint. “You were on your way to…” He clenched his fist. “A date?”

“No. Not really. I was—” A sudden memory caught me. “I did lock it. I remember. I was getting out. I dropped my keys and bent to get them. The kid behind me…” Jealousy and anger burned in his eyes in sufficient amounts to make me decide to withhold the story of the wolf whistle. “I picked them up by the remote. The button was right under my thumb. I'm sure I locked it."

He nodded brusquely. "When you got back, was there any sign that the door had been tampered with?"

I shook my head. "Not that I noticed. But I wasn't looking. I mean—"

"How about later?"

"What?"

"Did you notice anything later?"

I shook my head.

"When you leave here, I want you to check."

"Time's up, Rivera," the guard said.

"Look for any new scratches, gouges. Any sign that force was used to pry open the door," he said, rising to his feet.

I did the same. "Why? What difference does it make? I can't—" I began, then fell into his eyes. "If there's no sign of entry, it was a professional."

"What did he strangle you with?"

I put my hand to my neck, feeling nauseous, but he pushed on.

"Did he have a rope? A cord?"

"I don't know. I didn't—"

"You do know," he insisted.

"It's…" I stopped suddenly as another fresh memory stormed in. I shook my head at the onslaught. "His hands were empty."

"Are you sure?"

“Yes. They jerked up when he fell out. They were pale." I scowled. "Or he was wearing gloves. Rubber gloves. But there was nothing in them.”

“Maybe he dropped the garrote in the backseat.”

“I don’t think so. I would have seen it.” I barely breathed the words.

“If you’re right—”

“He used something that was already there.” I finished the thought for him.

“The seat belt, maybe.”

“Which means…”

We stared at each other.

“He didn’t plan to kill me.”

He nodded once, expression unreadable.

“Just warn me, maybe,” I reasoned. “But I kicked him and he got mad.”

For a second I would have sworn I saw pride fire up in his eyes, but then it was gone.

“Is Elaine still in Matamata?”

The guard stepped up behind Rivera. “Time’s up.”

I nodded. “But how did you know—”

“Go stay with her,” he said. His voice had gone very soft, very low, almost pleading.

“What kind of therapist would I be if I ran out every time things got a little…” I stopped, mind jumping. “Andrews is in intensive care," I said. Or at least he had been when I'd called that morning. "So it couldn't be him, but-"

“Take what you know to Captain Kindred. Don’t do anything on your own.”

“But he owned an auto repair place in Commerce." My late night communions with Google hadn't been a complete waste of time. "There were allegations that it was a chop shop. So he could easily have had an employee who would be able to-"

“Let’s go, Rivera.” The guard nudged him from behind, but he remained where he was.

“Do you hear me?” he asked. “Forget it.”

“He would have had the tools to get into my car and…" I paused, mind spinning. "But maybe I'm looking at this upside down.” I was excited now, talking fast. "Maybe the same guy who shot Andrews was after me. Maybe he was trying to keep me from learning the truth. To make sure I didn't-"

“Dammit McMullen! Tell Kindred you want police protection. Do you hear me?"

“Rivera…" The guard nudged him again. “Don’t make this difficult.”

“This isn’t something to mess with. It’s out of your league.”

“If I could find out who attacked me maybe I could link it to Andrews's hit and prove that you're-”

“Fuck it!” he swore, leaning in. “Listen to me.”

“Code red,” the guard said into his radio.

“Don’t get messed up in this,” Rivera growled. “Leave it alone. Do you hear me? Leave it alone.”

"Trouble in the visiting room!"

"Or if Andrews's did order the hit on me, that could shed light on your case. I mean—"

"Fuck that! Fuck the case."

"Rivera!" the guard warned. "I'm giving you one more chance."

"Fuck chances," he snarled, swinging toward the guard. "I want to talk to—" But before he could finish his sentence, he was zapped with a Taser.

Chapter 20

If God wanted me to be brave, why'd he give me so many legs?
—*Harlequin, the thinking girl's companion*

For the remainder of the day, I considered what I had learned about the Backseat Bastard: He had left no marks on the door of my Saturn when he broke in, which implied that he was good at the task. But did that mean he was a criminal or a cop or neither? He had come to threaten me, but not necessarily to kill me. He had a temper, but he was cautious. He'd worn a mask of sorts, and the more I thought about it, the more I believed he had been wearing rubber gloves. Did that mean he was a known criminal? And if so, did that even narrow down the field?

In the end, I called the hospital again. The bubbly soul on the other end of the line was thrilled to tell me he had been moved out of intensive care and could accept visitors in room 324. I digested that news slowly, changed into a pair of jeans and a baggy T like one in a trance and drove west, knuckles white against the steering wheel.

I turned onto Beverly Boulevard, took a left on George Burns Road and parked in the lot beside a monstrosity with a wavy metal exterior. Once there I sat unmoving in the Saturn for what seemed forever. But finally I unlocked my knees, quieted my weak bladder and shambled into the hospital.

It didn't take me nearly as long as I had hoped to find Jackson Andrews's private room. I stood in the doorway, heart in my throat, looking inside. He was lying in bed, sipping juice from a bendy straw and chuckling at something he was watching out of sight. I could hear a television laugh track. His right hand, complete with IV, rested on the remote. It took a matter of seconds before his gaze shifted to mine.

Life stood still around me. Only my heart continued to beat.

"Ms. Christina McMullen, PhD," he said finally, and zapped the TV into silence.

I stood frozen to the spot.

He smiled. The swaddling around his head looked very white against his dark skin. He was a little leaner than I remembered, but he was still James Trivette handsome. He even grinned like Chuck Norris's sidekick. "How nice of you to come by."

I didn't respond. Couldn't.

"Come on in," he said and motioned with his free hand. "I won't bite."

It took every ounce of courage I had to step through that door, even more to approach his bed.

He raised his chin a little and narrowed his eyes, studying me in the harsh, overhead lights. "You look like you've had a hard day, Christina McMullen."

I said nothing.

"What happened to your face?"

I couldn't seem to force myself to speak.

He sighed, smile dimming a little. "It wasn't me."

"What?" My voice sounded rusty, like an old hinge too long unused.

"You're looking for someone to blame for your current troubles. But it wasn't me."

I had almost forgotten his singsong voice, his eyes that never seemed to blink. The first time I had met him I had attributed it to drugs. But I was beginning to believe he didn't need a hallucinogenic to be spooky weird.

His lips lifted a little as I stared at him. "I've been in a hospital bed longer than those bruises have been on your pretty face," he said.

I swallowed my bile. There was something about being flattered by the man who had kidnapped my best friend that made my stomach clench. "Who'd you hire?"

His dark brows rose slightly beneath the white bandages.

"Who'd you hire to do this?" I asked and lifted a hand vaguely toward my face.

He shook his head, smiling wistfully. "I'm certain I seem like a likely culprit. But you're a smart girl. If you think about it I believe you'll realize the likelihood that our assailants…" He motioned to his bandaged head. "…may very well be one and the same. Amusing isn't it, that we have a mutual enemy."

I shook my head, more than willing to deny anything he said, but he continued.

"I can understand why you would choose to disbelieve me, Christina. But the truth is this..." The faraway look was amplified in his eyes. "I no longer tell falsehoods, for I have found Christ."

I blinked at him and he laughed.

"I fear your beau may be just as skeptical as you."

I stared at him blankly, though I probably should have been able to follow his logic.

"Lieutenant Rivera," he said. "I believe I have him to thank for this opportunity to rest and rejuvenate."

I shook my head. "He didn't do it."

"Then why is he being detained at MCJ?"

I felt myself pale. The fact that he knew Rivera's whereabouts made me want to vomit. "He didn't do it," I rambled. "I know you think he did but I swear to you—"

"I forgive him," he said.

I narrowed my eyes, calmed my breathing, and tried to articulate a question.

He smiled. "Once upon a time I was an extremely deviant person. A despicable person," he said. "When I think of the lives I have ruined..." He shook his head then brightened, "but that's all in the past. I have paid my dues to society and some day I will have to explain myself to a higher court. A celestial court. But that time has not yet come. God has saved me for a bigger—"

"Rivera didn't do it," I repeated.

He laughed. "You may be right, Christina McMullen. But you see, it doesn't matter. I will not seek retribution. That was the old man. The new man has learned to lay down the sword, to turn the other cheek. Unfortunately…" His smile dimmed a little. "Not all my former disciples have seen the light."

"You think one of your friends did this to you?"

"As I said, it doesn't matter. To err is human. To forgive, divine. I'm hoping for the divine, Christina McMullen."

"Who? Who did it?" I asked and took a step toward his bed. "Do you know an officer named Joel Coggins? Do you think he could have been involved? Or was it someone who worked in your chop—"

He laughed. "You are much like I once was. Intense. Focused. Angry." He tightened his left hand into a fist then loosened it against the powder blue coverlet. "But anger is the devil's doorway. Do not go there."

"Someone framed Rivera," I said. "Someone tried to strangle me in a car wash."

"In a car wash." He sounded introspective and maybe a little sad.

"Who was it?"

He shook his head. "I've no way of knowing, Christina. But he who has great capacity for evil, also has great capacity to do good."

"Who are you talking about?" I demanded but in that instant a nurse stepped through the door behind him.

"Is this a good time for your sponge bath, Mr. Andrews?" She was blonde and pretty, with a light in her eyes that suggested she had no idea she was about to bathe a man who would just as soon kill her as speak to her.

"Never better," he said, then shifted his gaze back to me. "I will pray for you, Christina McMullen," he said.

I woke up hours later in the dead of night.

My heart was pounding. So was my front door, or so I thought. But in a minute I realized it wasn't the door at all, it was the phone ringing beside my bed. I sat in the darkness waiting for my breath to come in a more even cadence, pondering whether I should answer.

My hand shook when I lifted the receiver.

"Hello?"

"Hey, Doc."

I sat frozen, imagining a half-dozen crazed killers on the end of the line. Harlequin blinked at me, looking worried. I should make him quit reading the headlines.

"Who is this?"

"It's Micky."

“Micky?” My voice probably sounded a little strained. But that’ll sometimes happen when you've just been prayed for by a homicidal lunatic.

“Yeah. You okay?”

“Sure.” I reached out to reassure Harley. But he was already snoring softly, eyes twitching. “Sure, I’m fine.”

“You sort of sound like you’re about to have a heart attack.”

“I don’t usually get calls in the middle of the night.” To my own ears, I sounded kind of pissy. But that’s how it is when I’m angry…or awake.

“The middle of the night. Hell,” he said and laughed. “It’s not even eleven yet.”

“Oh, well…” I glanced at my wrist. Still nothing. “I had a busy day.”

“Really? Your kid get you up at five A.M., too?”

“What’s going—” I began, but premonition struck suddenly. “You haven’t shot someone again, have you?”

He laughed. “Holy shit, Doc, you make me sound like a fucking…sorry…” Ever since Jamel had come to live with him he’d been trying to clean up his language, at least while his son was within hearing range. “Frickin’ gang banger. No. I haven’t shot anyone. I just thought I'd give you a call. Make sure you were all right.”

“At eleven o’clock at night?”

“You’re a wild one, aren’t you, Doc?”

"I can be." I'd gone from pissy to defensive…with maybe just a little raw terror left over for good measure.

"How you holding up?"

"Me? I'm doing okay. Why?"

"No one giving you any trouble?"

"No, why do you ask?" My heart rate tripped up a couple beats. I glanced at Harley. Still sleeping like an inebriated infant. Not that my parents had ever spiked our bottles or anything. What kind of under-educated rednecks would do that to their own children? "What have you heard?"

"Nothing. I just wanted to make sure you were all right."

I tried to relax. Not so much.

"I've been thinking about that car wash shit," he added after a moment.

"Yeah." I took a deep breath. "Me, too."

"I was thinking it probably doesn't have anything to do with Andrews."

"What do you mean?" I remembered the weird light in Andrews's eyes with heart-palpitating clarity, but didn't bother to tell Micky I had gone to visit him. Sometimes people yell at me when they think I take dumb ass risks. I wasn't up to being yelled at.

"There are a butt load of crazies in this burg. No reason to think it wasn't just someone out of the pile."

I would have liked to believe that. "He said my name."

“Oh. Well, hell.”

“Yeah.”

“Well, it’s not like you work with the best and brightest, is it? Look at me. Give me fifty bucks, I’d do practically anything."

“I’m pretty sure it wasn’t you.”

“Golly, I feel special. Maybe it was one of your other clients.”

“Is that supposed to make me feel better?”

“Does it?”

“No.”

He chuckled. Compared to his usual grimness, he was Mr. Giggles tonight. I wondered vaguely if he had been drinking. I also wondered if I should start. “Listen, Doc, I think maybe you should get some protection.”

I scowled into the darkness. “Like a gun?” Harlequin paddled weakly on the bed and whimpered a little.

“I’m not talking about condoms.”

“That’s good. Because they’re only about ninety percent effective,” I said, glancing at my purse, where Shirley’s Glock resided.

“I could hook you up.”

I drew a deep breath. “Thanks Micky, but I’m not really comfortable with firearms.”

“That’s too bad, 'cause I’m thinking the car wash son of a bitch might not be so squeamish about them.”

I felt the shiver start at my clavicle, but contained it before it got to my toenails. It was at that second that my mind kicked in. I drew a cautious breath. "You know something, don't you?" I said.

"What?"

"It's Andrews, after all, isn't it? He's gunning for me."

"Gunning for you? Hell, woman, have you been out branding cattle or something?"

"I just..." I felt weak. "What do you know?"

"Me? Nothing. And I think you should just let it go."

"Let what go?"

"Don't go poking into this, Doc. Please. Leave Andrews alone. Leave Lavonn alone."

I remained silent for a moment, letting the facts click slowly into place. "You found her."

I could almost hear his scowl. "You know that shit-pile of crazies we talked about? She could be at the top of the damn heap."

"Where is she?"

"You're not listening."

I had heard that sentiment quoted since I was old enough to not listen. "I just want to talk to her."

"You might be the pushiest woman I ever met."

"It's possible. Do you have her phone number?"

He sighed. "I got an address. Don't know if it's current, though."

"What is it?"

After a little more pushiness on my part, he rattled off digits and words while I found a pen between Francois and a brightly colored novel called One Night With a Knight. I scribbled down the address and swallowed. “Westlake?” My voice sounded a little raspy. “That’s not necessarily the best part of town.”

“Shit,” he said. “It’s not even the best part of hell.”

I tried to laugh but my face was frozen.

“I don’t want you going there alone.”

“No,” I said. “Of course not.”

“I mean it,” he said. “Lavonn used to be real sweet when she was a kid. Had a crush on me for a while I think. But she was gone for a few years and when she came back she got mixed up with Andrews. I’ve got the feeling that maybe she’s a little tougher now.”

“Are you just saying that because she tried to kill you?”

“Listen,” he said. “She’s been through some bad shit. Half of it's my fault…what with her sister and all." He cleared his throat. I could sense his gut-gnawing guilt. I'd spent the first several months of his therapy trying to convince him not to take his own life. "I don’t want to make things any harder for her.”

“I don’t plan on—”

“And I sure don’t want to be telling my son that his aunt killed some crazy-ass chick who didn’t know when to leave things alone.”

I sat there with my mouth open for a couple seconds, then closed it and scowled. "You really know how to make a girl feel special."

He laughed quietly. He did that more than he used to, despite the fact that he was raising a child alone and professed every day that he needed a lobotomy because of it. I'd have to analyze that sometime when I wasn't worried about getting dead.

"I mean it, Doc. I said I'd find her for you and I did, but I don't want you going there alone."

"I won't," I promised.

It wasn't that I lied…exactly. On the other hand, I didn't exactly inform Micky about my impending sojourn to Westlake. It's not that I didn't want his company. I did, but I had once thought that he and Lavonn simply hated each other's guts. After my conversation with him, however, I was beginning to believe he wanted to protect her almost as much as he wanted to protect me. Maybe their relationship was a little more complicated than I had realized. And I really didn't need more complications. So after a good deal of agonizing, I slipped Shirley's Glock into my purse and drove south on Sunland Boulevard.

Lavonn lived in a two-story house built somewhere around the turn of the century. Several of the windows were broken. At least two of them were boarded up.

I sat in my Saturn for five minutes, waiting for courage to find me. But it seemed to have gone the way of the dodo bird. Finally, though, I cranked myself up and got out of the car.

A dog barked as I clattered up the sidewalk. The sound was deep-throated and serious. I could see him through the torn screen door. He looked to be half as big as Harley and twice as mean. Cropped ears were laid back against his square head. Serious-looking canine teeth were showing above crinkled-up lips.

I slowed my pace as I neared the stoop. Cujo fell silent, a condition twice as terrifying as the barking. His hackles were raised from his shoulder blades to his tail. And then he lunged. His paws struck the screen like wooden mallets. I screeched and jumped back.

"What you want?"

By the time my life was done flashing before my eyes, a woman had appeared beside the dog. Dark skinned, tall, and pretty, she looked vaguely familiar.

I screwed up my courage. "Lavonn?"

She scowled, etching a single crease between her brows. "Who are you?"

I cleared my throat. This is where it could get tricky. "I'm um…my name is Christina McMullen." I waited for the name to sink in. Nothing registered on her smooth-skinned features. "I'm a psychologist from Eagle Rock." Reaching into my purse, I pulled out a business card and thrust it carefully in between her door and the jamb. "We met ahh…once."

She cocked her head a little.

I searched for words that wouldn't make her let the dog eat me. "I'm a friend of—" I began, grappling weakly, but at that second a phone rang from the bowels of the house.

"Shit! Now what does he want?" she said, and turned from the door. The dog remained where he was. "Come in if you wanna."

I stared at the dog. He stared at me. Turns out I didn't wanna. I really didn't wanna. And Cujo looked like he wanted me to even less. But I was dying (maybe literally) to find out why someone had attacked me in a car wash.

"Ahh," I spoke a little louder. "What about…" My voice failed me for a second. I cleared my throat. "What about your dog?"

"Charlie! Come here," she said, and was gone.

In a second the dog left, too, clicking across the floor after her and leaving me to stare at the screen that had been mutilated earlier, probably during Chuck's last visitor attack.

It took me a full thirty seconds to ramp up enough courage to put my hand on the doorknob. When it wasn't ripped off by a rabid dog, I turned it cautiously and stepped inside.

The foyer was as neat as a pin, devoid of a single speck of dust. I walked into the interior like I was stepping on glass, waiting to be brought down like a weakened wildebeest, but the coast was clear.

Lavonn was in the kitchen. A drawer beside the sink was open, exposing a couple dozen neatly aligned cleaning products: liquids on one side, powders in the middle, rubber gloves rubbing elbows with a half a dozen scrub brushes of varying sizes. She had a cell phone clasped between her shoulder and her cheek. A rag was clutched in her hand, though I hadn't seen a rogue dust mote since my arrival. "I was just about to clean the toilets," she said. "Yeah. You know I will. Okay," she said, and snapping the phone shut, stared out the window. Charlie stood immobile, head lowered as if contemplating whether to swallow me whole or enjoy me at his leisure.

Lavonn's expression was unreadable, but there was something in her eyes that made my heart ache, and in that instant I thought, Micky was right; she had seen enough shit. I glanced out the window to see what had snagged her attention. Two kids were playing in the front yard. One wore nothing but a pair of blue socks. The other wore considerably less.

"Hey!" she said suddenly.

I stabbed my gaze back to her and noticed that the heartbreak was gone from her eyes, replaced by something grittier and far more dangerous, but I had very little time to contemplate the sudden mood swing because in that instant the dog growled. I jerked my attention to him. His hackles were rising.

A double threat. The truth was, I felt like I had a decent chance of beating Lavonn to the door should the need arise, but I didn't feel so great about Charlie. Charlie looked like he could bring down a Hummer.

"Hey," she said again, eyes narrowing. "Ain't you Micky's bitch!"

My heart hammered one hard beat in my chest and threatened to stop dead. "What?"

She turned in my direction, and in that instant it occurred to me that she looked exceptionally fit. Maybe my chances weren't so good with her after all. "You're the little shit that got Jackson put away."

"No, I—"

"The hell you ain't," she said, and the dog lunged.

Chapter 21

Sometimes even dogs can't make up for the crap life shovels at you. And if that's the case you might as well pack it in, 'cause you're up shit creek and you ain't got no paddle.
—Lavonn Amelia Blount, owner of Charlie the pit bull

"No!" I said, and jerked backward. My shoulders slammed against the wall. Charlie hit me in the chest and snapped at my ear. I tried to scream, but before the sound left my paralyzed throat he had me pinned, forepaws on each side of my body, crazy-Cujo gaze holding mine.

I waited for him to tear out my larynx, but he remained where he was, demonic rumblings issuing from his throat. "Call him off," I whispered.

Lavonn stood a few yards behind him. I was pretty sure of that, though I didn't have the nerve to shift my gaze from her killer dog. "Why should I?" she asked.

A thousand possible answers whirled through my mind. I pulled one from the maelstrom. "So Jamel won't be embarrassed."

The room went silent. Even the dog was frozen.

"What the hell are you talking about?"

I refrained from closing my eyes. I didn't want to pass out. I was afraid if I became unconscious Charlie would tear out my gizzard before I hit the floor. “How do you think Jamel will feel if his aunt gets put away for murder?”

“I ain’t gonna murder you,” she said. “Charlie is.”

“Involuntary manslaughter,” I said. “Ten to life.”

“What?”

I had no idea what I was yammering about, but the fact that I could still yammer made me feel a little better. “Jamel needs a mother figure. You’re the closest thing he’s got.”

“What’s wrong with you?” she asked. “You too good for a little black kid with pokey-out ears?” That gave me pause. I thought for a second. It was probably about time. “You think Micky and I are together?” I remembered, a little belatedly, maybe, that she had shown signs of jealousy in the past. Perhaps coming here hadn’t been the best idea I’d ever had. And let me tell you, that is saying something.

“When he called you that night, you come running like a greyhound on the track. Why do that if you wasn’t his bitch?”

“I was his therapist.” That sounded weird even to me. I mean, really, is that in the job description of a licensed psychologist?

She laughed out loud, maybe thinking the same.

“I haven’t seen him in months,” I said.

She snorted, the dog growled. I swallowed.

"I mean, before yesterday I hadn't seen him for…" I took a deep breath, trying to rejuvenate my brain cells. "I'm not his bitch." I was stammering a little. "Not that there's anything wrong with bitches," I whispered, and dared to eyeball the dog. It might, after all, be female, though I wasn't entirely sure if demon dogs had gender.

"Why you here, then?" she asked. "Haven't you done enough? Look around you, girl; I ain't got nothing left. Even this shit hole ain't mine."

I raised my eyes to hers. She laughed and indicated the empty walls, the threadbare carpet. "It's all gone. The house, the car. My pretty rosewood. All 'cause of you. There ain't nothing else to take, so why you here?" she asked again. It wasn't until that moment that I noticed the bruises under her left eye.

The world slowed to the speed of a dirge. Thoughts tumbled quietly into place. "Because I've been hit, too," I said.

She stared at me for a full seven seconds before she pulled her gaze away. "I don't got no idea what you're talking about."

"Who hit you?"

"Nobody hit me," she said. "Do I look like the kind of woman that'd let herself get knocked around?"

I took a deep breath. The dog was still standing guard between us.

"Was it Andrews?" I asked.

"Andrews! He's found Jesus. Haven't you heard?" She snorted. "Why the hell do you care what happens to me, anyway?"

"I don't," I said. "But I care about Jamel and he cares about you."

When she turned around, her expression was defiant but her eyes were suspiciously shiny. "Yeah, well, I don't have no time to worry about somebody else's kid."

"Because you're too worried about how to keep him from hurting your own?"

Her eyes snapped to mine. "He wouldn't hurt no kid," she said, but her tone was tight.

"Just you, then," I said.

She wiped her nose with the back of her hand. "Get out of here," she ordered.

"I would," I admitted, and nodded cautiously toward the dog.

"Down, Charlie." Her voice was little more than a grunt, but the dog dropped almost gratefully to all fours.

"Kennel," she said, and he padded away, quiet as a lamb. "No reason for you to stay now."

I had to agree, and yet I remained. Sometimes I'm not known for my stellar ability to think things through. "Who hit you?" I asked again.

Tears filled her eyes, but she held them back. "I didn't say no one hit me."

"Girls usually don't," I said. "They just show up at the morgue."

Our gazes met.

“You don’t have to take that, Lavonn.” My own voice had gone soft, almost steady.

Hers was practically inaudible. “Where would I go?”

“There are shelters, homes—” I began, but she coughed a laugh.

“You think he wouldn’t find me there?”

“He’s not all-powerful. He might think he is, but he’s not.”

She smiled dismally. “Even Jackson was scared of him.”

My mind was spinning, but I didn't want to look too curious. Didn't want to frighten her off. “They know each other?”

“He worked for Jackson."

"Where?"

She shrugged. "Took care of his cars and stuff."

“At his chop…" I stopped myself, though my heart was thumping with excitement. Or maybe it was terror. "At his car repair shop?"

She shifted her eyes away. They were full of guilt and more. “I don’t know. He don't work there no more anyway and he’s real private about what he does. He don’t like no one messing in his business.”

“Even you?”

“Especially me. He don’t trust nobody.” An edge of frustration sharpened her tone, and she shifted her attention momentarily to the cabinet with the cleaning products.

“Who is he?” I asked.

She zipped her gaze to the door as if she might conjure him up by speaking his name. "They call him Drag. He don't live here all the time. Just when he wants. But I gotta make sure it's spotless twenty-four-seven or…" She swallowed. "He got high standards. Likes his clothes pressed just so and such. Nothing wrong with that."

"He could probably learn to turn on the vacuum if he tried really hard."

She almost laughed. "Drag clean something?" She shook her head and glanced toward the cabinet that made Proctor and Gamble a multibillion-dollar industry. "I can guarantee that won't happen anytime soon. He's tough. Real tough. And I thought…" She shrugged. "Thought he could keep me safe. You know…from the world."

"But who's going to keep you safe from him?"

She cleared her throat. "You'd best get going before he comes home."

I could see her point. It was an excellent point, but for reasons entirely unknown to me I remained where I was. "Where was he a week ago Tuesday night?"

She stared at me.

"August 29th," I said. "Where was he?"

She watched me a moment longer, then laughed out loud. "How the hell would I know? I'm just glad when he ain't here."

"Was he here?"

She scowled, but a noise sounded from the front of the house. She snapped her attention in that direction, then rushed it back to me. “Get out!”

The desperation in her voice made me jerk toward the door. Or maybe it was my own terror that caused my attempted exit, but she stopped me.

“Not that way.” She clutched desperately at my arm. “Out back.”

“Lavonn…”

“He don’t like no one in this house.”

“Come with me,” I said.

Something fired in her eyes but it was gone in a second. “Leave,” she ordered and I did.

Chapter 22

The rich get richer and the poor get pissed.
—Micky Goldenstone, one of the poor

“It wasn’t him.” Those were the first words out of D’s mouth.

“What?” I like to think I’m pretty quick on the uptake, but sometimes I could use a hi or how are you? or even a have you been attacked in any car washes lately? before one launches into the topic at hand. Especially first thing in the morning. I tried to rub the sleep from my eyes, but it turns out it went all the way to the back of my head.

“Andrews wasn’t the guy who attacked you.” He sounded dead-shot sure. And according to certain sources, D knew criminals like the pope knows sin, but even though I tended to agree with him after my visit to the hospital, I had to ask.

“Are you sure?” I sat up in bed. Harlequin put a paw over his eyes. It was as big as a mammoth muffin. Oddly enough, the sight of it made me hungry. "I mean, I know he's been shot and everything. But maybe it's just a front. Maybe he's not too badly injured. Maybe he snuck out for a few minutes to… kill me." And maybe I was crazy as a loon.

"He was in the chapel from seven o'clock Wednesday night to seven o'clock Thursday morning. Took his IV with him like a puppy on a leash. Guess he's been born again." There was a shrug in his tone. "I would have thought once would be enough."

"Maybe he snuck out for a while."

“At 2:45 he used the restroom.”

“How long was he gone?”

“Two minutes and fourteen seconds. He urinated in the second stall from the end closest to the door.”

“You’re making this up.”

“I am not.”

“Weren’t there urinals available?”

“There were.”

“Maybe that tells us something.”

“It tells us he’s a squatter. He’s always been a squatter.”

“You know that?”

“You don’t get to be the number one collection engineer in Chicago without finding out who squats and who stands.”

I shook my head, trying to negate the images. “He could have—”

“You want to know what I’ve learned about you?”

“No!” I said then winced and weakened. “Okay. What?”

“You let your dog poop in the park without picking it up.”

“I do not.” I made my voice sound shocked even though I was immensely relieved it wasn’t something worse. Believe you me, there is worse.

"And you have a fondness for French…tools."

I closed my eyes and tried to pretend that wasn't so bad either. It was. But I moved on. "Have you ever heard of a guy named Drag?"

"Andrews's number one gun?"

I felt my face twitch. "What else do you know about him?"

"Of the two of them, Andrews is the warm, fuzzy one."

I swore silently in my head. If the fuzzy one had held my best friend hostage, what would the prickly one do? "How loyal is he to his boss?"

"Are you asking if he would attack you in a car wash if Andrews ordered it?"

"I wouldn't have said it in terms that make me want to hurl."

"He'd pee on Mother Teresa," he said, "but only if it suited his mood."

"So he's not a puppet."

"Truth is, I don't expect Andrews to live much longer now that he's out of the pen."

I thought about that for a second. "You think Drag was the one who shot him?"

"Could be."

"Do you think he'll try again if he was?"

"He didn't shed any tears when the kingpin was put away, and there's talk that Drag might have been the one that killed Andrews's former number one."

"I thought there was loyalty among gang members."

"You must have seen too many mafia movies before you got hooked on westerns."

"I'm not hooked on westerns."

"Whatever you say, Pilgrim." His impression of John Wayne wasn't too bad. I closed my eyes for a moment.

"How do you know what movies I watch?"

He laughed, but I asked again.

"How do you know?"

"I'd like you to remain alive for a while, Miss Chris. I mean…we haven't even slept together yet."

"That doesn't give you the right to spy on me."

"If it doesn't, I don't know what does," he said, then continued before I could come up with a logical retort. "Stay away from Drag, Christina. He's no knight in shining armor."

"What do you—" I began, then changed course as I realized what his statement implied. "You know what books I read, too?"

"I won't tell anyone you've watched Stage Coach three times in the last four months if that's what you're worried about."

It wasn't. Well…it kind of was. I was a classy broad these days. Classy broads don't become obsessed with the Duke. They watch films like Doctor Zhivago and Reds, then sit around and pontificate about the meaning of life. But sometimes…just sometimes…I thought the meaning of life might involve…say…a guy like the Duke who was hell on wheels where bad guys were concerned, but gentle with women and horses.

“What about Andrews?” I asked.

“What about him?”

“Does he know Lavonn is shacking up with the guy who may have put a bullet in his head?”

“Not yet.”

“What’ll he do when he finds out?”

"I don't know. What would Jesus do?"

"Probably not make a fortune on mind-altering drugs in the first place."

"Seems kind of likely, I guess."

"What'll he do to Lavonn?" I asked.

“Can't say for sure. But if I was her, I’d take the first train to Patagonia."

"Even though he's found Christ?"

"I'm told it's pretty easy to lose Him in a crowd."

I thought about that for a second. “I don’t think the Metrolink has a direct route to Patagonia.”

“Then I’d shoot Andrews in the kneecaps and run like hell,” he said.

The phone woke me up again. It was 2:10 in the morning. legitimately the middle of the night this time. I answered on the umpteenth ring, breath held, mind muzzy.

“Christina?”

I blinked. “Marcus?”

“Christina. It’s so good to hear your voice. How are you?”

I winced, wondering where to begin. “To tell you the truth…”

“You’ll have to speak up, sweetheart. I’m in Mazyr. It’s not a very good connection.”

“Mazyr?”

“Belarus. Darndest thing, my book was such a huge success in Pinsk that they wanted me to come to Mazyr. Like a flash signing or something.” He laughed. “I guess L.A. isn’t the only place that has a plethora of secondary narcissists.”

I drew a deep breath. “Speaking of psychological disorders—”

“They’ve done extensive tests regarding the effects of cannabis sativa on a number or psychosomatic conditions.”

“What?”

“That’s right. They have an impressive amount of data suggesting that using marijuana in moderate amounts, and under the care of a licensed physician, of course, can significantly improve the prognosis of those affected by several different types of psychological ailments, such as—”

I interrupted him before my eyeballs rolled back into their sockets. “That’s nice, Marcus, but I haven’t had much time to consider the effects of pot lately…what with the car wash attack and everything.”

“What’s that?” His voice seemed to be coming from the other side of the solar system. “I think we’re breaking up.”

I winced and thought he might very well be right.

"Dr. Carlton, it is time," someone said. The voice was soft, cultured, accented and as sexy as dark chocolate.

"I'll be right there," he promised.

"Who was that?" I asked.

"Oh, that was just Sam."

"Your publicist?"

"We should not keep them waiting much longer," Sam said.

I closed my eyes for a moment. "Sam sounds very…female."

He laughed. "If I didn't know better, lovey, I would think you were jealous. But as you're very well aware jealousy is just a manifestation of one's latent insecurities. And I know you're not insecure."

I couldn't help but wonder what other misconceptions he harbored regarding my shortcomings. "What's that noise in the background?"

"I'm sorry." His voice had risen a little. "It's extremely loud in here. They're throwing me a little celebratory soirée . The executive vice president of Colfax Publishing is here. I should get back to it. They think the book might be the number one best-selling medical paperback regarding secondary narcissists with latent somatic narcissistic tendencies next week."

I cut through the crap and said, "I thought you were going to be home next week."

"I can't leave the tour now. The first month of sales significantly impacts the longevity of the book."

I stroked Harlequin's paw and subsequently caught a glimpse of Shirley's Glock on my night stand.

"Speaking of longevity—" I began, but he interrupted me again.

"Listen, I have to go. I simply needed to hear your dulcet voice before—"

"Marc, I've had a little trouble," I said. I didn't want to worry him, but I wasn't quite sure how to make a car wash attack sound innocuous.

"Trouble?"

"A couple days ago."

"Not another bipolar schizophrenic with a hypersensitivity to clothing, is it?" he asked. "Take my advice, honey; get out of Eagle Rock. Burbank has a much more favorable clientele. The wealthy have schizophrenics, too, you know."

"It wasn't a client."

"Dr. Carlton—" It was the very feminine voice with the masculine name again.

"I'm sorry. I really must go. We can talk shop upon my return. I can't wait to tell you my ideas for the next book. I'll be home before you—" And suddenly he was gone.

"Marcus?" I said, but we'd lost the connection.

Leather Italian Oxfords.

I sat in the dark and stared at the phone, thinking that that was how we'd met. I had gone to a symposium on transference-focused psychotherapy. Marcus had been the guest speaker. It had only taken me a few minutes to realize he was classy and intelligent. Less than that to see that he had really great shoes. I'd always been a sucker for leather Italian Oxfords, and he seemed to like me, too. Found my sense of humor unique and my outlook on life refreshing. Okay, so sometimes he could be a little snooty, but he was always well groomed and intellectually stimulating. Maybe he was a little self-centered, but what genius isn't? A man's intellect was of paramount importance to me, I thought, but just at that second a picture of Rivera's ass flashed through my mind like a lightning bolt on crack. It may not be as intelligent as Marc's brain but it was as hard as a—

The phone rang again, nearly jolting me from the mattress.

I yanked up the receiver, ready to apologize for the steamy thoughts that were streaming through my head. "Marc?"

"He's coming." The words were a raspy whisper.

Each one of my less-than-hard muscles froze in instant terror. "Who is this?"

"I didn't know who else to call." A rising moan issued from the background.

The sound made my hair stand on end. I was gripping the telephone cord like a lifeline.

"Are you there?" Her voice quivered, but there was something in the tone that I thought I recognized.

"Lavonn?"

"He was high. Higher than Jesus on the Mount. So I says he couldn't sleep in this house." A tiny whimper escaped her. She sniffled it back. "He come after me."

Holy God! "Are you alright?"

"Charlie…he jumped him."

Charlie's fangs flashed in my mind. "Is he dead?"

"Drag? Dead! Shit!" Her voice trembled in earnest now. "I ain't that lucky. He scrambled outta here, but he says he's gonna come back. Gonna come back and kill the dog."

"Where are you now?"

"He loves that dog."

"Are you in the house?"

"Course I'm in the house. I don't have no—" She gasped. Something clattered in the background. I could imagine her spinning toward the door.

"Lavonn?"

"Jesus save me."

"Can you get to a friend's house?"

"I don't know no one here."

"Where are you at?"

"I already told you, I'm in the damn house."

"Kitchen? Living room?"

"Bedroom."

"Upstairs?"

"Yeah."

"Is there a window?"

"Window?" Her voice had become increasingly shrill. "I can't jump out no window." Another gasp, quieter now, almost silent. "Shit," she whispered.

"What's wrong?"

"He's here."

"Did you call the police?"

"Jesus. Oh Jesus!" she said, and then the phone went dead.

I stood frozen in terror for a good five seconds, then I was out the door before I had time to think. My little car revved and fishtailed as I swung onto Vine. I punched numbers into my cell with manic speed.

"911."

"There's an assault taking place at…" I searched for the address that remained on a scrap of envelope on my seat and read it in a bluster of noise. The dispatcher repeated the address, then asked my name. I rattled that off, too.

"Stay on the line, please," she said, but at that exact instant we lost contact.

I tried to renew the connection, but it seemed to be only a matter of seconds before I turned onto 6th Street. I had no idea how I had gotten there so fast. I slowed down, heart pumping, wondering what to do next. That's when I saw them in the headlights.

Lavonn stood in the middle of the street, eyes rimmed with white. A skinny guy in well-pressed chinos and a fedora stood with his back toward me, legs braced apart.

I slammed to a halt while rambling prayers to every saint who'd ever shown mercy on lunatics and fools. Then, popping my door open, I stepped into the opening like I'd seen the cops do in movies where the police don't usually end up dead. "Drag!" I yelled his name. He turned his head toward me. The upper portion of his face was entirely shadowed. Only his grin could be seen. It looked demonic. Something lay flat out at his feet. It took me a minute to realize it was Charlie. I felt my stomach lurch, but Drag was already taking a step toward Lavonn. "Leave her alone!" I ordered, but my voice was quaky.

He didn't so much as glance toward me.

"Drag!" My tone was frantic, echoing in the silent darkness like a fire alarm. "The police are on their way."

He didn't turn around, just lifted his hand. Light gleamed off his pistol. He pulled the trigger. A bullet whizzed past the Saturn.

I shrieked and ducked behind my door. When I got the nerve to peek through the window I saw that Lavonn was running away. I could trace her progress in the glare of my headlights. Could see Drag following her. Charlie raised his head, and in that moment I imagined Harlequin lying there, imagined him bleeding into the asphalt. But Lavonn's shriek jarred something loose inside of me and suddenly I was back in the car. I punched the accelerator like a soccer ball. If I could get to her first, there was hope, but Drag was already raising his hand toward her back.

Leaning to the right, I grabbed my purse, pawing for the weapon Shirley had given me. In that second Drag turned toward me. We were only two feet apart. "Fuck you, bitch," he said, and swung his weapon toward my window.

I jerked the wheel in one spastic motion. In all honesty, I'm not sure what my plan was, but my bumper struck him. I shrieked as he fell. A bullet pinged through the rear window. I screamed, but I was almost even with Lavonn. She spun toward me.

"Get in!" My voice was nothing but a wild screech.

She pawed at the passenger door, jerked it open and dove inside, already twisting around to stare behind us. I never stopped the car as I careened around the next corner. The tires squealed. Lavonn was shrieking. It took me a full fifteen seconds to realize she was saying actual words.

"Turn around. Turn the fuck around."

"What the hell are you talking about?" Turns out I was shrieking too.

"I can't leave him. He's hurt."

"Are you nuts? He tried to kill you."

"He never did!"

"He has a damn gun!"

"Not him!" She was sobbing. "Charlie."

I was shaking and sure…absolutely sure I should keep hightailing it out of there as fast as my little Saturn could go. But I could still imagine Harley lying alone in the street. shivering with fear, his last thoughts of me.

I whipped the wheel around, did a skidding U-turn and careened back onto 6th Street.

In the white glare of the headlights, Drag was just rising to his feet. He'd lost his hat and was relying heavily on his right leg. But I wouldn't have cared if his head had been missing; he was raising his weapon. I shrieked as I zipped past him. He swung the gun toward us, but I was already even with the dog. I slammed on the brakes. Charlie didn't even lift his head as Lavonn stumbled out of the car, sobbing as she tried to drag him toward the Saturn.

Swearing and praying, I lurched up beside her. Charlie growled as I lifted his front end. A bullet zipped past my ear. The dog was slippery with blood. We almost dropped him on the pavement, but Lavonn yanked the back door open and tumbled inside with him.

"Fuck you, bitches!" Drag was almost on top of us. Light from a lone street lamp glowed in his eyes. As he pulled the trigger again, something seemed to snap loose in Lavonn. She screamed like a banshee and lurched out of the car. I don't know how long it took me to realize her intent but the second I did, I sprang forward and grabbed her by the back of her shirt.

"Let go! I'll kill the bastard!" she shrieked, but adrenaline had overpowered my system. I hauled her backward, pushed her in beside Charlie and slammed the door.

Drag pulled the trigger again. It snapped emptily. He glanced at the weapon, then cursed and staggered toward me. His fist hit me like a freight train, driving me back against the hood of the car. My head was reeling, but I was lucid enough to realize he was coming at me again. Gripping the edge of the Saturn in clawed fingers, I swung my legs up and kicked with all my might. I would like to say I planned to strike his leg wound. But that was just dumb luck. Still, he stumbled backward, hissing and cursing. I reeled around, but he was already rising, supporting himself on the bumper.

I tumbled into the driver's seat and yanked the car into gear. There was a grunt, a bang, and then silence.

My foot slammed onto the brake without my permission. Reflex. It took me a moment to realize the car had been in reverse. Longer still to comprehend that Drag was already pulling himself from beneath my bumper.

I didn't wait around to see if he was seriously injured, didn't have time to hope he was. Instead, I wheeled onto Wilton and got the hell out of Dodge.

Chapter 23

Some days you're the dog. Some days you're the hydrant.
—*The Hydrant*

I was shaking like a true believer, Lavonn was moaning, when suddenly the passenger seat began to sing. I shrieked and jerked the steering wheel, nearly skidding off the road before I realized the noise was nothing more terrifying than my phone. I snatched it up in trembling figures.

"Hello?" My voice shook.

"This is 911. We received a call from this number at 2:23 this—"

"Where have you been?"

"I beg your pardon?"

"Where have you been? I could have—" I was breathing hard. "I ran him over with my car!"

"I'm sorry, ma'am. I think I misunderstood you. Repeat that, please."

Lavonn's moaning was rising in volume. Her voice sounded past hysterical and into scary-as-hell. "He's dying."

"Is this an emergency, ma'am?"

"You're 911!" My own voice didn't sound all that calm. "Of course this is an emergency."

"Please explain the situation clearly and slowly."

"He shot Charlie." Let me say at this juncture that those words may neither have been clear nor slow.

"Please calm down, ma'am."

"I am calm!" I yelled.

"I think he's dead," Lavonn moaned.

I twisted toward the backseat. Her eyes were glowing in the darkness, showing the same kind of rabid fear I had felt during a dozen harried trips to the veterinarian.

"Are you currently in a safe location?" The woman's voice was über calm. Deadpan, even. It made me want to beat her within an inch of her life. But I suspected, even then, that that might not be the correct response to the situation.

"Ma'am, are you in a safe location?"

I glanced out the window. I had no idea where I was, but just then I zipped past a billboard for Disneyland. Nothing could go wrong in Disneyland.

"Ma'am?"

"Yeah," I said. "Yeah, I think so."

"Very well. Now, ma'am, there was a vehicular accident, is that correct?"

"It wasn't an accident," I said. "Aren't you listening? He shot Charlie."

"Where?"

"In the chest I think, but I'm not—"

"What street?" Her tone had gone from deadpan to patient. I hate patient, but I gathered my wits and rattled off Lavonn's address.

“Can you give me a physical description of the victim?”

“I don’t know.” I felt crazy and shaky and scared shitless. “He’s black, maybe seventy pounds, small ears, short tail. He has a—”

“Ma’am!” Her voice had gone clipped and chilly. Patience had disappeared. I kind of missed her.

“Are you aware of the penalty for prank calling an emergency number?”

“This isn’t a prank call.”

“The victim has a tail?”

“Just a short…” I don’t know why I didn’t realize the problem before this. “Charlie’s a dog. A pit bull, I think.”

“So it's the dog that has been injured."

"And maybe Drag."

“Is Drag a dog?"

"No, he's a man." I remembered what he had done to Lavonn. "Kind of."

"And where is Mr. Drag at this time?"

“Probably on 6th Street.” I didn’t repeat that that was where I had run him down with my car. But I wasn’t ashamed of the fact.

“I’ll need a physical description of Mr. Drag.”

“He’s the asshole with the gun that shot the dog and was chasing Lavonn down the—”

“Is there someone else there who might be able to give me a concise report?”

I glanced over my shoulder. Lavonn was on her knees in the backseat, singing lullabies to the dog. "I don't think so."

"Very well. We'll send an officer to the scene of the crime. You will be required to come in to the station to speak to an officer and fill out a report. Can you get to—"

"I don't think he's breathing." Lavonn's voice was little more than a hiss. "'Cause of me, he ain't breathing."

"Ma'am," the woman said. "I need you to go to—" she began again, but my attention had been snagged by the tragedy in the backseat.

"It ain't fair," Lavonn moaned.

"Ma'am? Can you do that, ma'am?"

"No," I said, and wheeling onto Vineland Avenue, snapped my phone shut.

In less than seven minutes, I had slammed the Saturn to a halt in front of the veterinary emergency hospital. I was out of the car and racing through the front door in a heartbeat.

"I need help," I gasped.

Jenny was behind the front desk. She looked up, startled, blond pony tail swinging as she jumped to her feet. "Ms. McMullen."

"Outside." My voice was raspy, my pulse jittery.

She pressed a button on her phone. "Dr. Kemah, Christina McMullen is here. Yes, ma'am. Yes. I think we'll need all hands.

"What happened?" Jenny was already hurrying out from behind the reception desk into the waiting area. "Chocolate chip cookies again?"

"Gunshot."

"Gunshot?" She drew back in surprise just as Dr. Kemah strode around the corner. Dark skinned and serious as an aneurysm, she was already pulling on a pair of latex gloves.

Our gazes met as they had during a dozen other canine emergencies.

"Harry!" she yelled, not bothering with the intercom. "We need you now!"

Harry appeared like an oversized angel as we rushed outside.

Lavonn was still moaning when we opened the Saturn's back door.

"This isn't Harlequin," Kemah said, and shot her gaze to Lavonn.

"He was just trying to save me." Her voice was velvet soft, her hands bloody as she cradled the dog's head.

The doctor stared at her for a full three seconds, then yanked her attention back to the dog. "Bring him in, Harry," she said.

In a half a second he had Charlie cradled in his arms. Cujo didn't bother to try to bite him. I thought it was a bad sign. Even on the stainless steel exam table, the dog lay perfectly still. His ribs were rising and falling, but the rhythm was slow and I could see no other signs of life.

Kemah shoved a needle beneath his glossy hide and cranked open an intravenous drip. Pulling up one lip, she checked the dog's gums. They were as white as a KKK hood. Whipping on her stethoscope, she checked his pulse, his breathing, the seeping entrance wound near his flank. "When did this happen?"

I glanced at Lavonn. She looked defensive and shocky. "He was just trying to protect me," she said again.

The vet turned toward me.

"Half an hour ago, maybe," I said. I wasn't sure when my hands had begun to shake.

She nodded. "He's lost a lot of blood." She probed the wound with a latex finger. The dog growled.

I winced, maybe because of the dog's pain, but maybe because the animal scared the bejeezus out of me. "Can you save him?"

"Maybe, but it won't be cheap. We'll need x-rays, possible surgery, antibiotics, pain killers. The bullet may have hit the spleen." She tapped a finger to the corner of the dog's eye. Its blink reflex seemed slow. "But he looks like a fighter."

Lavonn was rocking back and forth. "He wasn't five weeks old when I got him. He was the runt baby. Skinny as a string bean. I fed him from an eyedropper." The corner of her mouth twitched.

It was that twitch that sent me soaring over the edge of sanity and into the abyss of financial distress. "Do what you need to," I said.

Kemah nodded briskly, then started snapping off orders. We were banned to the waiting room.

Fifteen minutes later, Jenny reappeared. She was the approximate age of my freshest produce, but much cuter. "I have a preliminary bill for you," she said. I bobbled to my feet and went to the desk, where she spread out an itemized invoice the length of my femur. She explained it in detail, but I didn't hear a word. Not until she got to the price.

"Seven hundred now and the balance when you pick him up will be fine," she said.

I looked at Lavonn. She looked at me. Shame and worry flared in her eyes.

"I was lucky to get out of there with my damn life," she said.

I swallowed. "Can you bill me?"

"Well…" Jenny scowled, trouble-free brow furrowing in concern. "We usually require payment at the time service is rendered, but…" She glanced toward the back, then shook her adorable head. "For Harley's mom we'll make an exception."

Thirty seconds later, Charlie was being prepped for surgery while Lavonn and I sat in my car like war victims. I was staring out the windshield. Lavonn was looking out the passenger window. "I suppose you think I should be grateful." Her voice was low, steady, and absolutely devoid of gratitude. I kind of wanted to hit her on the back of the head with the steering wheel.

I think it's a testimony to my self-restraint that I did not.

"Is there someone who can take you in for the night?" I asked.

"Take me in!" She scoffed. "If it wasn't for you, I'd be in my own house right now. I'd be there with my kids and my rosewood banisters and—"

"Are you nuts?" I asked, voice rising. "If it wasn't for me, you'd be stoned out of your mind and living with a kidnapping drug dealer."

She stared at me a second as if trying to decipher my words then shook her head. "I wouldn't be stoned. I don't do that no more. You're the one that—"

I held up my hand. But not to slap her, I swear. I just wanted to make her stop talking.

"Where should I take you?" I asked.

She stared at me a moment. "I wanna see my babies."

I nodded and started the car. It rattled a little more than usual. Apparently running men over in the street isn't very good for the…something or other. "Where are they?"

She swiped her knuckles beneath her nose. "With my aunt."

"In…" I gritted my teeth, patience ebbing.

"Cleveland," she said.

I killed the engine and turned to her. "Cleveland."

"I miss 'em something terrible," she said, and started to cry.

By the time I pulled up to my curb, Lavonn had fallen asleep. I glanced toward my little house. Every light was blazing and that was all right by me.

I woke her up none too gently. She sat up like an inebriated rock star, swaying a little.

"Where are we?"

"My place."

She scowled at my humble edifice. "You live here alone?"

"Yes. I mean…" I'm not sure why I hedged. "I have a boyfriend, of course. He's big. He's very big."

She stared at me as if I'd lost my last marble, but I couldn't stop my ramblings. Sometimes when folks try to kill me I get kind of freaky.

"And a doctor. A psychiatrist. He wrote a book. It's going to be a best-seller."

She shook her head and got out of the car. Her steps were kind of unsteady as she wobbled toward my stoop.

It took me a little while to hustle up the wherewithal to beat her to the front door. When I did, I pushed my key into the lock only to learn it wasn't locked at all. My breath caught in my throat.

"What?" Lavonn sounded as if she had had about all the bad news she could handle.

"The door's not locked."

"Maybe your big doctor boyfriend is inside."

"He's in Pinsk."

"Do you mean Minsk?"

"Hell if I know."

"You sure you locked it?"

I thought back, retracing my steps, but my mind was a jumble and in that moment Harley whimpered. He was inside, and suddenly it didn't matter if the Bloods had taken residence in my kitchen and were duking it out with the Crips. The memory of a dog bleeding to death on the asphalt made me yank out Shirley's Glock and push open the door like Dirty Harry on an estrogen high.

Lavonn remained exactly where she was. "You had a piece?" she asked, but I barely heard a word she said because in that moment I saw Harlequin.

He was standing in the foyer, boxy head canted to the side. His eyes lit up with love when he recognized me. My heart lurched back into action. "Hey, handsome," I said, and sinking to my knees, wrapped my arms around his neck. He licked my ear, sighed, and rested his muzzle on my left shoulder. For several seconds all the world was right.

And then Lavonn spoke.

"You had a damn gun the whole time and you didn't shoot his ass? Why the hell didn't you shoot his ass?"

I gave Harley a kiss on the snout and rose reluctantly to my feet. "I ran him over with my car," I said, and dropped the Glock back into my purse. "Isn't that good—"

"What's going on?" a voice asked.

I squawked like a distressed chicken and swung toward the intruder, hands raised like machetes.

Officer Albertson took a step back and stared at me, brows raised.

"I was just curious," he said.

I let my air out in an explosive rush. "What are you doing here?"

He shrugged. "You didn't pick up your cell."

"I was…" I was trying to breathe properly. It wasn't as easy as it usually was. "I was out of range or something."

He nodded and shifted his eyes to Lavonn. They were unusually somber. Their gazes locked. She said nothing, just examined him.

I vaguely considered introductions, but explanations seemed ungainly.

"You a movie star?" she asked finally.

He smiled his Hollywood smile. There was more than a little relief in it. I was happy to see that I wasn't the only one intimidated by Lavonn. "I'm Officer Eric Albertson," he said, then turned back toward me. "You okay?"

"Yeah." I shrugged. The effort was strangely taxing. "Sure."

"You can probably put your lethal weapons away, then."

I blinked.

He nodded toward me. It wasn't until then that I realized I was still in kung fu position. I cleared my throat, feeling like an idiot. The only thing I knew about martial arts was Chuck Norris jokes. I lowered my hands. "Where can I sack out?" Lavonn asked.

"Upstairs," I said, refusing to be embarrassed by the mess she would find up there. "Second door on the right."

She trudged up the steps without another word. The word I was thinking of being thanks.

I turned back toward Albertson. Exhaustion hit me like a wave, but I tried to be social. "So what are you doing here?" I asked. Harley was sniffing my leg and giving me the stink eye as if I had been cheating on him with a Maltese. It wasn't until that moment that I realized there was blood smeared across my bare thigh.

My eyes met Eric's. He raised his brows.

"It's not what you think," I said.

"Really?" he asked. "Because I think I let you down."

I exhaled carefully, trying to keep up. "What are you talking about?"

He shrugged. "I'm a police officer, Christina. It's my job to serve and protect."

And suddenly, though I don't know why, I was crying.

Eric folded me into his arms like well-beaten egg yolks, and I went blubbering and sobbing.

"It's all right. Shhh. You're safe now," he said, and when I was sane enough to walk, he eased me over to the couch and sat me down. His body felt warm beside mine. "Shh, honey, shh," he said. "Tell me what happened."

I was getting his shirt wet. I eased back a little and wiped my nose. "I was so scared."

"I'm sorry," he said, and stroked my hair. "I should have known you were in trouble when I saw you weren't home." He pushed a few tear-stained strands from my face.

I tried to follow the mood, but generally when people try to kill me Rivera has been there accusing me of some heinous crime. It was hard to adjust.

"What happened?"

I hiccupped once, then shuddered and told him the story.

He shook his head when I was finished.

"Really," I said. "It wasn't my fault. He had a gun. I just didn't know what else—"

"Christ, Christina." He scowled, brows beetling over beautiful sea-foam eyes. "Of course it wasn't your fault. Drag's a certified nut job."

"You know him?"

"I know of him. Everyone on the force knows of him."

I nodded. "Lavonn's his…" I searched for the proper word. "Girlfriend." It didn't seem quite right. The term made it sound as if they would be attending the sock hop together.

"Seriously?"

"She used to be with Jackson Andrews."

"No fuck?"

"None," I said, and wondered if that would change any time soon.

"Are all your friends this interesting?"

I sighed, kicked off my sandals and tucked my feet under my butt. "I don't think she's my friend."

"You kidding? If half of what I've heard about Drag is true, you just saved her life."

Yeah, so shouldn't she have been nicer to me? I gave a mental sigh and a physical shrug. "Sometimes individuals feel guilty for being with partners who abuse them. Often they then blame others in an attempt to alleviate that guilt."

He stared at me. "You may be the nicest person I've ever met."

I stared back, thinking of how I'd just wanted to slap an abused mother across the back of her head. "I hope not," I said.

He laughed a little as he smoothed a few hairs behind my left ear. "And the most modest."

Wow, I thought, and cleared my throat. "What are you doing here? Really."

"I was driving by your house, saw the lights on."

"You were driving through Sunland at three o'clock in the morning?"

He stared into my eyes, expression sober again. "I know you're still hung up on Rivera."

Why did people keep saying that? "We broke up," I said.

He smiled. "Oh, that's right. You're with someone else now."

"Marcus," I said, and found I was inordinately proud of the fact that I'd remembered his name.

"He's a lucky man."

"He's in Pinsk."

"Do you mean Minsk?"

I shrugged. "He's a very important psychiatrist."

"Did they have a mental health emergency in…wherever the hell it is?"

"He's signing his book."

"Ahhh," he said, and stroked my cheek with his knuckles.

"It might be a best-seller."

"Meanwhile, you're here all alone?"

"I have Harley," I said, and stroked his ear. He'd placed his head on my knee, apparently forgiving me for my suspected liaison with the Maltese.

"Nice dog," he said, leaning in. "But don't you get lonely?"

I swallowed. "I have Francois."

"Francois?"

My eyes locked on his. Turns out I would rather be accused of any number of heinous crimes than have to explain why I had given my vibrator a French name.

I cleared my throat again, ready to make up some outrageous lie, but just then he kissed me.

Chapter 24

Thinking; it's not for everyone.
—Chrissy McMullen, age seven, cognizant of such things at an early age

Heat steamed through my body. I once heard that near-death experiences make people want to copulate, that awareness of their mortality makes them need to feel alive. Personally, I always thought that orgasms alone would be a big enough motivator. But right then I really did need to feel alive.

At least that's what I told myself as I kissed him back.

His hand scooped around my neck, drawing me closer. I was breathing hard by the time he lifted me into his arms. I didn't resist.

"My God, you're beautiful," he said, and kissed me again. It was a good thing he was carrying me, because I was too weak-kneed to speak. Not only was he not accusing me of murder, he was alleviating the necessity of walking and telling me I was pretty. The three steps to guaranteed sex.

He carried me to the bedroom and kicked the door shut with his foot. I sighed as he laid me down, moaned as he cupped my breast.

"Christina," he whispered, and kissed my neck. "You have no idea how long I've been wanting to do this."

I closed my eyes as he opened my blouse. His hands felt warm against my skin, and then he lay down beside me, long and firm. I arched against him.

"Jack," I whispered, and suddenly the world stopped.

I snapped my eyes open.

He stared at me. I stared at him. He blinked.

"Eric," I said. "I meant Eric."

Something sparked in his eyes, but after a moment he shook his head. "It's all right." His voice was nothing more than a murmur.

"No. It's not. I'm—"

He put his fingers on my lips. "You've been through a hell of a lot in the last couple weeks."

"That doesn't mean—" I began, but he kissed me again. His body felt hard against mine. My own revved up. A man. A living breathing man who was neither in jail nor in some country I couldn't locate without a magnifying glass. I had hit the mother lode. But guilt and shame were alive and well even at the mother lode. I put a hand on his chest, but my ovaries, suspecting treason, began sending dire warning to my fingers.

Don't do it, they said. Don't you dare do it.

"I'm sorry. I can't." I whispered the words, but my female parts heard me and immediately began screaming obscenities.

"Are you sure?" he asked, and gave me that smile that had certainly made stronger women offer to bear his babies.

"No, she's not fucking sure. The bitch is nuts!" Turns out my female parts can be pretty rude.

"I'm sure," I whispered.

"I'm not trying to take Rivera's place, you know."

"Marcus. I'm dating Marcus."

"That's right," he said, and smiled.

I winced. "It wouldn't be fair to you."

"Would you think less of me if I said I didn't give a flying fuck about fair when you look at me like that?" He stroked my cheek. I managed not to erupt into multiple orgasms and wriggled. He raised his brows, but I was just trying to wiggle out from under him. I swear I was.

Eventually, he slid off me. I sat up and put my feet on the bed. He swung his over the side and stared at me. There was no anger in his eyes. Only disappointment.

"So how did you get mixed up with a bottom feeder like Drag?" he asked.

I exhaled carefully. "I went to see Lavonn. We met a while back when…" I began, but I wasn't ready to relive those memories. "She used to live with Jackson Andrews. I thought maybe she could help me figure things out so I went to see her."

"At two o'clock in the morning?"

I shook my head. "No. A few days ago. Turns out she's living with Drag now. When she called me, she was pretty…" I steadied my hands on the mattress. "Distressed."

"Distressed. No shit. She's living with a fucking lunatic."

"Not anymore."

He snorted.

I raised my eyes to his. "She left him," I said.

"Oh, come on. You know as well as I do that she'll be back with him before breakfast."

"That's not necessarily true."

"You're right. She might find someone even worse."

"He shot her dog," I said. Harley whined at the door. "I'm not sure there is anyone worse."

His shrug suggested he was less than convinced. "It's nice of you to try to save her but…" He shook his head.

"You don't think people can change?"

"I do if you do."

I thought about my own high school years, during which I had participated in belching contests on more than one occasion. "I hope they can."

"Tell me the truth, Christina," he said. "Is it that same kindness of yours that makes you try to exonerate Rivera, or is it something else?"

"What are you talking about?"

"Come on, look at yourself, honey. You're…" He skimmed his gaze down my body. "Well, Lavonn doesn't exactly look like she'd be your sorority sister."

"What do you mean?"

"I mean, the only reason you were in that neighborhood is because you're trying to get Rivera off the hook."

I considered denying it, but I was too exhausted. "He's innocent."

No one spoke for a moment. His eyes were very steady on mine. "A man will do a lot when he's in love."

I stared back, but I wasn't ready to explore that option or debate the possibilities.

I shook my head. "He didn't do it."

"Tell me the truth. What has he done to earn such loyalty?"

"It's not loyalty. It's realism. Emotions have no part in this. I'm with…" Aw, fuck. Not again."…Marcus! I just know Rivera didn't shoot anybody."

He laughed a little. "Well," he said, and sighed as he rose to his feet. "Maybe you're right. Imp seemed to think the same thing."

"What?"

He looked momentarily chagrined, then shook his head, seemingly at his own absentmindedness. "Never mind. I'm sorry I got overly"—he nodded toward the bed, looking sheepish—"enthusiastic. I hope this won't stand in the way of our friendship."

"What's an Imp?" I asked.

He laughed and turned toward the door. "Next time you have a friend in trouble, call me instead of charging into the fire, will you?"

I stood up. "What did Imp say?"

His shoulders slumped a little, and for a moment he looked infinitely sad. “I’d give my right arm to have that kind of loyalty.”

“It’s not loyalty!” I repeated. “I’m with…” I really think it was just fatigue that made me forget that time.

“Marcus?” he suggested.

I shook off the pesky forgetfulness and forged on. “Who’s Imp?”

He stared at me for a few long seconds, scowled and stepped back toward me. “Forget I said anything, Christina. Please.”

“He knows something about Rivera, doesn’t he?”

He shook his head slowly, ignoring my question. “He doesn’t deserve you.”

“What does Imp know?’

He exhaled heavily, then glanced toward the door as if expecting to see Drag come barging through with a battering ram. There was another prolonged silence then, “There’s talk that she has information.”

“Imp’s a she?”

“Forget it. Please. You don’t have to worry about Rivera. He’s a big boy.”

Did all these cops shower together or what? “I know he is,” I said.

“But you’ll worry anyway.”

“No. I mean…where would I find this Imp?”

“You wouldn’t.”

“Where—”

“Christina…” He took my left hand in both of his. “You can’t. Drop it. Please. I don’t even know where to find her myself since she quit per—”

“Quit what?”

“Leave it alone.”

My mind was spinning wildly, trying to patch the clues together in an attempt to form the next question. “Is Imp her first name or—”

He laughed out loud. “Jesus, woman, word around the station was that you were a tiger. I was kind of thinking they meant it in a different way.”

I was too revved up to be embarrassed.

“Help me learn the truth, Eric,” I said. “For Rivera’s sake.”

He shook his head.

“He’s a fallen officer. A brother. A—”

“I’m sorry.”

“Then do it for me,” I said, and stepped toward him, looking up through my lashes as I slipped my hands around his biceps. They were pretty good biceps. “Please.”

Our lips were inches apart.

He kissed me, then he stepped back and shook his head as if awakening from a dream.

“He doesn’t deserve you,” he said, and whipping the door open, left me alone with my frustrations.

Chapter 25

Babies are God's way of saying, "What the hell were you thinking?"
—Connie McMullen (Chrissy's mother) while intoxicated and unforgivably honest

Fueled by terror and hormones, I didn't sleep for the rest of the night.

The Westlake cops showed up on my stoop sometime before dawn. I gave them as detailed a report as I could then woke Lavonn so she could add her two cents. She was atypically subdued, and after learning that Drag had not yet been apprehended, she went back to bed.

I would have liked to have done the same, but there was still a good dose of craziness swimming around in my head. I was close to finding the answers that would prove Rivera's innocence. I knew it. But first I had to form the right questions.

For instance, this Imp…who was she? What was she? I checked the internet first, but my Google results, while intriguing, were unhelpful. I waited until seven o'clock in the morning to begin phoning everyone I knew: cops, attorneys, beggar men, thieves. But even my friends hadn't heard of an Imp.

By eight I was wound as tight as a rubber-band plane and had learned approximately nothing. Three people had hung up on me, seven hadn't answered, and one had cast aspersions on my mother's origins. Two hours later I was back at the computer in my little office. My eyes felt like they had been sautéed in battery acid.

At eight thirty-seven Jenny called from the emergency clinic to say that although Charlie had survived surgery, his condition remained guarded.

"Who was that?"

I jumped at the sound of Lavonn's voice and twisted about intending to scold her for scaring the crap out of me, but the sight of her puffy eyes and grim expression stopped the words before they escaped.

"It was the animal hospital. Charlie made it through surgery," I rushed to add, "but his condition's still…well, he'll need some time to recover."

Her lips trembled before she turned away and hurried into the kitchen.

"But Dr. Kemah is an excellent veterinarian." I rose to follow her. "I'm sure—"

"Don't you have nothing to eat around here?" Her tone was gruff as she shifted through my cupboards, but I wasn't forgetting the misery I'd seen on her face only moments before.

"You don't have to be so tough, Lavonn. I'm your friend. You can—"

"My friend!" She pivoted around, eyes blazing. "If it wasn't for you I'd still be living in Glendale. Still have my babies and my car and my—"

"And your drug-dealing maniac!" I snarled.

"Jackson wasn't no—"

I held up my hand to ward off any possible histrionics…or facts. "My apologies," I said, determined to take the high ground. But high ground or not, there might have been a bit of snootiness in my voice. "I didn't mean to impugn Jackson Andrews's stellar reputation."

She looked at me with crafty eyes. "Do you have any idea what the penalty is for defamation, either libel or slander, in the state of California, Ms. McMullen?"

I stared at her, brows shooting through my hairline. Her Ebonics had been replaced with tight-assed diction and a holier-than-thou expression. "What?" I asked, tone flat.

She snorted softly and propped a hand on her right hip. "You think you're the only one in this house that can talk snotty?"

"Yes?"

"Well, you ain't. Not after twenty-eight months at Southwestern," she said, and turning on one bare foot, started looking through my drawers.

I stared at her for a good ten seconds before, "You have a law degree?"

She didn't bother to quit rummaging through my stuff long enough to answer me. "I didn't say I had no degree."

"You went to college for"—I waved my hand dramatically—"forever…and you didn't graduate?" It was entirely possible that she was even dumber than I thought. Then again, it was far more probable that she was much, much smarter than I had anticipated. “Why? What happened?”

“Life,” she said, and reaching up, began shuffling through a jungle of sugary cereals. “Life happened.”

“How long before you would have graduated?”

She shrugged and pulled a box of crispy something-or-other off a shelf. “Year. Maybe two.”

“Why in the world didn’t you—” I began, but she whirled around and slammed the box down on the table, jolting my words to a halt.

“I guess you never spent nine months puking up your guts, huh? You never cursed the little shit inside of you, only to push it into the light of day and realize you never loved nothing like you love it. I guess you never been awake thirty hours straight waitin’ for teeth to come in or prayin’ he’ll get over the colic before you cut your wrists.“ She tilted her head at me. “I guess you never had no babies, huh!” she said.

I blinked at her, deflated but not sure if I should be. “Well, no, but surely—”

“Then you got no idea what you’re talkin’ about.”

I stood there speechless. I mean, I’m all for women’s rights and brave mother bears and all that, but she seemed to be impugning my chosen path, so I girded my loins and marched out my professional tone. “I realize it can be quite difficult to juggle a family and a career, but if you had just—”
“Juggle!” she snarled, leaning so close to my face

that I could see the pores on her nostrils. My professional tone may have pissed off the mother bear a little. "They ain't grapefruit. They ain't…" She waved a hand vaguely…possibly toward Cleveland, where her own non-grapefruit were supposedly stored. "Baseballs. Maybe just 'cause they's black, you think they can be tossed around like so much garbage. Like they's—"

"Holy shit!" I yelled. Professional was long gone. Keep an eye out for stark raving mad. "What the hell's wrong with you? I saved your ass last night. Hell," I said, remembering back, "I saved your nephew's ass. Black, white or frickin' magenta!"

We faced off like mad dogs, and for one wild second I thought it might come to blows. Hell, for one second I hoped it might. But finally she drew a deep breath through her nostrils and nodded.

"Try the Blue Fox," she said.

I tilted back slightly. "What?"

"If you got the balls to try to find Imp," she said, snagging the chosen box of cereal under one arm and heading back toward the stairs, "try the Blue Fox."

At 12:47 P.M. I was on the phone with Julio Manderos. Julio is a good-looking Spanish gentleman who owns a little establishment called the Strip Please. Besides participating in a couple other less-than-perfectly-legal activities, he had, at one time, made a decent second income by being Senator Rivera's body double.

I kid you not. I can't make this shit up.

"What do you know about the Blue Fox?" I asked.

There was silence on the other end of the line for a good five seconds. "Why do you ask, Christina?" Even his voice sounded like Miguel Rivera's.

"I'm looking for someone," I said.

"And this someone, he has a name?"

I hesitated a second, though I didn't know why exactly. "Imp."

I could hear him draw a heavy breath. "I know of no one by that name."

"I think he might be a snitch for the police."

Another silence. "This has something to do with the senator's son, si?"

I considered denying it, but there wasn't much point. "Si," I said.

"Christina, I do not think it a good idea for you to get involved in a situation of this sort."

"Rivera's innocent."

"Perhaps so, but it is not for you to prove. He is a big boy."

Seriously? Again with the size?

"Well, his father doesn't seem to be doing much of anything to help him," I said, feeling, irrationally, perhaps, that since the two of them looked alike, the senator's parental neglect was somehow Manderos's fault, too.

"I cannot speak for the senator, Christina," he said. His voice was sad.

I drew a deep breath and sighed. "I know. I'm sorry. So you don't know anything about an Imp?"

"I do not."

"Okay. Well…thank you anyway," I said, and prepared to hang up. "I'll talk to you—"

"Christina."

"Yes?"

"The Blue Fox is no place for a lady such as yourself."

I considered asking him what kind of lady it was suitable for, but I wasn't in the mood to be clever...or enlightened. "I'll be fine," I said instead.

"You must promise me you will not go there alone."

"I'm afraid I'm not swamped by offers to accompany me just now."

"Then I shall come with you."

"No," I said, though honestly, the idea of having someone with a little testosterone on my side did give me a boost. "You can't."

"I can."

"Julio," I said, more grateful than I had expected to be. "Thank you. I appreciate your offer. But think about it. I'm not going to be able to get any information from anyone when I have an ex-senator sitting beside me."

"I am not an ex-senator."

"But no one will know that."

"Good. Perhaps then they will not bother you."

I sighed. "Okay, I'll call you if I decide to go there."

"This you promise?"

"Yes."

"Very well. We will talk soon."

"Sure," I said, and prepared to hang up again.

"And Christina..."

"Yes?"

"There is a special place in hell for those who lie to people who care for them."

"I'll call," I said, and hung up.

Seven hours later, I was on my way to the Blue Fox. I had Shirley's Glock in my purse, my pepper spray on my key chain and 911 on speed dial by the time I parked by the curb outside.

It was a long, low building with an asymmetrical roof line and a tilted sign. The street was set in semidarkness. Off to my left, a couple was making out on the hood of a Mazda. Up ahead, a trio of boys were playing music and talking trash. I drew a deep breath, steadied my nerves and stepped out of the car.

The man appeared out of nowhere. One moment I was alone and the next he was right behind me.

"You shouldn't have come," he whispered.

Chapter 26

The last thing I want to do is hurt you. But that doesn't mean it's not on my list.
—*Christina McMullen, to about thirty-seven ex-boyfriends*

I gasped and spun around, grappling for my pepper spray, but I was too slow. My spastic fingers connected with the canister just as he grabbed my hand.

"Christina." The voice was soft, the hand gentle but firm. "You promised." It took my palpating heart several seconds to slow down enough to allow me to recognize my attacker.

"Julio!" I exhaled his name like a prayer. "What are you doing here?"

"I am hoping to not get myself killed." We stared at each other from inches apart. "Perhaps you could tell these fine people that you are well."

"What?"

He tilted his head toward the onlookers. As it turned out, the couple making out on the Mazda were both male. Or… I stared at them a moment longer. Perhaps they were both female. Either way, both had pulled out pistols.

My hands were shaking. My voice, too. "I'm okay." I cleared my throat and tried again. "Just startled. There's no problem here." I gave them a wobbly smile. "We're friends."

A boy in low-slung jeans stepped away from the trash-talking trio. Even in the dim light I could see he was barely old enough to shave. "You sure you okay, girl?"

"Yes," I said, and slipped my arm around Julio's waist. "I'm great."

"He kind of old for you, ain't he?"

Julio's eyes glowed a little. I didn't know if it was fear or anger.

"Tell you what," said Slung Low. "You come with me I'll give you some fresh meat for dinner."

My heart did a nosedive toward my stomach. I felt Julio's biceps twitch and knew beyond a shadow of a doubt that he was about to reach for a gun of his own. I pulled myself closer, blocking his motion.

"No thanks," I said, and snuggled under Julio's left arm. "Age doesn't matter with a love like ours, does it, Honey Pot?"

He turned his head toward me. And now I recognized the emotion. It was fear. Not for himself but for me. Years ago, he had vowed to care for me for as long as he drew breath, but perhaps I hadn't realized the depth of his emotions.

"None," he said, and gently slid his hand down my waist. I stiffened, but his kiss was soft and pure and full of caring. I opened my mouth to protest, but he pressed his fingers to the small of my back and deepened the kiss.

By the time he pulled away, my head was spinning like a globe.

Neither of us looked back as he turned us toward the club. His arm around my waist was all that kept me upright, and even then I wobbled a little.

"Holy shit," I said.

"We must keep walking," he ordered.

When we stepped into the building, the musky smells and pounding music were almost overwhelming, but I was too buzzed to worry about either of those details.

"Julio," I said, leaning forward and finding his eyes in the dim lighting. "I didn't know."

He glanced right and left, dark eyes gleaming. "You did not know what?"

"About your feelings for me."

He turned slowly in my direction. "Christina," he said, worry edging his sweet accent, "you do know what I do to make my living, si?"

"What?"

He scowled a little. The ambient noises seemed to dim. "For many years I was…I am in the business of pleasure."

I blinked as formerly known facts came flooding past the hormonal wall that had momentarily barricaded my brain; Julio Manderos had not always been a business owner and senator look-a-like. He had once been a paid companion. "Oh. Yes. I know. Of course. I know that. I just—" I jerked my head to the right. "Look! An open table," I babbled, and sped through the mob toward the stage.

A pretty couple was dancing there, but I barely saw them. My face was on fire. I stumbled into a chair.

"Christina," Julio said, and seating himself gracefully, took my hand in both of his.

"What do you think?" I asked.

"Christina, we must discuss this."

"I know," I whispered, and forced a lopsided grin. It was the best I could do. It was sobering and somewhat frightening to realize I was still an idiot. "So what's your guess?"

"I beg your pardon?"

I nodded surreptitiously toward the pretty couple. My movement was the physical equivalent of a stage whisper. "Do you think they're male or female?"

"Christina, I did not mean to give you the wrong impression. I only wished to—"

"Listen, I've got to pee. When I get back, I want you to tell me their genders," I said, and stumbling to my feet, hurried toward the back of the building.

The restroom was small. It had two stalls, one free-standing metal cabinet with listing doors, and enough graffiti to fill a novel. It was also unoccupied. I have never seen such a beautiful sight in my life. I made it to the only sink, splashed water on my face and stood staring down at the drain as if life's many mysteries would be answered there. But they remained hidden. I mean, seriously, what was wrong with me? Julio was a friend. A good-looking friend, true. A tall, dark, handsome suave friend, but a friend nevertheless. Not to mention the fact that he was, as often as not, a paid friend. Was I so hard up that I needed love in all the wrong places?

I glanced at the mirror. The face that glanced back was okay. Not glamorous. Not heart stopping. But not hideous either. My skin was kind of pasty, my hair a little messed, as if I'd had a run-in with an opinionated dry vac. But no one was perfect. And I had a boyfriend. My face flamed red again as I thought back to some of my recent exploits. So what if I sometimes forgot his name? So what if he was in a country I had never heard of while I was being attacked in my car? So what if—

The door opened. I turned back to the sink, hiding my reddened cheeks. "It's so hot in here," I said, and splashed more water on my face. "But I'll be done in a minute."

"You sure as hell will."

I jerked around at the sound of the guttural voice. Drag stood between me and the door. Bruising showed around his right eye as if he'd recently been hit in the face. My mouth went dry. My knees went weak, and when I looked down, my breath stopped dead in my throat.

He held a pistol in his right hand. I staggered backward, bumping into the sink.

"You can't come in here." They were the first words out of my mouth, barely audible, completely nonsensical. You can't come in here? Like social etiquette was the reason he couldn't kill me?

He laughed, low and mean and self-assured.

"I can do anything I want," he said, and took a limping step toward me. I jerked my purse up to grab Shirley's gun, but he snatched it out of my hand and flung it across the room. The Glock flew out and skittered against the wall. My arm screamed in pain. I was breathing hard now, wide eyed as he grinned at me. I backed away, skirting the sink, but the space was limited.

I shook my head, grappling for something intelligent to say, but all that came out was, "You don't have to do this. Andrews doesn't own you."

"Fuckin' A," he said, and lunged toward me.

I shrieked, grappled behind me and tore the cabinet away from the wall. It toppled forward, almost striking him. He jumped back just as I leapt for the door, but he was already blocking that route. Turning wildly, I dashed into the stall, but he was right behind me. I spun around and slammed the door with all my might. It smashed into his arm. I was sobbing as I yanked the door toward me and slammed it again, but he had already drawn back.

I fumbled for the latch just as his shoulder hit the door. I flew backward, landing on the stool.

"Where is she?" he growled, and yanking me to my feet, drew back the gun as if to strike me. "Lavonn, where—" But he never finished the sentence.

"I'm right here," she snarled.

Drag half-turned, and in that instant, Lavonn leapt toward him. She shrieked as she swung. The tire iron hissed past his face. He shoved me backward and stumbled out of the stall, dodging her blows. I fell back against the wall, dazed and terrified. I heard iron strike flesh, but Drag grabbed her weapon and yanked her to the floor. Her head struck the tile with sickening finality.

“Fucking bitch!” he snarled, and stumbled toward her. But there was a pop of noise. He jerked as if yanked by a cord. Flinging his arms wide, he turned and stumbled three steps in my direction. He raised his gun, growled a threat, then crumpled slowly to the floor near my feet.

It took me a long time to realize I was unscathed, longer still to understand that Eric Albertson was standing by the door, legs straddled, gun still trained on his target.

I watched woodenly as he closed his stance and strode forward to gaze down at Drag. He was lying on his side, pistol half-hidden beneath him, eyes wide and staring. Blood seeped from his neck onto the grimy floor tiles. Eric held his gun outstretched, but knelt and touched his fingers to a spot just below Drag’s jaw. Nobody moved.

“Is he dead?” Lavonn’s voice was no more than a raspy whisper, but it seemed to bring Eric out of his trance. He looked up. The door creaked open. A face appeared momentarily, then disappeared. Footsteps could be heard skittering away.

Eric blinked once and glanced at me.

“You okay?”

“Sure.” I was still sprawled on the floor like a broken doll. I didn’t even try to change that situation. “I’m fine. Lavonn…” My voice was unsteady. “Lavonn got here just in time.”

She was already struggling to her feet, eyes wide. “You bet your white ass I did,” she said.

“How did you know?” I asked. “Why did you come? How did you get here?”

“I took a damn taxi,” she said. “You owe me forty-two bucks.”

Chapter 27

A true friend will stab you in the front.
—Oscar Wilde

It was hours before the police allowed us to leave the crime scene. But finally we were back home. Lavonn trekked immediately into the kitchen.

Eric watched her go, then sighed and stared down into my eyes. “Are you sure you’re okay?”

“No,” I said, and drew a ragged breath, “but I will be.”

He shook his head, kissed my forehead and said, “You’re amazing.”

I was, kind of. “So you think Drag was the one who shot Andrews?”

He exhaled slowly, as if just beginning to relax. “That's my guess."

I thought about that for a moment. “He probably planned to take over the sale of Intensity.”

“That seems likely. But maybe he just had a grudge. We’ll probably never know for sure now.”

I nodded, feeling numb, and a little less amazing than I would have liked.

“I’m sorry I was late.”

I pulled my gaze back to his face. He wasn’t the first person to apologize to me that evening. Julio had been beside himself when he’d realized I’d been attacked under his watch. But he’d allowed

Eric to drive me to the station and eventually take me home.

“I should have been more careful,” I said.

“Yes, you should have,” he agreed, and sighed. “So maybe you want me to stay the night?” He looked hopeful, and I have to admit I was tempted. But I had a boyfriend.

Rivera’s dark features flashed through my mind, followed languidly by Marc’s blander ones.

“I’d better see to Lavonn,” I said. “She’s probably more shook up than she seems.”

Eric chuckled a little and squeezed my hand. “An army boot would seem more shook up.” I glanced at him and he shrugged. “I don’t think you have to worry about her too much,” he said. “At the end of the world it’ll just be her and the cockroaches left.”

“She’s probably a marshmallow in—” But just then she yelled from the kitchen.

“Don’t you ever have no damn groceries in this house?”

“Probably just hiding her sensitivity,” Eric said, and turned to go, but he paused for a moment. “Hey, Lavonn doesn't have Drag's phone does she?"

“Not that I know of.”

He nodded. “Well, if it turns up, make sure she doesn’t mess with it, will you? It wasn't on the body and we’ll need it for evidence.”

“Okay.”

He nodded and prepared to leave.

“Eric?”

He raised a brow at me.

"Thank you again."

"To protect and serve," he said, and left.

I walked into the kitchen, only to find Lavonn munching on a PB and J sandwich.

"I thought you couldn't find anything to eat," I said.

She shrugged. "I been eatin' since I walked through the door. I just couldn't stand the thought of you suckin' face with that pasty-faced do-gooder."

"What are you talking about? He saved our lives."

"He saved your life. He woulda just as soon I was drowned in the toilet."

I scooped up a spoonful of peanut butter and sat across the table from her. "I take it you don't care for Officer Eric."

Another shrug, but then she snagged her sandwich and stood up. "Come on," she said.

"Where?"

"You're going to take me to get my shit."

"What?"

"My shit," she said, "In Westlake."

I was shaking my head even before she quit speaking. "Now's not the time. The police aren't going to want us messing up the crime scene."

"It's not a crime scene, Sherlock. Case you forgot, Drag tried to kill us at the Blue Fox."

"Technically that's true," I admitted regretfully. "But I still think they won't want us to—"

"Technically I saved your ass," she said, "so go get your damn keys."

I considered arguing, but I've never been comfortable being the sensible one. It had rubbed me wrong since the day I shed my diaper and took off across Fernbrook Avenue at warp speed. The ensuing spanking had taught me little.

In a minute we were in my car.

Outside the little Saturn's windows it was blacker than sin.

"I still don't understand why you decided to go to the Blue Fox," I said.

"You think I'm illiterate?" she asked.

"What are you talking about?"

"I saw your doodling by the phone. Julio. Imp. Blue Fox. All that."

I nodded, but I really wasn't following her line of thinking very well.

"It's a major hangout for folks who are looking to get themselves killed," she added.

"I didn't want to get myself killed."

"Well, you sure as hell act like it. When you come running that time Micky shot Jackson…" She shook her head. "I thought you must have had a thing for him. But then you do the same thing when I call."

I gave her a nonchalant shrug.

She scowled, seeming to try to figure me out. "You come running when every nigger bitch calls?"

I raised my brows. "It's not emotionally healthy to call yourself names."

"Yeah, well…" She sighed and glanced through the windshield, peering into the night. "You call me that and I guarantee it won't lengthen your life."

The hum of my engine was all that was heard for a while. That and my own roiling thoughts.

"Thank you," I said finally, and turned to look at her.

She shrugged. "Could be I owed you one."

"Could be you owed me a couple," I said, and she snorted. "So what now?"

"Now I go pick up my stuff."

"You won't stay there?"

She shuddered visibly. "Drag, he got friends round therc."

"You're welcome to stay with me until you get on your feet."

She chuckled. "If you knew how unsteady my legs was, you wouldn't offer."

The little Saturn hummed on. No one spoke for a moment, then, "But I did," I said.

She shook her head. "You and me, we don't sing in the same choir. This time next year you'll probably be on some big-ass book tour with…" She paused. "What the hell's his name?"

I sighed. "Damn if I know."

She chuckled. "Well…you'll be with some rich somebody, and I'll be poppin' out a new kid."

"Tired of your old ones already?"

She laughed. The sound was a little off. I glanced over, but she was staring out the passenger window again. The neighborhood was deteriorating rapidly. I took a right onto Wilton.

"I'm good at making babies."

"Maybe you'd be good at practicing law, too."

One shoulder lifted a little. "Folks from the hood stay in the hood."

"That doesn't seem to be what Micky Goldenstone thinks."

She was silent for a moment. "Micky ain't got no time for me."

It took nearly a half a minute for reality to finally strike me. When it did, I felt a little bit like an idiot. I mean, it didn't take a genius to realize she had feelings for him. "How long have you been mooning over Micky?"

There was a long pause, then, "God, I hate this neighborhood."

"Lavonn—" I began but she interrupted me.

"Pull up here and let's get this over with."

She seemed a little jumpy as we traipsed up the walkway to the door. Jumpier still as she shoved her key into the lock. In a moment we were inside. She had only been absent a few hours, but the place looked the worse for it. Dirty dishes had been left on the table. Broken shards of glass lay on the floor, only half swept up by the nearby broom. Towels, several of them spotted with blood, were heaped on the counter, and the all-important cleaning drawer was open, showcasing enough chemical cleansers to cause an asthmatic epidemic.

I swallowed my revulsion and turned my gaze away from the towels. “What are we taking?” I asked.

“Anything we want,” she said.

“Are you sure that’s legal? Maybe the police will want to have a look at things first.”

She stared at me. Her eyes showed a lot of white around the irises, making her tough-guy act seem a little suspect, but she marched into a little room off the kitchen. Returning with a laundry basket of neatly folded clothes, she dumped the contents onto the floor. “You trying to be a saint, or what?”

In the entirety of my life I was pretty sure I had never been threatened with being canonized. Threatened with being shot out of a canon, sure. “Yes,” I said, “Saint Christina.”

She chuckled as she headed toward the stairs. “Well, Your Sainthood, you start in the kitchen. Pack up anything that ain’t growing fuzz.”

In the end, that didn’t amount to too much. But I did find an un-fuzzy box of Whoppers in the cupboard above the stove. I had just popped a pair into my mouth when a torpedo erupted from the counter. I jumped and squawked, spewing gobs of chocolate and malt.

“What!” Lavonn appeared in the doorway, eyes wide as softballs, but I was frozen in place. She shot her gaze to the offending counter, then strode purposefully across the floor to dig around under the mess of towels. A cell phone lay there buzzing like a bee.

Our gazes met.

"It's Drag's," she said, and lifted it from the counter.

"You're not supposed to touch that."

"Uh huh," she said, and turned it face up.

"Who's it from?" I asked.

Her brows lowered. "Vanessa."

I watched her, breath held.

"Vanessa Valdez." She put down the phone, stared at it. "When he'd get high, he'd accuse me of fooling around on him."

The phone quit ringing. The house was silent as only a dead house can be. Somewhere outside, an engine revved.

"I always thought he was seeing other girls on the side. But when I said as much…" She paused, absently rubbed her arm. "Funny thing was, I didn't even care."

"People often project their own sins onto others," I said.

She raised her brows. "What the hell's that supposed to mean?"

"Perhaps he felt guilty for cheating on you and allowed himself to believe you were the guilty party, thus—"

She coughed a laugh. "You get paid for shoveling that shit?"

"It isn't—"

"How much?"

“What?”

“How much you get paid?”

“It’s not shit.”

She snorted. “First off, Drag never felt guilty a day in his life. Second…” She picked up the phone, snapped it open and pressed a button. A moment later her scowl deepened. “Hell. There must be five calls here from that Vanessa chick.” She scrolled down. “Two from Aggie. And three from some poor fool named Erica.”

“Put it down, Lavonn. Eric said it’s evidence.”

“Well, Eric…” She scowled. “Eric Albertson.” Our eyes met with a snap.

“Eric A,” I said, staring at the phone.

“Shit!” She breathed the word.

My muscles were frozen but I forced my hand to dig my cell from the back pocket of my jeans. “What’s the number?”

Her hand was shaking as she punched a button and read off the digits. It took me a moment to scroll down to the last call I’d gotten from Officer Albertson.

“It’s a shame,” someone said from the hallway.

We jumped in unison. Lavonn squawked. I bumped into her, backing away just as Eric Albertson stepped into view.

Chapter 28

Most folks are just alive 'cause you get in deep shit when you shoot 'em.
—Dion Templeton, minutes before his mother confiscated his Glock

"I was hoping you wouldn't find out." Eric stood very still, his handsome face calm, his beautiful eyes sorrowful.

"Holy shit!" Lavonn jerked back, then steadied herself on the open cleaning drawer.

"What're you doing here?" My words weren't quite as articulate as Lavonn's. Maybe it was because he was holding a gun in his hand.

Lavonn was also staring, but her mind seemed to be clinking along at a faster pace than mine. "You was Drag's ace, wasn't you?" she asked.

He tilted his head at her. "What's that?"

"Drag said he had an ace in the hole. That was you, wasn't it? The reason he always knew when to pack up the drugs and get out. When to shut down an operation."

"What?" I backed up a step, shock shimmying through my system. "What are you talking about?"

Eric gave me his million-dollar smile, then shrugged at Lavonn. "Your boy was useful. But he was volatile and unpredictable. Hell, you never knew when a simple mugging was going to turn into a car wash murder."

I swallowed. "You made him do that?"

He lifted one shoulder. "I thought if anybody could scare off a nosy bitch like you it'd be Drag. I can't tell you how relieved I was when you said you didn't have a clue who attacked you." He chuckled. "He was a mean little bastard. But"—he stared pointedly at Lavonn's still-healing bruises—"you already know that, don't you? Hell, I'd think you'd be kissing my ass for getting rid of him instead of snooping through his stuff."

"Was you the one shot Jackson then?"

He shrugged. "If I had known he was going to find religion in the pen I maybe would have let things slide, but after all the work I've done to build up Intensity's clientele it just wouldn't be right for him to take over my territory. I didn't want to waste any time. Wanted to get to him right away. You know what they say about the early bird." He laughed. "I got a clean shot through his window. Got away. If some fucking neighbor hadn't called in a disturbance I would have done us all a favor. Course, I guess it was the same nosy bastard that reported seeing Rivera's Jeep parked around the corner. So I can't be too steamed." He laughed as if we were discussing a missed appointment or a tennis match.

"You framed him," I said, but he shook his head.

"Coggins hates his guts and had gotten some of the other guys a little fired up. He was being favored because of his old man. That sort of thing.

Personally, I always thought your boyfriend was an okay guy. He'd just been asking too many questions. Wondering why the drug raids weren't turning out to the department's satisfaction. I thought I might have to put a bullet in his head, too, but this'll turn out all right. Hell, maybe he and I can bond while mourning your death together. You and your little black nemesis there. See?" He tilted the pistol a little. "This is the same gun that shot Andrews. Looks like Lavonn got her hands on it and killed you so they'll figure it must have been Drag's. But you're a scrapper, aren't you, Christina? You won't go down without a fight."

"You can't kill us," Lavonn said.

He canted his head at her as if he were merely inquisitive. "Why's that?"

"Yeah." My voice was little more than a squeak to my own ears. My neck creaked when I turned toward her. "Why is that?"

"Because no one will never believe it."

"Oh, they will," he said, smiling at her for the first time. "It's common knowledge that your change in fortune is her fault."

She stared at him.

"If she hadn't gotten involved, you would still be with that good-looking and newly religious Jackson Andrews."

She glanced at me, brows lowering.

"Still have that snazzy little sports car."

She tightened her lips. "I loved that car," she said.

"Still have that house in Glendale instead of slumming it like an eastside whore."

"It had rosewood banisters," she said, and turned toward me like one in a trance. "I picked out the stain myself."

Fresh panic sizzled through me. "Listen, Lavonn—"

"You know that?" she asked, and took a step toward me. "I picked out the damn stain myself."

"Lavonn, what are you doing?" I asked, and sidled away, but my back was already against the wall. "It's not—"

"I got nothing left."

"Lavonn..."

"I got nothing!" she shrieked, and lunged at me.

Her shoulder hit my left boob like a freight train. The air left my lungs in a hard whoosh of pain. My ass hit the floor a fraction of a second later. She yanked at my hair. I rolled over and pinned her for a second. But she was as wiry as a jacked-up terrier. A jerk and a screech and she was on top again. Screaming. Flailing. Fingers tearing. Fists flying. I rolled again, fighting my way to the top.

She lay beneath me, panting hard, and in that splintered second our gazes met. Something flashed between us, something as primitive as fear, as deadly as PMS. There was the slightest pause. I held my breath, unsure, and then I dove at Albertson. I hit him in the knees with the full force of my weight. He staggered backward, trying to bring the gun to bear, but Lavonn was right behind me, snatching up the broom as she leapt. She struck him with the handle. The pistol soared from his hand. She lunged after it, but so did he. I grabbed his arm. He swung toward me. His fist exploded against my left ear. I staggered backward, head spinning. My hip hit the floor a second before a gun fired. I jerked. Lavonn screamed.

Albertson grunted. Then he stumbled lethargically backward. It took me a lifetime to realize Lavonn had pulled the trigger. Longer still to understand that the bullet had plowed a harmless path into the wall behind him.

"Stay where you are!" she shrieked. Her hands were shaking like leaves in the wind.

He laughed. I stabbed my attention from her to him as he took a step forward. "You're lucky you didn't hit me, Lavonn," he said. His voice was singsong. "You know what happens to little black girls who injure police officers."

"Don't you come no closer!" Her voice was shrill, her body stiff.

He smiled his beatific smile. "They'd throw you in jail for the rest of your life," he said. "What would happen to your precious babies?"

She shook her head, looking wild.

"Come on," he said, still advancing, "we can work something out. You're a smart girl and I bet… I just bet you can keep your mouth shut."

"I don't wanna lose my babies."

"I know. I know you don't," he said.

"What about her?" she asked, and jerked a nod toward me.

He shrugged. "She's a nosy bitch," he said. "And she did cause the trouble between you and Jackson."

"She did that."

"Lavonn…" I said.

He smiled again. "I'd understand if you had to get rid of her. Hell…I'd call it self-defense. We could say she was having an affair with Drag and got jealous. With her gone, we could split the full profits."

"So you got control of the goods?"

"Every ounce."

"Don't lie to me," she said. "What other cops got dibs?"

He snorted. "The whole fucking force is a bunch of pansy-asses."

"So with Drag gone, Intensity's all yours."

"That's right. But I'm willing to share. You could have your house back, Lavonn. Your babies. Your life."

"You'd protect me if I take her out?" she asked. Her eyes were as steady as steel on me. I was frozen in place.

"You have my word. Do it," he crooned, but in that second she glanced toward the cleaning cabinet.

"I hope to hell you guys heard that," she said.

He stared at her. "What are you talking about?"

"Get down on your knees," she ordered, raising the gun a little.

"What's going on?"

"The cops are on their way right now."

He stared at her, face blank, and then he went pale. "You're lying."

She swallowed, adjusted her stance. "I got a little unit taped right there beside the Pledge," she said. "Only place Drag would never look."

"You're fucking lying!" he screamed, and then he leapt at her.

She didn't flinch. Didn't move. Didn't make a sound. Just shot him dead center through the forehead.

Chapter 29

Breaking up is like being pooped on by a wood duck. Divorce is like being pecked to death by the wood duck.
—Donald Archer, shortly after his first divorce

My throat hurt and my eyes stung.

"So…did you love him?" Lavonn asked. She was sitting at my kitchen table, eating my ice cream…again.

"No."

"How come you're crying then?"

"I'm not crying."

"Then your eyeballs are leaking."

"That's because you're eating my ice cream," I said, and snatched the carton out from under her spoon. "What are you doing here, anyway?"

She watched me in silence for a second. "I just wanted to make sure you were okay."

"I'm fine," I said, and stabbed the unoffending ice cream with my fork.

"It's hard to get dumped."

"I told you, I didn't get dumped," I said. "I broke up with him."

She smiled a little. "What was his name, anyway?"

I shoved the spoon into my mouth and spoke around it. "Dr. Marcus Carlton." And all of a sudden his name was clear as a bell. "He's an author."

"So you said." She tried to look impressed. It wasn't enormously successful. Perhaps she had known a few too many authors. "Better than an ax murderer, I suppose."

"I guess I should have realized it wasn't going to work out when I could never remember his name."

"Might have been a sign," she said, and reaching into my freezer, rummaged around until she brought out a Snickers bar.

I scowled as she tore it open, but managed not to break into full fledged sobs. "I mean, I always knew he wasn't the love of my life." I took another chunk of ice cream. "But I guess I was just kind of hoping…" I shrugged.

"That you were the love of his?"

I sighed, not quite ready to admit it. "I suppose I—" I stopped abruptly. "Wait a minute. Why are we talking about me?"

She smiled around the candy bar. "I always wanted to be a therapist."

I shook my head, trying to adjust to the facts. "But…you're not a cop, right?"

"Hell, no."

"Then…" I paused, not quite sure how to formulate a question.

"I attended Southwestern, like I said. Met a man there. And he…" She inhaled deeply. "He seemed like a nice guy. Intelligent. Classy. Rich. You know?"

"Yeah," I said. "I know."

"It was tough going to school. I never had any time for the kids. And he offered… Well…he offered everything. A nice house. Nannies. Vacations abroad. But it turns out…Turns out I was his mule."

"And the police found out."

Her eyes were distant. "They said I'd have a get-out-of-jail-free card if I'd do a little work for them. There was talk even back then that there was corruption in the department. So no one could know about me. Not even my family." Her eyes were dark, her expression pained. "I thought it'd just be a couple months." She winced, seeming to see the march of time in her mind's eye.

"But you're done now."

Her face lit up from within. It wasn't quite a smile. It was bigger than that. More hopeful than that. "I'm going to pick up my kids tomorrow."

"Are they really in Cleveland?"

"Andrews was dangerous, spooky, a fanatic. But Drag…" Her eyes went flat. She glanced toward my darkened window. I could still see remnants of the bruise high on her left cheek. "I told the chief that if he didn't get my kids out L.A., I was done." She shrugged. "My aunt was willing to take them. She wasn't so excited about Charlie."

"Charlie." I had almost forgotten about her dog. "How's he doing?"

“Good. The bullet just missed some pretty important organs, I guess, but he's tough."

"Yeah," I said, remembering our introduction with a shiver, "I noticed."

"He's waiting in the car. Would you like me to bring him in so you can say goodbye?"

"No! I mean…" I cleared my throat. "I wouldn't want to bother him," I said, and she laughed.

"Well thanks," she said. "For what you did. For saving his life." She tilted her head a little. "For saving my life."

I shrugged, humble as pie as I stroked Harley’s ear. He reciprocated by licking my knee. “So now Micky can tell Jamel his aunt is a hero.”

She laughed, then glanced toward the window again. “About Micky…”

I waited, and suddenly I saw it, that girlish expression emblazoned on her hard-ass features. I opened my mouth, closed it, opened it again.

“You really do like him.”

“I do not.”

“Do, too,” I said. “You’re crushing on Micky Goldenstone.”

“Listen. I’m a grown woman. And a mother. I don’t—”

“You loooove him,” I said.

“Oh, for God’s sake, what are you…a two-year-old? I—”

“Holy crap!” I said, and sat back suddenly, as if struck by a revelation. “You’re human.”

She stopped, looking embarrassed as she scrubbed her hand across her face. “Well…he is hot,” she said, and peeked through her fingers at me.

I laughed out loud.

She exhaled heavily, dropping her hand and looking sheepish. “I wouldn’t mind if you’d put in a good word for me.”

“Seriously?”

She rolled her eyes, then glanced away. “I just… Kaneasha, my sister…”

I nodded, sobering at the mention of the woman who had overdosed shortly after Jamel’s death.

“She adored him. And I know…Micky’s got issues. He’s moody. And he carries around a shitload of guilt. Maybe for good reason.” She glanced at me. I neither denied nor confirmed so she drew a fortifying breath and shook her head. “You really are a shrink, aren’t you?”

“For quite a while.”

She nodded, then stood up. “Listen, I’ll get out of your hair. I really just came to apologize.”

“For…”

“For getting you involved,” she said. “I should never have called you. But Drag had gone nuts, and I was so close to the truth. I couldn’t call the cops and blow my cover.”

“Well…” I took another bite of ice cream. “…try not to do it again.”

“It’s a deal,” she said and headed toward the door, “if you promise to be more careful.”

"What do you mean?"

"I mean, if some crazy bitch calls you in the middle of the night yelling about men with guns and bad tempers, you keep your ass out of it."

"Where's the fun in that?"

"I'm serious," she said, sounding more like Rivera by the second. "Jackson may have found religion." She made air quotes with her fingers. "But don't trust him. Not ever. He's a nut job, and Drag's friends…a few of them have been indicted. But there are still some serious head cases out there. One in particular." She scowled. "They call him Coke. He idolized Drag. If you even hear that name mentioned you run like hell."

"What about Pepsi?" I asked. I'd always wanted to be the class clown. But no one had ever taken me seriously enough. "Is he okay?"

"Listen, I don't care how suicidal you are," she said, smirking a little. "You don't want to get involved with him. Sometimes there really is loyalty amongst thieves. Well…" She rose to her feet. "I'd better get going."

I glanced toward the outside world, wondering about head cases and guys with soda pop names. "Now?"

"Lock your doors."

"Geez, you sound like a cop," I said.

She laughed as she stepped outside.

I sighed, locked the door and traipsed into the kitchen.

The phone range just as I reached the table, nearly scaring me out of my skin. I stared at it, the thought of head cases making me nervous.

"Hello?" My voice was tentative when I answered.

"You okay?"

"Laney." I felt my shoulders slump with relief.

"You should get caller ID before you have a heart attack," she said.

I slipped into a chair, feeling floppy and old. "I think terror is good for my heart. Keeps it pumping."

"Good thing you live in L.A. then."

I smiled. It seemed like forever since we'd spoken, though honestly, it hadn't been more than a handful of hours. "How'd filming go today?"

"All right until it rained."

I glanced outside. The temperature had dropped into the double digits. "I've heard of rain."

"How are you doing, Mac? Really."

"I'm good." I was lonely and tired and a little depressed, but I straightened my spine, remembering I should be pretty thrilled just to be breathing. "Excellent."

"You don't miss…" She paused.

"Marc?" I guessed dryly, and she laughed.

"Yeah."

"I think I'll live without him."

"I think you already were," she said.

I shrugged. "I guess. It's just… it was nice to say I had somebody."

"You have somebody."

"Somebody with testicles."

"So now I'm not good enough for you?"

I smiled, letting a little contentment steal in. "Have you told Solberg yet?"

"No. I'm waiting for the perfect moment."

"When there are no hard surfaces so that when he faints he won't hurt himself?"

"You're funny."

"I know."

"You sure you're okay?"

"I will be," I said and almost believed myself.

We hung up a couple minutes later. I glanced around the kitchen. The empty ice-cream tub remained on the table surround by a bevy of dirty dishes, but I wasn't very motivated to clean up. Classy hadn't worked out very well for me. Snoopy tended to get me killed. Maybe Sleepy and Dopey were more my—

A noise sounded from the entry, a creak of something so faint that it made my breath lock tight in my throat. The name Coke was conjured up like black magic in my brain. My hand dropped to the silverware drawer without an order from its command center. I wrapped my fist around a steak knife and turned to face this new threat just as a man stepped into view.

Lieutenant Jack Rivera stood in the doorway. He was silent and dark and bigger than life.

He hadn't shaved in days. His hair was a little longer, his body a little leaner. But his eyes were the same shade of mesmerizing intensity as always.

It took a lifetime for me to find my voice and when it came it was little more than a croak. Even I didn't know what I said, but his words were perfectly clear.

"I'm sorry."

I shook my head and glanced behind him. I'm not sure what I intended to see. Perhaps I thought there might be a ventriloquist throwing his voice, but he seemed to be alone and absolutely sincere. "For breaking into my house?" I was trying to play it cool. Struggling to play it safe.

"No," he said and took a step toward me.

I lifted the knife slightly, remembering a thousand reasons why he should be sorry. "For letting me believe you were really under arrest?"

He shook his head. "I was as much in the dark as you were."

I considered calling him a liar, but his expression was too angry, his eyes too direct. "How about the senator? Was he in on it?"

"If I say yes will you make him suffer?" The first tiny flicker of humor shone in his dark-shadow eyes.

"I'll do my best."

"Turns out the old bastard knows more about my department than I do."

"Damn him!" I breathed.

"Already done."

I scowled, fighting the softness that threatened to well up inside me. "Why'd you go to Andrews's house in the first place?"

He shook his head as if seeing his own foolishness for what it was. "I was just planning to check things out." A muscle jumped in his cheek. A new ember of anger flamed in his eyes. "Maybe put a little fear of God in him, but he didn't answer the door, so I went back to my car, waited around a while, fantasized about beating the hell out of him. It wasn't until the next day that I heard some guy reported seeing me sitting out there in the dark."

"He recognized you?"

"Got my license. Said I was a suspicious looking character." His lips quirked up a little at the corners. "I didn't know anything about this deal they had brewing with Lavonn. I guess the captain was afraid I'd fuck up their setup if I was left at large once Andrews was released. Could be he thought I really would kill the son of a bitch if he…" He fisted his hands then inhaled deeply as if steadying himself. "…if he touched you."

It was a pretty good explanation, but I pulled myself out of the grip of his gaze, holding strong. The knife was impressively steady in my hand.

“Then your apology must be for cheating on me.” My voice broke. I cleared my throat.

“I never cheated on you, McMullen. Not with that woman in the car. Not with Coggins’s girlfriend. Not with anyone.” He chuckled with dry humor and glanced at the steak knife. “I’m not that brave.”

I almost laughed. Relief threatened to flood my good sense, but we still had unresolved issues. Though for the life of me, I couldn’t remember what they were.

“Why are you apologizing then?”

His eyes were dead steady. “For making you turn to Marv,” he said.

I blinked back tears. Bloody traitors. “His name’s…”

“I don’t give a fuck what his name is!” he said, and suddenly I was in his arms. But the steak knife was between us.

“I have a new boyfriend,” I lied, and pressed the blade against his ribs. “He’s—”

His lips descended on mine for one long, hard, brain-stealing kiss. I tried to keep my head, but my knees felt saggy and my heart overtaxed. He drew back, eyes blazing.

“—wonderful,” I breathed.

“He’s an idiot,” he growled. “Or he wouldn’t leave you alone. Wouldn't let you take such dumb-ass risks.”

My mouth felt dry. My resistance weak. “I was scared,” The words were a whisper.

"I'm sorry." He gritted his teeth against the force of his emotion. "Sorry you were hurt. Sorry you were threatened-"

"Scared for you," I corrected. "I didn't know where you were. Didn't know if you were safe.

Didn't know if you were—" I rattled, but he bent his corded neck and kissed me again.

Heat sizzled through my system, setting any hitherto un-torched organs ablaze.

"I can take care of myself, McMullen," he said, and lifting me into his arms, carried me into the bedroom.

The mattress felt soft against my back, his body hard against my front.

"Holy crap!" I breathed as his belt came loose in my hands. "They were right. They were *all* right."

Lois Greiman was born on a cattle ranch in central North Dakota where she learned to ride and spit with the best of them. After graduating from high school, she moved to Minnesota to train and show Arabian horses. But eventually she fell in love, became an aerobics instructor and gave birth to three of her best friends.

She sold her first novel in 1992 and has published more than thirty titles since then, including romantic comedy, historical romance, children's stories, and her fun-loving Christina McMullen mysteries. A two-time Rita finalist, she has won such prestigious honors as Romantic Times Storyteller Of The Year, MFW's Rising Star, RT's Love and Laughter, the Toby Bromberg for most humorous mystery, and the LaVyrle Spencer Award. Her heroes have received K.I.S.S. recognition numerous times and her books have been seen regularly among the industry's Top Picks!

With more than two million books printed worldwide, Ms. Greiman currently lives on the Minnesota tundra with her family, some of whom are human. In her spare time she likes to ride some of her more hirsute companions in high speed events such as barrel racing and long distance endurance rides.

http:/www.loisgreiman.com
http://www.facebook.com/lois.greiman
http://www.facebook.com/ChrissyMcMullenMysteries
Blog with Lois at ridingwiththetopdown.blogspot.com
Follow Lois on Twitter @loisgreiman

Other Chrissy McMullen Mysteries
by Lois Greiman

Unzipped
Unscrewed
Unmanned
One Hot Mess
Not One Clue
Unfortunate (short story)

Romance Novels by Lois Greiman
Highland Jewel
Highland Flame
Highland Wolf
Beloved Beast (short story)

CPSIA information can be obtained at www.ICGtesting.com
Printed in the USA
LVOW06s1557091113

360677LV00001B/78/P